The Bishop in the West Wing

"In his own bumbling, inimitable style, Blackie once again proves to be a loyal friend, a formidable foe, and a gifted spiritual advisor. An entertaining romp through the West Wing." —*Booklist*

"Fun is the word for bestseller Greeley's latest, lively Bishop Blackie Ryan thriller. . . . [Readers] will appreciate the well-drawn characters, swift action, and logical resolution." —*Publishers Weekly*

"It's an especially enjoyable tale for a mystery fan on a hot day when murder is just too heavy to deal with and a poltergeist's antics can be just the thing." —*Abilene Reporter-News*

"Given the success of "West Wing" (the TV Show), those who are not fans of Greeley will pluck this book up quickly. And they will love it. . . . The book will also delight . . . because it follows his near-perfect formula of adventure and amusement, mystery and mastery of the English language. Enjoy this one—*The Bishop in the West Wing* is a winner." —*Star Newspapers*

The Bishop and the Beggar Girl of St. Germain

"Full of unexpected turns and twists." —*Publishers Weekly*

"For the reader who enjoys clever dialogue and a thought-provoking story as much as a roller-coaster action thriller, Greeley continues to deliver." —*The Tampa Tribune*

"Fine for a day at the beach or a bistro on the Boulevard St. Germain." —*The Star-Observer*, Hudson, WI

D0250812

The Bishop and the Missing L Train

"The lighthearted Bishop Blackie returns with this beguiling entry in Greeley's series detailing the misadventures of venerable Bishop John Blackwood Ryan." —*Publishers Weekly*

"The inimitable Bishop Blackie Ryan resurfaces in fine form to solve another new mystery set on the streets and in the parishes of Greeley's native Chicago. . . . As usual, the author interweaves the central plot with a couple of tangential romances cleverly designed to culminate with the resolution of the mystery. Vintage Greeley fare." —*Booklist*

THE BISHOP
IN THE
WEST WING

THE BISHOP
IN THE
WEST WING

A BLACKIE RYAN STORY

ANDREW M.
GREELEY

FORGE®

A TOM DOHERTY ASSOCIATES BOOK
NEW YORK

This story is a fantasy set in a future White House administration. All the characters in it are fictional. Even the two seemingly nonfictional characters, Bill Clinton and Rich Daley, are fictionalized versions of themselves. Its major premise is that the fanatic partnership which marks comtemporary America gets worse and that therefore the determination of a radical minority that no Democrat can legitimately serve as President increases.

Quod Deus Avertat

THE BISHOP IN THE WEST WING: A BLACKIE RYAN STORY

Copyright © 2002 by Andrew M. Greeley Enterprises, Ltd.

Interior illustration by Heidi Hornaday

A Forge Book
Published by Tom Doherty Associates, LLC
175 Fifth Avenue
New York, NY 10010

www.tor.com

Forge® is a registered trademark of Tom Doherty Associates, LLC.

ISBN: 0-812-57598-9
Library of Congress Catalog Card Number: 2001058284

First edition: July 2002
First mass market edition: June 2003

Printed in the United States of America

0 9 8 7 6 5 4 3 2 1

For President William J. Clinton,
who invited me to the White House three times,
twice for the solemnities of St. Paddy's day
and once for an overnight because he liked
Blackie Ryan and Nuala Anne McGrail

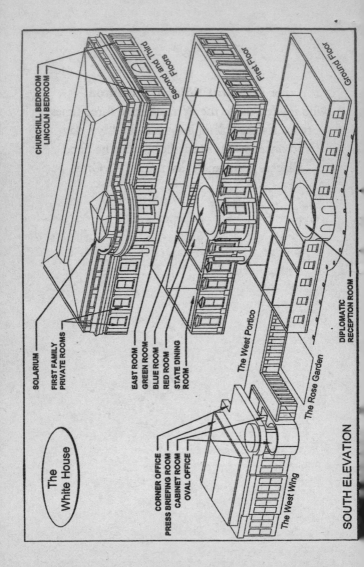

The White House

CHURCHILL BEDROOM
LINCOLN BEDROOM

Second and Third Floors

First Floor

Ground Floor

SOLARIUM

FIRST FAMILY PRIVATE ROOMS

EAST ROOM
GREEN ROOM
BLUE ROOM
RED ROOM
STATE DINING ROOM

The West Portico

The Rose Garden

DIPLOMATIC RECEPTION ROOM

CORNER OFFICE
PRESS BRIEFING ROOM
CABINET ROOM
OVAL OFFICE

The West Wing

SOUTH ELEVATION

1

"*Your good friend was on* the phone earlier this evening."

Cardinal Sean Cronin leaned casually against my doorframe as though he was posing for a fashion magazine shoot, in light blue pajamas and royal blue robe. He had never appeared at my doorway in such array. I noted with some pleasure that he did not wear his cardinalatial ruby to bed at night and that his slippers were also royal blue, not crimson.

"Ah," I said as I turned away from the purgatorial task of catching up on my e-mail. Naturally I had no idea who the friend was—a beautiful but troubled woman, a penitent Mafioso, a haunted priest, someone from Rome, a mystic with revelations that must be passed on instantly to the Pope. The rhetoric of Chicago discourse, however, required that he begin with such an indirect approach, as though all the rooms of the Cathedral Rectory were wired by hostile law enforcement agencies.

"The Megan thought I should talk to him since you were not around."

It was therefore a serious matter. None of the four porter person Megans who presided over the entrances to the Cathedral Rectory from after school to 9:30 would dream of disturbing the Cardinal

Archbishop (whom they adored as "extreme cute") unless some important game was afoot.

(One must understand that for the younger generation "extreme" has become an adverb.)

"Indeed!"

"We have you on the 6:00 flight. Your friend Mr. Woods will pick you up at 4:30."

"P.M.?" I said, knowing full well that it was not.

Milord Cronin permitted a frown to furrow his handsome brow.

"The monks get up a lot earlier, Blackwood."

"Such as they are these days. However, patently I am not a monk."

"He was going to send Air Force One to pick you up, but I said it wouldn't look good for a lowly auxiliary bishop to fly around in that. Create a lot of comment, which he doesn't need right now."

"Arguably," I conceded.

So that's who "my good friend" was—John Patrick McGurn, POTUS, aka to the media "Machine Gun Jack."

Without asking my permission—he never does—Milord Cronin opened the secret cabinet on the wall of my study (hidden behind a portrait of our currently gloriously reigning Pontiff), removed a bottle of my precious Jameson's Twelve Year Special Reserve, and poured himself a good-size splash into one of the attendant Waterford goblets.

"You're proposing to assign me to the White House," I protested. "That won't look too good."

"You always say that you're the little man who isn't there. They won't notice you." He leaned against the door and sipped complacently from his goblet, looking all the more like a cover for *GQ*.

"The Nuncio won't like it."

"I'll worry about him."

If he did worry about the reaction of the ambassador of the Holy See's reaction to my translation to the White House, it would be the first such worry in his career.

"Why is it necessary that I abandon all my serious responsibilities here in your Cathedral parish?"

A weak argument, I acknowledge. Yet the game had to be played out.

The Ryan family has a gene that inclines them to resist travel. In my own case the power of the gene is primordial. The upper limit of my tolerance is the drive from Chicago to South Bend, Indiana, home of the fighting Black Baptists. However, the apparent need of the first South Side Irish Catholic from Chicago to become president of the United States overrode my reluctance, though not without a loud west of Ireland sigh which might suggest an attack of asthma.

John Patrick McGurn indeed needed help, though he would have been the first to deny it.

The media, especially the *Wall Street Journal,* the *New York Times* and the *Washington Post,* hated President McGurn. They persisted in calling him "Machine Gun Jack" because the name broadly hinted of the Capone era and Chicago Irish political corruption. So deep in the subbasement of Chicago memory is the name of that alleged perpetuator of the St. Valentine's Day massacre that Jack McGurn had never been identified with a machine gun during his brief career in Chicago politics.

"He has some serious problems," the Cardinal continued with a sigh as loud as mine.

"Surely not the sexual harassment charges!" I protested.

Milord waved his hand in a graceful, dismissive gesture.

"Those go with the territory if you're a Democratic president. Jack will survive them."

"Arguably," I said without much conviction. The top national media hated Irish Catholics, especially from Chicago. They were determined, even though they would piously deny it, to drive Jack McGurn from office. Such assaults sold newspapers, increased TV ratings, satisfied needs to experience pious self-righteousness. Typically Jack did not shy from the Chicago identity, though he and his family had been at best minor figures in the various Daley administrations.

"Though I deserve little credit for it"—Jack would smile and his blue-green eyes would glitter with mischief—"I am proud to be identified with the most effective municipal administration in America."

"Why then," I persisted, "this late-night emergency call for the lowly sweeper to the Cardinal Prince of Chicago?"

This was a none-too-oblique reference to my conviction that an auxiliary bishop's main *raison d'être* is to sweep up his Ordinary's messes, as the worthy Harvey Keitel had done for the Outfit in the film *Pulp Fiction*.

"Ghosts," Sean Cronin said in his most gloomy apocalyptic voice.

"Ghosts!"

I warned myself mentally that I must not seem too enthusiastic.

"Ghosts. Or psychic phenomena or whatever."

"Legend has it that Mr. Lincoln's ghost haunts the building."

"It's more than that."

"Ah?"

Sean Cardinal Cronin hesitated, something he almost never does.

"There are psychic phenomena happening all over the White House—in the West Wing, including the Oval Office, in the bedrooms, in the family quarters on the third floor, in the various museum rooms on the first and second floors, in the basement offices under the West Wing, in the guest bedrooms like the Lincoln Bedroom and the Queens' Bedroom, even out in the Rose Garden and the South Lawn . . ."

"Appalling!" I murmured with little conviction. "Of what sort are the phenomena?"

"The usual junk—doors slamming, chains rattling, paintings falling off the wall, vases flying across the room, windows springing open during snowstorms, thermostats going crazy, televisions switching on and off . . ."

"Nothing ever breaks, I presume?"

"No."

"Poltergeists," I said with some disappointment.

"Presumably . . . There's a twist to it . . ."

"Ah?"

The Cardinal hesitated again.

"The rumors around the White House, which still includes some service personnel who worked for the last president, are that Ellen has come back to harass Jack over the sexual harassment."

"Absurd!" I said hotly. "Ellen was not and is not that kind of woman! She might burn the White

House down if she were sufficiently angry, but poltergeist phenomena are beneath her."

"Steady, Blackwood! You and I know that and so do most people in this city. However, the media have stirred up so much hatred for Jack and his family that the public is capable of believing anything about them. Irish Catholics from Chicago are capable of bringing every kind of evil to the White House, even ghosts. Many people will think that the ghosts are proof that he did mess around with those campaign bimbos."

The harsh truth about political campaigns that you will never read in the papers is that they are airborne orgies, traveling brothels in which boredom with the political rhetoric provides an excuse for the hangers-on, including the self-righteous journalists, to indulge in day and night promiscuity. John Patrick McGurn's campaign was, heaven knows, not boring. Nonetheless, the habits of promiscuity continued. Sex on campaigns is far more important than the issues that allegedly divide the candidates. If the candidate's wife is not with him, then speculation erupts about whom he is sleeping with. In the bawdyhouse atmosphere of a campaign it is taken for granted that everyone is committing adultery, especially a candidate who has recently lost his wife. It is alleged indeed that some young women, one might call them groupies, join a campaign so that they can sleep with world-famous journalists and even perhaps spend a night with a man who may be the next president of the United States. Two such young women, who might not be utterly innocent of Milord Cronin's accusation that they were bimbos, filed sexual harassment suits against him three days before his inauguration, alleging that they had not received promised White House jobs because they resisted the candidate's sexual advances.

Those who did not know John McGurn as we did could easily have believed the charges. Most Americans did not know him very well. Indeed they were surprised that he was sitting in the Oval Office and had begun to wonder if they had made a serious mistake.

"Poltergeist phenomena," I observed, "are usually associated with an early adolescent, especially of the female variety. Does not the President have two such in his family?"

"It may surprise you, Blackwood," the Cardinal said with a touch of superiority permissible in an encrimsoned prince, "to learn that I know that about the playful spirits. However, Deirdre is back at Notre Dame and Granne is living with her aunt in Chicago until she graduates in June from St. Praxides Grammar School, your alma mater, if I'm not mistaken."

His Eminence had begun to talk like Sherlock Holmes, which was my role not his.

"Then our mutual friend needs an exorcist. If I am not mistaken, you have one such on your staff, against my advice I might add."

"You've been working too hard lately, Blackwood," he said with mock disappointment. "What would the *Washington Post* do or the Calvinist Vatican on Forty-second Street should they find out that the Catholic Church had sent an exorcist into the White House?"

Milord was always amused to describe the *New York Times* as a Calvinist newspaper.

"Especially one as eager to appear on television as your staff exorcist."

He ignored my sally, which was all he could do under the circumstances.

"Besides, we know from past experience that all you have to do is to walk into a haunted house—or aircraft carrier as far as that goes—and the playful spirits go out of business."

That lamentably was the truth. The adolescent who was, not altogether consciously stirring up trouble, knew better than to mess with Father Blackie.

"You yourself have observed that I have been working too hard," I said, knowing that the battle was lost. These battles were always lost, but it was nonetheless necessary to play out the scenario.

"The *Post* and the *Times*," Sean Cronin continued implacably, "know about the phenomena from their spies inside the administration. They are hesitant to use it because of their ideology that there is no such thing as the supernatural."

Having conducted a token search for a coaster, he placed his empty goblet on top of a stack of computer output.

"So they will wait till the supermarket tabloids run it and then they'll play it as a media story," I observed.

"And the sharks will swim in from all sides for a feeding frenzy."

We were both silent for a moment. American journalism had come a long way from its assumption that major public figures were entitled to their private lives. Even the most responsible media outlets would salivate at the prospect of poking into a president's parapsychological life.

"Blackwood," the Cardinal intoned, "John Patrick McGurn is a good and worthy layman of this great Archdiocese. I baptized him, I officiated at his marriage, and I baptized his kids. I said his wife's funeral Mass. Now that he is also president of the United States of America it is unfitting, offensive, and intolerable that he be haunted by ungodly spirits, especially when a revolution is sweeping China."

"Ah," I murmured.

"Moreover the bimbos that are suing him are also ungodly spirits. I expect that you will be able to deal with them too."

Swept by the power of his prose, Milord had just doubled my assignment.

"I won't have it," he said solemnly. "I simply won't have it."

"Indeed."

"See to it, Blackwood!" he ordered as he turned towards the dark corridor whence he had come to disrupt my late-night tranquility.

He departed from my study with the swoosh of a passing but lordly hailstorm.

"Tomorrow!"

2

After Mr. Woods delivered me to O'Hare and I managed with some difficulty to find the 6:00 plane to Ronald Reagan Washington National Airport (one president apparently not being enough for its name) I settled back in my seat and began to ponder the man who had summoned me to the Beltway as it is called with notable lack of poetic sensibility.

"How did this man get to be president?" the *New York Times* had demanded in a stiff and somewhat offended editorial on Inauguration Day. (The *Wall Street Journal* demanded, "Who is Jack McGurn?") The answer to the question from the point of view of Chicago politics is that he won because he got more votes than the other man, indeed 53.7 percent of the popular vote and 413 electoral votes.

"Do you consider your victory a mandate, sir?" a reporter asked him the day after the so-called upset.

"No, only a license to negotiate with Congress."

However, even if you patiently explain to the *Times* editorial writer that he won because he received the most votes, you must still answer the question of why he got the most votes. What kind of man is John Patrick McGurn, Ph.D. LL.D?

If you know many Irishmen, you know John McGurn, aka Machine Gun Jack. He is the kind of

slick, smooth, witty Irishman that might be your parish priest or your undertaker or your cousin the
mildly psychopathic wheeler-dealer or your com-
modities broker or your local barkeep or your precinct captain or your tort lawyer or your political
science professor. Jack had in fact been the last three,
but he could have fit into any of the other roles with
the ease of interchangeability.

He is at best of medium height, perhaps five feet
ten. His square, dimpled face seems impeccably honest. His blue-green eyes dance with charm and sometimes gentle mischief. His black kinky hair, parted in
the middle over a low forehead, edges into silver,
suggesting a mix of youthful vigor and mature wis-
dom. He's in excellent physical condition and exudes
kinetic energy. He is spontaneously funny so you
don't notice that the one-liner covers a question he
does not want to answer. You'd want him on your
side if you were in trouble. You know you can count
on his loyalty. He speaks quickly and thinks even
more quickly. If you're wise, you won't get into an
argument with him because he will mop up the floor
with you and you'll both end up laughing at your
folly. He can greet three people at a time and make
each one of them think he's talking directly to them.
Yet beneath all the contagious wit and exuberant
charm, there are layers of reserve and mystery that
you know no one will ever penetrate, save on some
occasions a determined spouse, one like the late Ellen
Fitzgerald McGurn. Many will count him a friend,
even a close friend. Few will really feel close to him.

You know the kind of person I mean?

The president of the United States is one of these,

the kind of man you can bump into on the streets of Chicago almost any day of the week.

John Patrick McGurn is like these men with two important exceptions, both of which contributed notably to his success as a candidate.

He is supremely intelligent, arguably the brightest man I know. He defines a problem, considers the data, ponders alternatives, then articulates solutions almost instantaneously whether the problem is why Lee and Longstreet fell out at Gettysburg or what to say about the current political crisis in Romania. He reads a situation the way Michael Jordan reads the basketball court. Moreover, he does not seem to have forgotten anything he ever read, no matter how long ago or how obscure it might have been. It helps that he has a photographic memory.

The second difference is that he is supremely self-controlled. Knowing that it's all a game he keeps his emotions under fierce discipline so that they will not get in the way of something more important—whatever that may be. In court and on the political circuit, he can be eloquent. Rarely if ever, however, does he lose his temper, save deliberately.

The only sign that he is indeliberately angry is a quick movement at one corner of his lips and a dangerous flash in his eyes. His late wife, with whom he had carried on a passionate love affair for almost a quarter century, once remarked to me, "It took me a year to catch the twist of the lip sign."

"Whereas in your case," I ventured to say, "it took only a nanosecond to disclose anger."

"If that long!" she laughed merrily.

Women find him very attractive, as you might imagine. Some of them tend to "hit" on him just to

see if they can get a reaction. His response is a polite
smile and a different flash of his blue-green eyes,
which say in effect, "I see right through you."

The hit person quickly backs off, unless her name
was Ellen Fitzgerald and she didn't give a damn
whether he thought he saw through her.

The McGurns are third-generation South Side
Irish professionals, doctors, teachers, lawyers, military officers, and traders, but mostly lawyers. They
have amassed substantial sums of money by these
activities though they would all deny that they were
rich. His grandfather, Black Jack McGurn made a
fortune in real estate. His father, Long Tom Mc-
Gurn, a red-haired giant (of whom Jack's son and
press spokesman Sean Patrick is almost a clone)
added to it with spectacular trades on the Board of
Trade. Each generation produced its own batch of
precinct captains, all of whom showed no interest in
moving up the political ladder. They were all Daley
loyalists, even during the years when the Daleys
were out of power, a loyalty which was not forgotten
when Jack ran his quixotic race for governor—though
he never called on the obligation of loyalty because
he knew he didn't have to.

He and his brother Tim joined their uncle Ted's
law firm and made a lot of money before they were
forty by, as he put it, "keeping the insurance companies honest." His sister Peg became a neonatolo-
gist. His brother Mike took over the clan's
construction company. All were notoriously honest,
despite repeated attempts by the media to find something amiss in their wheelings and dealings because
they were "big contributors" to and good friends of
the mayor. "Only idiots cut corners," Long Tom had

told me when I was but a callow seminarian.

"And only idiots don't cut the cards," I replied, quoting my father Ned Ryan, who repeatedly beat Long Tom at poker.

The old man threw back his silver-red hair and roared with laughter.

"You're your father's son all right," he bellowed.

Jack's career was typical of his generation, if brilliant—St. Praxides Grammar School, St. Ignatius High School, Notre Dame, Loyola Law School. There was nothing in his life when he celebrated his fortieth birthday that suggested that he would break the mold of three generations of Chicago Beverly Irish.

Except that he had married one of them who had never fit the mold. He and Ellen had been fierce rivals through grammar school, and constant verbal combatants through high school. At Notre Dame they studiously ignored one another. Ellen was from the east end of Beverly, where the "poor people" lived—though we would have never used the term. Her father was a fireman who rose to the rank of chief at the end of his career. She was the first one in her family to attend college—on a Merit Scholarship. She was firmly, if joyously, committed to transforming the world, your pragmatic Irish Catholic woman liberal activist.

They discovered one another again in the Contracts class of the first year of law school and promptly fell in love.

"Blackie," he said to me when he asked me if I would attend the wedding that summer, "she's smarter than I am. I never met a woman who was smarter than I am."

"If you can't beat em, join em!"

So they did. Sean Patrick was born a decent ten months after the marriage, Deirdre, the following year, and Granne nine years later. The whole clan did things like building homes in Appalachia, serving soup to the homeless, and flying to Peru to work with the Jesuits in the Altiplano. By Beverly standards they were a little crazy—an African-American couple were Granne's godparents—but since they were McGurns, whatever they did was all right.

Then at forty Jack retired from the practice of law, turned his money over to a skilled investment broker, and collected a degree in political science at the University. They wanted him to stay there on the faculty, but he chose Loyola and taught both law and political science. His first year on campus he was voted the best teacher, a prize he won repeatedly.

All right, he was not the first man from our neighborhood to change his career in midlife. Nothing much so extraordinary in that, was there? He was a great teacher, but he figured to be with his wit and his stories. Unusual in a lot of ways, sure, but not really unusual.

Then one night in the early spring of the off year election he was complaining to his wife and kids, the older ones of which were home from the Golden Dome, about the lack of quality in the four Democrats who were running for governor.

"It's too bad the primary isn't in March anymore," Jack had said. "Those clowns will bore us all summer long."

"Well," Granne piped up, "why don't you run for governor? You can tell your stories and make your jokes from now till the election. . . . When is it by the way?"

"September," Ellen had said uneasily.

"You really should, Daddy," Deirdre joined the emerging consensus.

"I could be your press spokesman," said Sean, a junior in Notre Dame's communications programs. "I wouldn't charge much, just room and board."

Silence around the dinner table on Longwood Drive.

"You think I should?" Jack asked uneasily.

"Why the hell not?" Ellen replied. Her characteristic reaction to anything that was a little zany.

So he did.

The media ridiculed his "belated entry" and suggested he stick to teaching law school. He had little campaign money, no fund-raisers, and no staff. Even his friends who chipped in money, usually unasked, told him it was too late.

"Do you think we're crazy, Blackie?" Ellen asked at the Cathedral Rectory the next night, her oval and very Irish face aglow with the light of battle. "Really crazy."

"Patently," I said. "Go for it."

On the day of his first press conference he laid out an unusual agenda—abolition of the death penalty, a progressive state income tax, aid for parochial schools, harmony between Chicago and downstate, more concern for the environment, and better salaries for teachers.

If the program was ideologically inconsistent, the persona was consistent through spring and summer—charm, wit, and laughter together with concise and intelligent arguments driven home by his stories.

Since he didn't have much money for advertising, he flew around the state almost every day, hitting the nightly news somewhere every night.

The press thought at first he was crazy, but then discovered he was good copy. The TV journalists loved him because he always had a sound bite and a one-liner. The crowds greeting him at the airports around the state grew larger. Somehow Jack Mc-Gurn was always on time and always spoke without notes. The idea spread that he was someone very special.

The people in the neighborhood began to think so too. More important, the idea reached City Hall, where the cautious rule had always been "Don't make no waves, don't back no losers!"

Jack had of course told the mayor he was going to run before he told anyone else. Typically the mayor praised him for seeking public office and wished him well. This was a standard reaction, since the mayor did not believe in throwing his weight behind anyone who would lose.

Sometime in August he must have decided that Jack was a winner, because the cautious and careful word went out, "We can work with Jack."

That may have done the trick all by itself. However, a debate among the five candidates on a rainy Labor Day Sunday evening also helped. The other four candidates went into the debate worried about one another, but not worried about Jack. He was an amateur, a newcomer, someone who didn't know the score.

He didn't rant, he didn't bicker, he was all charm and wit. He creamed the lot of them.

When it came to endorsements, the papers passed

him up, though they praised him as an original and creative candidate. How many votes can they deliver, Sean Patrick, now an accomplished press spokesman, demanded.

The pre-election polls showed him running a close third, five percentage points behind the two leaders with 20 percent of the votes statewide.

However, when the actual votes were counted, Jack McGurn was nominated with 32 percent, three percentage points higher than his closest rival, a shrewd and able and well-liked downstate politician. Almost all of his votes were from Cook County and the "collar counties" around Cook. Pundits observed that once again the Democrats had beaten one another to a pulp in the primary and would be easily routed in the general election.

The Republicans certainly thought so.

"Dear God, Blackie!" Ellen said to me on election night at their party at the Fairmont Hotel. "What if we win? It was all supposed to be a joke!"

"Keep it a joke," I said, trying to look preternaturally wise, "and you will win."

"I've loved him since grammar school, third grade," she said, tears streaming down her cheeks. "I'm responsible for getting him into all this social action stuff. He's doing it for me."

"Indeed?"

This was hardly surprising information.

"He didn't really want to run. He did that for me too."

"Did you urge him?"

She hesitated.

"I didn't have to."

"He seems to be having the time of his life." I

nodded towards the laughing nominee, who was bantering with the media.

"He's a great actor, Blackie," she replied. "You know that."

I didn't, not really.

The Illinois Republicans made the same mistake that Jack's Democratic opponents made. They didn't take him seriously. Nor did they pay attention to the political changes that were happening in Illinois. Clinton and Gore had both carried Illinois big because of the shift in the suburbs around Chicago from automatic Republican voting. The yuppie suburbanites, David Brooks's Bohemian bourgeoisie liked the New Democrats. Jack McGurn, idiosyncratic Democrat that he was, still seemed like a New Democrat to them. Suburban Cook County was now solidly Democratic. The collar counties were moving in the same direction. Rich Daley saw that even if the Republican leadership didn't. He threw his prestige behind Jack McGurn not only because he could work with him but also because he saw the wave of history. Somehow our neighborhood had caught up with the world. Or maybe the world caught up with us.

Jack had two months to convince metropolitan Chicago that he was one of them. It turned out that it was not a problem. He carried the state of Illinois by ten percentage points and carried the Democrats into control of both houses of the legislature. His brief administration was hailed by everyone as brilliant. He managed to get the new income tax bill and the prohibition of the death penalty passed with ease. He hung out at the capital, schmoozing with that strange collection of humans that the people of Illinois send to Springfield every year. He treated them with infinite respect, learned the names of their spouses and children and their birth dates, and charmed them into agreeing with him on all major issues. It was the first hint that any of us had that Jack McGurn was not only an able campaigner, but also a brilliant politician. He was having the time of his life.

"God had him in mind," Ellen told me, "when he created this job."

"Patently."

The good times came to an abrupt end three days before Christmas, when a plane flying from Springfield to Chicago with Ellen as a passenger somehow got lost in the rain over Lake Michigan and missed Meigs Field. It took them three days to find her body in the frozen waters of the Lake.

3

The cabin attendant wakened me.

"We're at Washington National Airport, sir."

"Indeed," I said, opening eyes that I had been resting. "Actually it is more properly called Ronald Reagan Washington National."

"I'm a Democrat, sir," she said with a pleasant smile.

"I also," I assured her. "However, by combining the two presidents on every possible occasion one emphasizes the absurdity of the name."

She laughed.

I sighed and added, to reassure the young woman, "It is not unlikely that they will reverse the names with the Democrats running Congress."

"Hopefully forever," she agreed.

There were patently some Democrats still around, despite the claims of punditry that the major Democratic victory in November was in fact a serious defeat (on the grounds that the Democrats would quickly split and the inexperienced president would make a mess of governing).

Because I had been resting my eyes I had not noticed the landing or the other passengers leaving the plane. However, with only one or two false turns I navigated my way out of the terminal. My instruc-

tions were to cross the inner lane of the roadway
and walk to the outer lane, presumably avoiding on-
coming traffic as I did so. I was then to glance to the
left and see a black car with two persons in dark
suits standing next to it. They would signal me to
join them.

That was where the careful plan went awry. The
persons (one of each gender) sent no signals. The
problem with being so nondescript that no one no-
tices you is that on some occasions you want to be
noticed.

I ambled over to the car, assuming that the agents
would realize that a little man wearing a black-and-
white Chicago White Sox windbreaker would certainly be a bishop from Chicago.

The woman agent pulled a photograph out of her
briefcase, glanced at me, and showed it to her colleague. He nodded dubiously.

By that time I had joined them.

"Call me Blackie," I said, extending a hand.

"Wholley," said the woman.

"Chick," said the man.

Was Wholley her first name and Chick his pa-
tronym?

Improbable.

Ah, for the days when girl children were given
respectable first names like Elizabeth or Mary or Ann
or Marilyn or Kathleen.

"You don't look like a bishop," the young woman
said, searching for a ring to kiss and finding none.

"Most bishops don't look like bishops," I responded. "I do own a ring, but my young colleagues
tell me that if I wear it, I will surely lose it and they
have to search for it."

It would seem that Secret Service agents do not smile.

In the car I tried again.

"Would it violate the national interest for you to tell me what code name you folks use for the president?"

Wholley, who was not driving, turned to look at me, and murmured, "Kerryman."

"How appropriate! I'm sure he's amused by it."

"He thinks it's a wonderful joke," Chick admitted.

"He finds jokes everywhere," the young woman added.

"The Irish are a strange people," I observed. "We tend to laugh even when our hearts are breaking, perhaps especially when our hearts are breaking."

They did not choose to comment on my explanation for Kerryman's laughter in the midst of tragedy.

Jack's State of the Union Address, the *New York Times* had informed a nation eagerly awaiting its opinion, was certainly the funniest such address in history. However, it would have been more appropriate, the *Times* observed, at a Gridiron Club roast than on national television.

"I'm so new at the job," he told the nation, "that I'm afraid every night that my good friend Mr. Justice Scalia will show up before morning with a writ telling me that I have to vacate at sunrise. I warned the vice president she won't even be able to take possession. They have a writ somewhere for her too."

Vice President Cruz was not amused, though she was the only one in the room who did not laugh. Even the Republicans laughed in spite of themselves.

The Democrats loved it. So, if the polls are to be believed, did the people.

He went through his agenda, being careful to say at every point that he needed the help of Congress at every step of the way. The Republicans booed at first and then, sensing that they were being mouse-trapped by a clever pol, locked their jaws shut.

At the end, Jack became very serious—perhaps the *Times* editorial writer had not stayed up to listen to it.

"I've told my staff and my kids that they ought not to take this president stuff too seriously. I admit that it is one of the most powerful jobs in the world, but we must always keep in mind how little a president can actually do. 'Hail to the Chief' can go to your head if you listen to it more than once. Yet the presidency can get you a ride on Mayor Daley's L trains only if you happen to have a dollar and a half in your pocket.

"I can issue some executive orders about the environment and gay rights. I can talk to the people of this country from the Oval Office. I can schmooze at international meetings. I can give State of the Union Addresses like this with a long list of wishes. In fact, however, a president has a lot of power and no power at all unless he can sell his program to his own colleagues, to the government offices and agencies, to these two distinguished Houses, and to the people—a daunting task.

"There is very little I can do to prevent global warming, to persuade Americans to stop using drugs, to bring lasting peace to the Middle East, to respond to the AIDS epidemic in Africa and Asia, to take guns out of the hands of teens, to make the highways safer, to help the very poor, to prevent airplane accidents. I can do a few things to correct some aspects of these problems with your help. Other than that I have very little power. I will keep telling myself that so I never take myself too seriously—though the Daughters will do their best to see to it that I don't. Many of you have been in Washington for a long time. You will be here long after I've left. At best I will be a transitory phenomenon. I will try to remind myself of that at least once a day. I pray that God will help me and that my wife will remind Him up in heaven that He owes me—as He owes all of us.

"The transitory phenomenon, however, will last eight years!"

Tumultuous applause.

We drove across the bridge behind which lurks the Lee-Custis mansion, Arlington National Cemetery, and the Kennedy monument. I made the sign of the cross and prayed for all the Kennedys, living and dead.

No other words were said as we approached the White House. A policeman in Park Service uniform checked us at the back gate.

"Bishop Ryan," Wholley told him, as the cop peered into the backseat. "He says that most bishops don't look like bishops."

Who else was due in on this particular pickup?

We then glided to the low-slung entrance through which foreign visitors are often depicted as entering or leaving the White House or from which the president emerges to board the Marine One helicopter.

"It's all right to let a bishop into the White House, but you have to sneak him in the basement back door," I observed.

"Standard procedure, sir," Chick explained apologetically.

"He's joking," Wholley explained. "He's one of them."

It was not necessary for me to ask what she meant by that.

"One of us would be more appropriate, Agent Wholley."

I heard a sound like a suppressed giggle.

I was ushered into the diplomatic lobby, whose low ceiling suggests it also could serve as a bunker should the Rebs try again to attack across the river.

There are three Ovals in the White House as residence, arguably four—the Diplomatic Reception Room on the ground floor, the Blue Room above it, the Yellow Oval on the second floor in the family quarters, and the Solarium on the extension of the family quarters created by Florence Harding.

A woman in her middle years and at peak efficiency introduced herself as the president's social secretary. She would have made a good mother superior in the old days.

"Welcome to the White House, Bishop Ryan," she said. "We hope you enjoy your stay here. This is your White House pass, which you must wear around your neck at all times . . ."

"I will endeavor not to lose it," I replied.

The letters on the pass were red.

"It is a high-clearance pass. It will get you anywhere in the building except the Oval Office."

I gave it back to her.

"It won't do," I said.

Time stood still in the diplomatic reception room. "Won't do?"

"It will be necessary for me to enter the Oval Office whenever I wish."

"I'm sure that I won't be able to arrange that."

"Then I will be forced to ask my good friends Chick and Wholley to take me back to National Airport."

I thought that I heard a snicker behind me.

If I were to war with the mischievous spirits who are badgering the Kerryman, I would have to be able to go anywhere I wanted. Besides, early on it was necessary to communicate to the diligent staff that I had clout.

The woman turned away from me and spoke into her cell phone. I retreated to an easy chair and rested my eyes again.

"We will have a pass for you shortly, Bishop."

"Excellent," I said.

An African-American gentleman with a flawless Harvard attitude appeared after several minutes with the pass. It was, appropriately, green.

"We don't give these out very often, sir," he explained.

"Most prudent," I agreed.

I shook hands with my two agents from the airport.

"It was an unnecessarily gracious ride," I assured them.

Agent Chick grinned in response. Agent Wholley tipped her head. Another victory for the harmless little bishop.

I was conducted by elevator to the second floor of the White House and then to a wide corridor which was arranged like a hotel lobby or perhaps the biggest drawing room in all the world.

"The suite on the right is the president's private quarters. This one here is the library which is usually the president's private office. On the right is the Yellow Oval room, it's been that since the time of Dolley Madison. The Christmas tree is usually here."

"An admirable and virtuous woman who saved the portrait of George Washington from the perfidious Brits who were about to burn the place down in a characteristic act of Brit barbarism."

That stopped her for a moment.

"At the end," she regained her composure, "we have the Lincoln sitting room and bedroom that is usually reserved these days for married couples . . ."

"No committed partners?"

"We don't ask," she replied primly.

"Ah."

"You will be staying across the hall in the Queens' Bedroom," she informed me, "so-called because five queens have slept there. Also Winston Churchill when he came here for his war meetings with President Roosevelt. Franklin Roosevelt that is."

"Patently . . . If it had been the earlier Roosevelt the visitor would have had to have been Lord Randolph Churchill."

I was showing off. In fact, Winston could have shown up in the era of Alice Blue Gown and the Republican Roosevelts.

"Feel free to use the phone. Just dial the operator and give them the number."

She took her leave, doubtless convinced that my first call would be to the Pope asking for further instructions. It was, however, Milord Cronin who was first informed that the White House was calling, but only after I had checked the walls for possible secret rooms and scanned them for bugs with a little toy that Mike Casey had given me.

"I'm impressed, Blackwood," Sean Cronin said with obvious lack of sincerity.

"Doubtless . . . I am ensconced in the bedroom Winston Churchill used when he was here during the War. I observe that with the exception of myself and the sheets on the bed, nothing is more recent than 1831, including the chandelier over the bed, which might collapse anytime."

"It's a museum, Blackwood. What did you expect? . . . Any emanations yet?"

"Only this orotund English gentleman who just emerged naked from the bathroom smoking a cigar."

"Very funny . . . have you barged into the Oval Office yet?"

"That's my next move. I am also engaged in a campaign to persuade the staff that I am a harmless eccentric."

"I'm not so sure about the adjective . . . Blackwood, I know it is beyond possibility that you look like a bishop as you wander around that place. However, do me a favor and wear a suit jacket instead of your damn White Sox windbreaker."

"The Secret Service call your friend 'Kerryman,' " I offered.

"I don't care what they call him, Blackwood. I want you to get those spooks out of the building. See to it."

The line went dead. Cardinals give orders. Auxiliary bishops carry them out. As Milord had commanded I donned a rumpled jacket which I found in my luggage. It did not, alas, match in color the black of my trousers. However, it would facilitate my storied invisibility.

If you approach the White House from the front, you think it has only two floors. In fact it has four. On the bottom is what can only be called the ground floor through which I had entered (heaven preserve us from suggesting that those ornate rooms with their china and silverware are in a "basement"). It is through this museum that the daily tourists enter to gawk—as I had gawked. Above that is the first floor, the White House of film and story—the East Room at one end and the State Dining Room at the other end and the Red Room, Blue Room, and the Green Room linking them on the south side of the corridor through the cross halls. On the other side one observes the entrance from the North Portico and the staircase down which the president and the first lady, should there be one, enter in solemn procession, accompanied by the distinguished foreign head of state of the moment—with perhaps the Marine Band playing "Ruffles and Flourishes: Hail to the Chief."

The second floor is the location of the Lincoln and the Queens' Bedrooms and the private apartment of the first family and is off-limits to the tourists, who are permitted to visit only the ground and first floors.

You have to peer very closely at the White House to discern the third floor, which was added during the Harding administration to provide extra room and more privacy for the family. It seems to crouch and hide behind the façade so that the observer won't know it's there, spoiling the appearance of the building. Harry Truman, when he rebuilt the White House (gutting the inside and introducing steel-and-concrete beams to hold it up), added a porch over the South Portico, much to the horror of the purists. Behind this porch is the Solarium, which is kind of a TV and dining room for the presidential family. I was told that's where I would eat as long as I was in the White House.

After my conversation with Milord Cronin, I continued my investigation of my room and its surroundings. I did my best not to stumble into something precious or historic lest by knocking it over I strike a severe blow to the nation's budget. I discovered a hidden staircase behind the wall outside my room. One merely pushed a panel of the wall aside and there were the stairs, innocent of dust and cobwebs and other phenomena one would expect in such a staircase. Obviously it wasn't very secret. Perhaps a president merely ducked into it and fled to his own suite when he wanted to escape for a few moments.

Not that the Secret Service would let him escape for even a few seconds.

I walked down the stairs and emerged around the corner from the East Room, where all the big parties occur. A Secret Service agent glanced at me, saw my magic talisman and nodded. I asked for directions to the West Wing.

As everyone who owns a television in the United States today knows, the nation is not really governed from the White House (the "Residence" as it's known) but from the West Wing, which is connected to the White House by the West Portico, inside of which is the zoo occupied by the media and outside of which there is a covered walkway along the Rose Garden and into the environs of the Oval Office. There were no roses blooming in February.

I entered the West Wing through a door at the end of the portico and promptly attracted the attention of two Secret Service men. They noted my talisman, smiled, and said, "Good afternoon, Bishop Ryan. The Oval Office is that way. Ms. Chan will take care of you."

I thanked them for their unnecessary graciousness and walked down the corridor into a series of small rooms that looked like the antechambers of a successful physician's office. Hardly anyone seemed to be aware of my passage until I arrived at the office of the president's secretary, an Asian-American woman with lovely eyes and a broad if opaque smile.

"Good afternoon, Bishop Ryan," she said with solemnity that would be appropriate if I were a chief of state. "You may go right in. The president is expecting you."

I thereupon entered the Oval Office, the political epicenter of the world. Given the number of times I had seen it on television it was a bit of an anticlimax.

The president of the United States, in a blue blazer, was sitting behind his desk, hunched over a couple of sheets of paper. Standing near him, but at a respectful distance, was a shapely woman with long black hair.

"I note with interest, Jack," I announced my presence, "that this place is a passable imitation of the set of your friend Martin Sheen's television program."

"Blackwood!" He erupted from his presidential chair and embraced me. "I hear you've been terrorizing my staff. It's great to see you!"

Such embraces are not fashionable among South

Side Irish Catholic males. The president of the United States, I thought to myself, is in deep trouble if he is so eager to see Sean Cronin's lowly sweeper, very deep trouble.

4

Jack McGurn, the **New York** Times had solemnly pontificated, was an accidental president. The good, gray *Times* as it is often called (I would call it the mean, gray times) added that he should act like he was aware of that fact. This was hardly a fair summary of the extraordinary circumstances that had brought him from his home on Longwood Drive to public housing on Pennsylvania Avenue. I would have preferred the adjective "providential," but I was obviously biased. Whatever adjective you might choose, his election was a surprise, so much a surprise that some Republicans demanded a national recount.

The Democrats had held their convention at the end of August in Chicago in honor of the new Millennium Park or at least I think that was the reason, although their candidate, Alabama Senator W. Robert Harris ("Billy Bob") had won the nomination in the spring primaries. Billy Bob, a mellifluous-voiced, white-haired, old-school populist, was as smooth as a water moccasin. He promised to restore the old Democratic coalition. He stood for all the right things—racial and gender equality, respect for the environment, improvement in education, the importance of unions, globalization of trade, protection of social

security, quality medical care for the elderly. Yet
somehow he seemed like a throwback to an earlier
era—or a bad imitation of the late Colonel Sanders
of Kentucky Fried Chicken. He won the primaries
because no other Democrat seemed to want the nomination.

The pundits said that his ability to bring the South
back into the Democratic camp would compensate
for his failure to appeal to the big-city Democrats
who had nowhere else to go anyway. Moreover, his
geniality would make him a "likeable" candidate.
Nonetheless, in the weeks before the convention, he
lagged behind the incumbent in the polls.

His only opposition came from a more "liberal"
candidate, Congressperson (sic) Eugenie Cruz of
California, a blond California surfer type whose
much noted "sex appeal" escaped me. It was understood that Billy Bob would choose her for his vice
presidential nominee. I was informed by one of our
political correspondents in Chicago that she was
given to towering temper tantrums and "moderate"
usage of "recreational drugs."

"No one will say anything about it because she is
a Latino and a woman."

"Until the Republicans find out," I had muttered.
Oddly they never did.

One afternoon that August, as I was poring over
the latest report on the Cathedral finances, the Megan buzzed me, "Bishop Ryan, Deirdre is on the
line."

The governor's elder daughter called the Cathedral so often that the Megan did not need to identify
her in more detail.

"Father Ryan."

"Bishop Blackie, you entirely have to like tell my daddy that he totally has to accept the vice presidential nomination."

"It has been offered to him?" I asked with some surprise. Perhaps "Ole Billy Bob" had more political smarts than I thought he had.

"That extreme terrible man with his cheap cologne was in our suite here at the Hilton for two hours, like trying to talk Daddy into it. He goes the ticket needs balance."

"Indeed! And your father is expressing some doubts."

"He goes he just doesn't want to do it. Like, Bishop Blackie, it will take his mind off Mom."

Typical girl child: her father's happiness mattered far more than a victory for the party.

"Does he want to talk to me?"

"I think so . . ."

"Blackwood? . . . The kids are trying to talk me into this, I don't really trust Billy Bob. Too much cornpone. I don't want to be vice president, much less president."

"What do the valiant young women argue?"

"They say their mother would insist."

Ah, from the grave Ellen would have the final word. The die was already cast.

"Would she have?"

Silence.

"I suppose so."

"Would she be right?"

Sigh.

"I suppose so."

Jack's acceptance speech was the high point of the convention, a comic masterpiece that should have told the nation that he was a very dangerous man. The Republicans, he warned, had never met a rich businessman for whom they didn't feel sorry. Nor could they overcome their deep compassion for tobacco companies and gun dealers. They wanted to protect the lumber industry, he suggested, from the incursion of gray wolves. They were eager to provide tax credits for those who owned mansions on the shores of the oceans so they could rebuild their homes farther inland before global warming inundated them. They thought it would be wise public policy to protect the mining companies from toxic waste—that is from suits based on the harm done by arsenic poisoning and other toxic chemicals. They had done such a wonderful job of being compassionate to the wealthy and to big business that they deserved every single vote from all those who earned more than ten million dollars a year.

There were complaints from the GOP spinmasters that he was stirring up class conflict. Yep, Jack replied, conflict between those who earn ten million dollars a year and those who earn twenty million.

Jay Leno asked him the following week who wrote his material.

"My younger daughter Granne tells me which jokes are too yucky."

"What does she think of my material?" Jay asked.

"She says that your jokes are all kind of yucky, but it's all right because they're for grown-ups with a yucky sense of humor."

There was only a slight "bounce" for the Democrats in the postconvention polls. They were still twenty points behind. However, while only 60 percent of Americans knew enough about Jack McGurn to have an opinion of him, two-thirds of that half had positive thoughts about him. "He makes us laugh," *USA Today* quoted a response from a woman in Canton, Ohio.

That should have been a warning too.

"We're not going to win, Blackwood," he told me on the phone. "This guy won't fly north of the Mason-Dixon line. But we'll have fun."

The national media were not happy with the choice. They had committed themselves heavily to Genie—a divorced "single mother" with "interests" in oil and real estate and a rich lover whom she had married early in the primaries. The *Washington Post* observed, "Though Senator Harris's health is reputedly excellent, one would worry that a political hack of the Daley machine and a man with an odd sense of humor and a year and half experience as governor of Illinois would be only a heartbeat away from the Oval Office."

A tidal wave of journalists descended on our city to "investigate" Jack McGurn (the title "Machine Gun" had yet to be added). They didn't find much of anything other than that he was a precinct captain for the Daley "machine." Jack didn't deny the charge. "I am proud that I was a tiny cog in the most effective municipality in America," he says with a grin and a wink.

Nor could they find much wrong with his year and a half as governor of Illinois other than to suggest that he was a "satrap" for Rich Daley. The latter worthy observed that he didn't think he had ever won an argument with Jack McGurn and that he didn't believe anyone else had either.

They covered the death of his wife over with the

snide observation that she had been the one with the political fire in her belly. All they could discover about the children is that they had no record of arrests for drunk driving or possession of narcotics or anything else. A Notre Dame classmate (gender unspecified) described Deirdre, accurately enough, as "cool, sexy, and a hell of a good golfer."

They missed completely the implications of the political miracle Jack had worked in winning the Illinois election.

He named his son Sean Patrick, two years out of Notre Dame with a degree in communications, as his press secretary, Conrad Ward, a professional political operative from New York, as his campaign manager, Tommy Horan, his chief of staff from Springfield (and from the Nineteenth Ward in Chicago), as his communications director, Jesus Maria Lopez, a Latino state senator, as chief of staff and counsel, and Mary Elizabeth Chan, from the north (Chinese-American) end of Rich Daley's Eleventh Ward, as his administrative assistant.

Before he could name anyone else, a rumor leaked from Mobile that the United States Attorney for southern Alabama was targeting Billy Bob Harris in an investigation of use of government money to support two mistresses. The U.S. Attorney had been investigating Senator Harris for months, it was said. Nothing more than an accident that he was asking a grand jury for an indictment the week after the Democratic convention.

Billy Bob blustered to no avail. The Mobile office leaked like the *Titanic* just before it went under. The principal witness against him was one of the two mistresses, who was jealous of the other. She was also the financial manager of his office, who diverted the government funds to his personal account.

The Democratic Party went into free fall.

When the National Committee gathered to select a new nominee on the Labor Day weekend, they were warned by the media that only Genie Cruz had a chance of winning. Moreover, they said, it was time for a woman. Those who knew a bit about her sex life were not so sure. Rich Daley was alleged to have pointed out to his colleagues that Jack McGurn was a winner, a characteristic that appealed at least to those Democrats who were interested in more than moral victories.

He captured the nomination, which was instantly pronounced "worthless," by a four-vote majority. Genie was given the vice presidency unanimously. She made it clear that she would run her own vice-presidential campaign, implicitly a dress rehearsal for her own presidential campaign in four years. It was whispered in my ear that Jack was delighted that he didn't have to put up with her.

"What do you think, Punk?" my sister Mary Kathleen Ryan Murphy asked as we watched the manic exchanges between anchorpersons at Grand Beach on Labor Day.

"All the wise people are saying that the nomination is worthless."

"They're idiots . . . I think I'm going to select my dress for the Inaugural Ball next week."

"I will tell that to the candidate. He will be reassured."

One notes that she didn't push her question about what I thought, as the point in that was to create an opportunity to tell me what she thought. I did not, however, disagree with her assessment.

So, on the Tuesday after Labor Day, Machine Gun Jack McGurn (the media had discovered the legend from Chicago's past) began his seven-week presidential campaign, down twenty-seven points in the polls.

His ideas in his first press conference were standard Democratic material. On the day of his inauguration he would reinstate all the executive orders about the environment and the workplace that the other side had rescinded, tax rebates for college education, the right to sue Medicare, some kind of health insurance for everyone, end of the second Cold War ("Republicans feel like they've lost their clothes if they are not muscling other countries around"), more concern about global warming etc. etc.

He also produced two new programs: rein in the Supreme Court and make everyone pay for social security, no matter how much money they made. Every dollar of income, he insisted, should be taxed for social security. If the cut off at $85,000 were abolished, then the Social Security Trust Fund would never run out of money. Would this raise taxes for the rich? They benefited from the social peace that Social Security made possible, they should pick up some of the tab. Moreover, he advocated eliminating payroll tax on all those earning less than $25,000 a year. He went into detail about the growing concentration of wealth in the country during the last quarter century and argued that the Social Security reform would level the playing field a little bit but not come near restoring the balance of 1975, in which there was still too much concentration of wealth.

"Will this hurt the very rich?" he asked rhetorically. "Not all that much. In fact they won't feel it at all, though they may complain like a kid who has lost her first baby tooth."

Then the Supreme Court. In our system of checks and balances, there was no check on the Supreme Court. In the interest of fairness some of the Court's power had to be taken away from them. "They are, after all, only nine lawyers. We know enough about lawyers to know that they are not to be trusted with absolute power. They play word games with the law, which is great fun, as I have reason to know, but someone should be able to say to them, if the law says that, the law is a fool! I don't want to tie the Supreme Court justices to the bottom of Lake Michigan—well I might make an exception for Mr. Justice Scalia and tie him to the bottom of the Lake—I just want to permit a vote of fourth-fifths of the House and four-fifths of the Senate to reverse a decision and to limit their terms to twelve years. Both of these reforms will require a constitutional amendment. Since that requires a fair amount of time, Mr. Justice Scalia won't have to invest in wire cutters just yet."

Milord Cronin was watching the press conference in his suite along with his sister-in-law Nora Cronin.

"Can anyone be more Chicago than Jack McGurn?" she asked. "Pure, unadulterated, quintessential Chicago."

"South Side Chicago," the Cardinal agreed. "Not civilized like we West Siders, right Blackwood?"

"No West Sider," I remarked, "would be crazy enough to try such a game."

"You think he will lose, Blackie?" the charming Nora asked.

"My sister, the virtuous Mary Kathleen, has already purchased her gown for the Inaugural, a sure portent of victory."

"As good a sign as any," Milord agreed.

He presented both proposals with charm and laughter; the light touch would mark his whole campaign. They got attention, lots of attention and lots of rage. The Chief Justice condemned him as wanting to destroy the constitution. He replied he just wanted to provide the Chief Justice with some well-earned retirement time. The Republicans condemned him as a socialist and he laughed.

He also promised that there would be no attack ads and no dirty tricks from his campaign. "I'd rather lose than do that," he said.

"Do you think you have a chance to win?" a reporter asked him.

"I am going to win," he replied firmly.

"He really thinks he's going to win!" the Cardinal said to me.

"Arguably."

"You think he'll beat these idiots?"

I had avoided any commitments on the subject.

"Not if the world comes to an end before Election Day."

He had drawn attention to himself and his proposals. He had made Machine Gun Jack McGurn the issue in the campaign. It was a risky tactic but, "Hell, Blackwood, we're down more than twenty points. Let them run against me."

The strategy behind the tactic was that the Democrats didn't need the "Crackers and the Cowboys to win" (though he never said that). They needed merely to carry the states Gore carried and Ohio "in case they steal Florida again." It was the same strategy that had elected him governor of Illinois two years before—carry the city and the immediate suburbs, break even in the collar counties, and sweep the Asians and the Latinos and the Blacks. It was a simple and elementary strategy that you didn't have to be a political genius to figure out. The Northeast, the North Central, and the Pacific Coast were solidly Democratic. Spend all your campaign time in your strongholds—and carry Ohio and Pennsylvania.

The "Daughters" lined up behind him at the press conference, ready if necessary to do battle to protect him. However, they managed to control their fierce loyalties during the campaign and to appear as nice, sweet, if witty, young women and not as the adorable smart-asses they really were.

"Do you think your father ought to remarry, Deirdre?"

"My daddy's too old to date. I think he ought to become a monk. Wouldn't that be extreme cool? A man in brown habit and sandals with rattling rosary beads wandering around the White House?"

"Are you serious, Deirdre?"

"Like totally. I'm always serious. Really, we want our daddy to be happy. Didn't God say that it was not good for a man to be alone?"

"Well, guys," said the candidate, "that's enough burning gasoline for this morning. We're now off on the yellow brick road!"

The daughters promptly began to sing "We're off to see the Wizard, the wonderful Wizard of Oz."

His whole makeshift staff joined in. It became the

theme song of what a seasoned political commentator called, "the most unusual political campaign in American history—and perhaps the most ingenious."

A reporter asked Sean Patrick about, "Your father's schedule."

That red-bearded young giant replied with the family's genial smile, "Let's call him 'the candidate', just so we look respectable."

Machine Gun Jack had virtually no money, a skeleton staff, and not much time. At first there were no crowds to listen to him either. Then the crowds began to show up, if only to listen to the jokes. As he crisscrossed the country in a dizzy and almost aimless fashion, he rode trains, trailers, riverboats, barges, and even a windjammer. He appeared on every local TV program that would have him. He played basketball with his three kids, he and Granne against the other two. Granne had, as he said, "the best jump shot of any going-on fourteen-year-old woman in the country. I hope she gets a scholarship to Notre Dame because I'll be paying off this campaign debt for the next thirty years."

"Genie Cruz," Deirdre complained to me in an e-mail, "is an extreme bitch. Daddy is totally nice to her. She pretends that he doesn't exist. Everyone says she's running for president four years from now after Daddy gets swept away by a tsunami—that's a tidal wave. I don't thing she's sexy at all, despite her phony blond hair and her horrid makeup. She never mentions him. She didn't show up twice when they were supposed to do joint appearances. Daddy just laughs. He's like hell hath no fury . . . And I'm who scorned her and he laughs again. But that's Daddy."

The candidate was hoarse and weary when he

called me just before the first debate to ask what I thought about the campaign.

I replied to him as I had to Milord Cronin.

"You will win if the world does not come to an end before Election Day."

He laughed like he used do before Ellen died.

"Wait till I tell the Daughters that!"

The Republicans at first flatly refused to debate him because, as they said, "he's a comedian, not a serious candidate."

"They don't understand us Irish," Jack replied. "The more we laugh, the more serious we are."

He won over the working press in the first two weeks. First thing every morning there was a press conference (before cameras of course) at which no one tried to protect him from the tough questions. He managed to finesse quite a few with a joke—"I don't know where Ms. Cruz is today. I do know that she's a veteran campaigner and I have complete trust in her political judgment. If any of you find out where she is, let me know. I don't want to bumble into her territory.

"My daughters have a leave of absence from Notre Dame and St. Praxides, though Granne has to be back for the basketball season. They're on the phone every night with their friends—on my credit card."

Moreover, he never developed a standard campaign speech. He had something new and different to say every day. The working journalists smelled good copy when they encountered it. Machine Gun Jack was good copy.

Two weeks into the campaign, he had cut the Republican lead to seventeen percentage points. The editorial writers began to call for three serious debates between the presidential candidates. The Republicans didn't want to do it, but their surveys and their focus groups warned them that the voters were unhappy over the stonewall. Perhaps they would have been much wiser to ignore the focus groups. Jack had no surveys of his own and no focus groups. He merely followed his instincts.

The Republican spinmasters said that it was impossible to have a serious discussion with Mr. McGurn because he was evasive and hid behind his jokes.

"They mean I'm Irish," the candidate replied. "We never say what we mean and never mean what we say."

Despite the charm and the jokes and the laughter—or rather inside them—he was deadly serious. Moreover, his years in the classroom had made him a superb teacher. Just as he had in Illinois between the jokes, he summarized concisely and fairly the major issues, giving the Republican argument a clear and accurate brief.

"Maybe if I lose I can get a job as one of their speechwriters."

So finally there were to be three debates, one at the end of September, one halfway through October, and one at the end of October. Jack refused to take time away from his campaign to practice for the debate.

"I'm a lawyer. I think better when I don't know what I'm going to say than when I do know."

"Is that not reckless, sir?" asked a reporter.

"It's not like I'm taking the bar exam."

The day of the first debate he was twelve percentage points down. In three weeks he'd cut the Republican lead in half.

He was charming and gracious during the debate, deferring to the other candidate politely on every possible occasion. The jokes were even more gentle and there weren't very many of them. He was establishing that despite his wit he had the intelligence and maturity to be president.

"Do you have the gravity, Mr. McGurn, to sit in the Oval Office?"

"Well I've put on five pounds in three weeks during the campaign, so I'll have more gravity than I used to. I've been a trial lawyer, a member of an ongoing committee with Russian lawyers, I've even learned their language, just as I've learned Spanish, I've taught school, I've been a governor and according to most people a pretty good one, I've raised three presentable children, I've lost the love of my life. I'll let the voters decide how grave I am. I can only promise that I will not stop laughing. As G. K. Chesterton might have said, the great Gaels of Ireland are the men that God made mad, all their campaigns are merry and all their songs are sad."

The spinmasters said that he had not established himself as the kind of man the American people would trust in the Oval Office. But the people, according to the polls, thought he had won the debate.

The phone rang in the Cardinal's suite right after the debate.

I picked it up because the Cardinal was standing on his feet in front of the television, a glass of Evian water in his hand, as if he thought Jack McGurn could hear his encouragement.

"The president is on the phone, Bishop Blackie," the relevant Megan informed me.

"The president wants to talk to you," I told the Cardinal, handing him the phone. "Megan said it was the president."

Arguably he wanted to talk to me. Yet encouragement from the major priest in his life had more clout, even if he were from the West Side.

"You creamed him!" the Cardinal shouted.

Jack McGurn was now only nine percentage points down.

"Peaking too early," the pundits said.

"I only got a month left," he said. "June is too early, not October."

On the strength of the debate the money and the help began to pour in. Various experts volunteered to join his staff, including a China expert from Stonybrook named Marianna Genovesa.

"She's like totally cool, Bishop Blackie," Deirdre assured me, on their nightly phone call. "She played basketball at Columbia."

"She helped me improve my jump shot," Granne added.

"We like her a lot."

"Does she know anything about China?"

"Who knows?"

"Who cares!"

The little demons had targeted her as a potential stepmother. I thought for a moment that I should warn them, then realized that I would be wasting my time.

The second debate may have been the turning point. The other side, the media reported, were ready to play hardball against Machine Gun Jack.

To which Jack replied that he hoped the pitches were high and fast.

The theme of the attack was that Jack was a "liberal." He opposed the death penalty, he favored abortion, he had visited Cuba and wanted to surrender to them, he was soft on China and Russia and North Korea, he wanted to tax and spend. Same old liberal nonsense. The American people were tired of tax-and-spend liberals.

He smiled affably and admitted that he was indeed a liberal. Liberal meant free. The American political tradition was liberal. He believed strongly in freedom for Blacks, for American Indians, for Hispanics, for immigrants, for poor people, for those who did not have health insurance, for those who weren't rich businessmen, for gay and lesbian people. He thought most Americans were liberal in those matters too. He did not advocate massive tax increases, he did not believe in solving problems by throwing money at them. He visited Cuba to find out what it was like, a nasty Communist police state. He would negotiate with Castro only if he was willing to permit free elections and no one should hold their breath till that happened.

Somehow the Republicans had managed to stack the audience with their people. They cheered enthusiastically after each point apparently made against Jack.

"They're playing all the old tunes," Milord Cronin snorted irritably as we watched the debate on the vast TV screen in his suite. "They must be desperate."

"Arguably," I agreed, more worried than I was willing to let on.

Then came the explosion.

A tall man with white hair rose and asked a question in Russian.

Jack didn't miss a beat.

"I'll translate that. He asked about future relations between America and Russia."

Then he launched into a brief answer in Russian.

"I told him that I thought that the relations between our two great countries could and should be much more relaxed and friendly than they are now."

The other candidate lost it.

"You've violated the rules of the debate by planting that question," he shouted. "You wanted to show the American people that you could speak a few words in Russian. I won't permit this debate to continue unless you apologize for breaking the rules."

The distant early warning flashed in Jack's eyes. I was afraid he might lose it too.

"I did not plant the question, sir," he said affably. "I gave strict orders to my staff never to do that. If they did, I will dismiss the one responsible. I am sorry if you're offended."

"That's not enough!"

"I'd ask you then to consider the possibility that someone on your staff planted the question to show that I really can't speak Russian. All that our little exchange showed is that my Russian grammar and accent need a lot of improvement."

Then the quick, self-deprecating grin.

"He's got him!" Sean Cardinal Cronin crowed like Notre Dame had won in the last seconds.

"Patently."

"We don't have to hide behind tricks and shallow humor!" the other candidate sputtered.

"I didn't think I was hiding behind the humor. I thought rather that I was showing the risks of electing a crazy Mick . . . However, it's up to you, sir. If you want to end the debate, it's your call."

The other candidate realized that he was blowing it.

"You're soft on Russia, you sympathize with the former Communists who are in charge now. You don't want to build a missile defense system. You want to pour millions of dollars of taxpayer's money into boosting their failing economy!"

"Russia is an ancient country with a rich cultural tradition and a profound religious faith," Jack said easily, now the political science professor. "Much to everyone's surprise, it broke free fifteen years ago from a terrible oppression which the Russian people never accepted. Since then, they've made their share of mistakes. On the whole, however, they have also made, all things considered, remarkable progress. In our work with the Russian-American Lawyers Group, my late wife and I were astonished at how open and eager they were to learn about the art of sustaining a civil society. They also had some of the same lawyers' jokes we have, which shows either that they surf the same net we do or that lawyers are incorrigible everywhere in the world. They're good people, not our enemies. We will have disagreements, but we have so much in common with one another that I see no reason why we should enjoy pushing them around or trying to intimidate them. Moreover, I haven't recommended any foreign aid legislation for Russia. I think informal, private initiatives like our lawyers group are much more effective."

"That just proves you're a soft-headed liberal!"

"Maybe only soft-hearted."

"He just won the election," Milord Cronin exulted.

"Arguably."

After the end of the debate the spin doctors went crazy. The Republicans insisted that their candidate had come out fighting mad and had won the slugfest. Our guys asked what all the rage was about. The press dug quickly and deeply into the twin issues of the crowd and the question. All the evidence suggests that the Republicans had planted the question to embarrass Jack—and had not told the candidate so he would have "deniability." A couple of their "operatives" had "requisitioned" more than their share of tickets. The candidate heatedly denied both charges and insisted that he had broken through the fog of silliness to nail Jack on serious matters.

"Well," said Jack, "I guess that means I've scared them a little . . . In the old days in Chicago we called it 'the voice from the sewers.' "

The polls show that the people (or those who had tuned in) thought by 70 percent that Jack had won but were still dubious about his "lack of experience."

The Republican lead had fallen to five percentage points where it hovered up to and after the third debate, a lackluster duel. The last few percentage points would prove the hardest. The race had to look "dead even" the pundits told us all for Jack to have a chance of winning. The "American people" would not vote for a candidate who looked like a loser.

Then, during the last week before the election, the polls turned volatile. Some showed the Republican lead rising to eight percentage points and others claimed that it had fallen to three points. One pollster said the magic words "It's dead even."

The Republicans responded with the mother of all attack ads. Its argument was that Jack was a Socialist and personally corrupt. He wanted to soak the rich and spread it out thin. Rich Daley's image was in the ad as much as Jack's. "Do the American people want the Daley organization running the country?"

Jack refused to take it seriously.

"That was a line from Huey P. Long, who was governor of Louisiana when Roosevelt was president," he said. "I'm surprised that anyone over there remembers it. They want to soak the middle class and spread it out thick on the rich . . . I'm sure Rich Daley is grateful for all the free advertising, but it's my campaign not his!"

Yet the talking heads on PBS hailed the ad as a "masterpiece" of its genre and observed that it had stabilized the GOP lead where it belonged, "about 4 percent."

A reporter cornered Sean Cronin coming out of the Chancery and demanded to know whether he would condemn Jack McGurn before the election.

"Why?" Milord drew himself up to his full six-foot-two frosty height.

"Because he supports abortion."

"He does not."

"Will he sign a bill forbidding partial birth abortions?"

"He said he would if such a bill passed Congress, a most unlikely event after the way the Court slapped down the previous attempt."

"He has not promised to appoint only judges who are committed to reversing *Roe v. Wade?*"

"He has promised to appoint good judges. I fail to see how he can do anything else. Fortunately or unfortunately *Roe v. Wade* is not going to be reversed."

"Do you think Jack McGurn will go to hell?"

"No, but I think you might for asking that question."

Back at the Cathedral Rectory he asked, "I suppose you saw the clip, Blackwood?"

"Indeed."

"And?"

"You could not have done better if I had been there to advise you."

He snorted and strode away down the corridor.

Jack continued his reckless dash back and forth around the country—Boston, New York, Cleveland, Columbus, Philadelphia, Pittsburgh, Detroit, St. Louis, Los Angeles, and even Miami all in one exhausting day.

"We're thinking of a side trip to Paris," Deirdre cracked to the exhausted reporters. "And then maybe Timbuktu!"

The press weighed in with its endorsements, as if what they said made any difference. Jack garnered only a few, from prestigious smaller papers like the *St. Petersburg Times*. Except for the *Wall Street Journal*, which damned him as the weakest political candidate since Benjamin Harrison, the editorials tended to take the high road. "An interesting man," the *New York Times* admitted "but lacking in the necessary experience." The *Chicago Tribune* seemed to think that it was their hated enemy Rich Daley who was running for president.

The polls remained stable until Friday morning, when they turned volatile again. The Republicans claimed that their polls showed that they would win by ten percentage points. One of the major polls showed them ahead by eight. The others trailed off towards "dead even."

Jack commented that he would wait for the voters to decide on Tuesday.

The Republican spinmasters repeated relentlessly the themes of inexperience, liberalism, corruption, not serious. Jack's people were too exhausted to reply.

He spun around the country again on Sunday.

That night, home in Chicago, he ad-libbed his final fifteen minutes on national television, most of which was a voice-over on scenes taken from his life.

"Wait till you see it, Father Blackie," Deirdre told me. "Dr. Genovesa helped me and Granne do it. Like totally awesome."

"I thought she was the Old China Hand?"

"Huh? . . . Oh, you mean an expert on China . . . Yeah, but she like had a minor in film at Columbia."

"People tell me that the public doesn't know who I am," Jack began with his Jimmy Cagney wink. "I thought I had made a fool of myself enough in this campaign so that they'd have no doubt. Anyway I'm going to talk about politics while on the screen you'll see enough pictures of me to make you forget that I'm a retired professor of political science.

As Jack summarized the issues of the campaign, succinctly and cogently, we saw him on the screen as a baby over whose head a very young Sean Cronin was pouring water, a toddler taking his first steps, at his First Communion, throwing a football in an eighth grade game against the hated enemies from St. Titus parish to the south of us, in his Notre Dame graduation robes with the Golden Dome glittering in the background. Ellen appeared for the first time in that picture and the nation grabbed for its handkerchief. She was so young, so pretty, and so bright through all the rest of the pictures that her death ate our hearts all over again. Then there were a few campaign shots, mostly of the candidate and his kids playing basketball, and finally of the first time the kids sang the Wizard song. The singing interrupted Jack's final sentences. He just lowered his head and listened as a crowd in the Daley Civic Center Plaza bellowed it out and the program ended. Not everyone in the country, I suspect, put away their handkerchiefs.

I wondered if they had shown him the tape beforehand. Probably not.

Would Ellen have approved of the exploitation of her tragic death?

Is the Pope Catholic?

I now had not the slightest doubt that he would win.

The next day the campaign spun around the country, beginning very early in the morning in Miami.

"Florida is not going to let them steal it this time!" Jack thundered to a tremendous dawn crowd. He appeared on the *Today* show and even braved the absurdity of Regis. Then he went across the country and back to Chicago. Here in the middle of evening of a gentle November day, he boarded a cruiser in Jackson Park and proceeded north along the Lake Shore to a glittering display of fireworks. He disembarked at the Michigan Avenue Bridge over the river and led a torchlight parade up the Magnificent Mile and then over to State Street, back to Michigan south of the river and then to the new band shell in the Millennium Park, where he entertained a cheering crowd for fifteen minutes. His opening line was "I want to thank the mayor personally for finishing this Millennium Park and band shell just in time for my campaign."

He was up at dawn to vote in the public school building across from St. Prax's, then raced downtown for an election-morning interview on *Good Morning America.*

"Still running, Mr. McGurn?" the interviewer asked.

"Can't help myself!" he said hoarsely.

"What do think about the polls taken last night?"

"I was shouting in the park last night, so I didn't hear about them. What do they say?"

"That you've caught up and that the momentum is on your side."

"Really?" he raised an eyebrow.

"Really."

"Maybe I should start to worry."

"About losing?"

"About winning."

We gathered that night in the big old Victorian house on Longwood Drive, his family, and friends, the inevitable Tommy Horan, and a harmless auxiliary bishop. The candidate himself was exhausted and silent, as were his children. The rest of the campaign staff was down at the Conrad Hilton, waiting for the results.

The early returns in the Northeast showed that Jack McGurn was doing well in most precincts, "as was to be expected," said the commentators.

Because of the fuss over the election in which the

Election News Service had correctly predicted the election of Al Gore, the predictions in the various states and in the nation as a whole were to be postponed till after the voting stopped in California. The commentators were supposed to be in the dark, but of course they weren't.

"Governor McGurn," one of them said, "is likely to carry many of the same states that the Democrats have carried in recent presidential elections. This will not be enough necessarily to win, but it does guarantee another close outcome."

Profound.

A phone, not the direct line to the Hilton, in another room rang ominously.

"You'd better get it, Sean Patrick." The candidate sighed.

A few moments later, Sean returned.

"It's our friend."

Jack forced himself out of the chair. "I guess I have to talk to him."

Someone with access to the exit polls. The silence of a wake descended on the room.

Tommy Horan raised an eyebrow. "What do you predict, Bishop Blackie?"

"Big!" I said.

He grinned slightly, the only facial expression he normally permitted.

"Yeah!"

Jack McGurn returned and sank into the easy chair.

"Well, Daddy?" Deirdre demanded.

"Hmn? . . . Oh, he said we won."

The Daughters jumped out of their chairs, high-fived one another, ran to embrace their father.

"How much?" Tommy Horan asked calmly as the room erupted in cheers.

"Pretty big. They say maybe four hundred electoral votes, though that seems too much. Good-size Democratic majorities in Congress. I don't know . . ."

Everyone rushed to embrace and to call him "Mr. President." Naturally the Daughters beat them all in saying it.

"Shall we call downtown, Mr. President, and tell them?" Tommy asked.

"Better not," Jack came alive again when faced with a political decision. "Someone might slip, and we'd be accused of trying to influence the California vote."

Then he turned to me, and murmured, "Blackwood, I never thought it would happen."

A jolly warrior on the outside and a fatalist on the inside. How very Irish.

Slowly the number of red states on the maps began to increase as the early returns began to pile up. The networks moved back and forth among the four campaign headquarters. Genie Cruz's crowd in Los Angeles seemed to be anything but delighted about what was happening.

"They'd better work on the joy of victory a little harder," the putative president-elect said. "People might get the idea she wanted to lose!"

We all laughed. Though the media folk never mentioned it, they all knew that this race was Genie's dress rehearsal for the next time. Now she was going to be stuck in the vice presidency for four and probably eight years.

Down at the Hilton, "Senator" Jesus Lopez, who

needed only the cape to look like Zorro, was smiling brightly.

"We're elated at the early returns," he said with just the right touch of a Latino accent. "However, we don't want to say anything until the California polls close. It will be a long night."

At one minute after eleven all four networks pronounced John Patrick McGurn as the winner with 54 percent of the popular vote and perhaps four hundred electoral votes.

Jesus could hardly be heard over the uproar of the Hilton crowd singing about the yellow brick road. Nor did his enormous smile require any words.

"We won!" he shouted over the din. "They said we couldn't and we did."

At the Republican headquarters the scene was somber, grim.

"We do not believe in exit polls," said the spokesman. "We will defer judgment until there are more actual returns."

"Will the candidate have anything to say tonight?"

"I hardly think so. Our information is that returns are close enough in perhaps a dozen states for us to ask for recounts."

Our bunch shouted their disdain at the television screen.

"Sir?" Tommy asked the president-elect.

"I think we'd better take a ride down there and talk to our people," he said.

"To claim victory?"

Jack McGurn's smile had returned.

"More or less."

The whole neighborhood had crowded onto

Longwood Drive to shout congratulations and sing about the "Wonderful Wizard of Here."

The red eyes of the television camera and the klieg lights turned the Beverly night into daylight.

"Are you going to claim victory, Mr. President?" a reporter shouted.

"Wait and see!"

Our bunch piled into the four Secret Service limos. All except the invisible auxiliary bishop, who disappeared into the night.

"He's coming on now!" Milord Cronin cautioned as I entered his study.

The crowd in the Hilton shouted for at least five minutes while Jack held up his hands like the prizefighter he might have been in an earlier era. Finally, the crowd calmed down.

"The Republican bastards are claiming vote fraud all over the country. They are refusing to concede," Sean Cronin protested.

"I've been advised," the putative president-elect said with a broad grin, "not to claim victory until the other side gets around to conceding . . ."

Cries of complaint!

"All I'm going to tell you is that we've won!"

More cheering.

"I understand their point," he went on. "They were sure they had it sewed up. Now they can't believe they've lost. They have every right to ask for recounts, though they weren't ready to let us have them not so long ago . . ."

Boos.

"They can have all the recounts they want. We will not contest them, though local Democrats might want to. I assure all of you that we've won, and even my good friend Nino Scalia can't steal this one from us!"

Cheers and sustained applause.

"I want to thank all of you here and all the voters around the country who responded to our campaign. You've shown enormous good taste!"

More cheers.

"No words can capture my gratitude to my family, the big redhead here who is the next presidential press secretary, my two gorgeous daughters who will continue to provide insightful criticism every day of my eight years in the White House . . ."

Laugher, applause, and beaming smiles from the Daughters.

"Also, I must report the gratitude of our family to Ellen Fitzgerald McGurn of whose absence and presence we were all aware throughout the campaign. When I considered declining the vice presidential nomination in August—how many centuries ago was that—the Daughters pointed out that their mom would be most displeased with me. They were right as the Daughters usually are. We dedicated the campaign to her. I'm sure she watched over and protected us on our way. We assume that she will continue to do so."

Both the Daughters were sobbing.

The next morning there was the usual press conference on Longwood Drive with the neighborhood all around. Deirdre stood in the background. Granne had already gone back to school.

"Mr. President, when do you expect the other side to concede?"

"I expect that they never will explicitly."

"Does this upset you?"

"No."

"Are you planning a vacation?"

"Certainly not. Tomorrow we're flying to Los Angeles for a joint celebration with the vice president–elect. I'll also want to talk to Martin Sheen about life in the White House. Then we're going on to Seattle and Portland to thank the people in those states. On the way back, we will stop in Tucson and Santa Fe. Then we'll head up to Grand Beach for a long weekend. Next week we'll hit Minneapolis, Des Moines, St. Louis, Indianapolis, Cleveland and Columbus, Detroit, Pittsburgh, Philadelphia, Newark, Boston, and the Big Apple. In the week before Christmas we'll stop in at Moscow, Berlin, Paris, London and, of course, Dublin. Then after the first of the year we'll go to Beijing, Seoul, and Tokyo. Then maybe a few days in Tucson to get ready for the Inaugural."

"Why all the trips, Mr. President?"

"In this country to thank the people that voted for me and in Europe so that the people there will get to know me a little bit."

"How will you fly?"

"Commercial. I don't think they're ready to give me Air Force One. The Secret Service can send along a skeleton crew and work out the security arrangements in the other countries."

"No rest at all?"

"None for the wicked . . . Maybe the kids and I can take a long weekend in Tucson when we get back from Asia."

"What about your transition team? Won't they miss you?"

"I doubt it. There's e-mail and satellite phones."

"You have given some thought to your transition team?"

"Certainly. I have asked Mayor Daley and President Clinton to head up the team. Tommy Horan will be the liaison with my staff."

Consternation.

"Will you offer President Clinton a cabinet level position?"

"I think he'd make a superb secretary of state . . . I haven't asked him yet."

"Do you have any other staff appointments in mind?"

"Of course. Conrad Ward will be my chief of staff, Tommy Horan deputy chief of staff, Jesus Lopez my senior counsel, this big redhead here the press secretary, Mary Elizabeth Chan will continue as my administrative assistant. Claire Jones of the University of Chicago will be my national security advisor; Dr. Marianna Genovesa of the State University of New York will be my advisor on China temporarily. Mae Rosen will be my communications director. Judge Ogden Jefferson will become counselor to the president to head up my antidiscrimination program . . ."

As usual Jack had no notes, he never used notes. The media people must have seen that, but no one commented on it.

"Aren't they mostly from Illinois?"

He raised his eyes as if counting the list.

"Dr. Genovesa is from Brooklyn."

"Who will be the first lady?"

"You mean the first gentlewoman, don't you? I don't have to have one, do I? It isn't in the Constitution, is it? Anyway there's no first gentlewoman in the offing. I have neither plans nor prospects."

"Don't you need a host person?"

Big grin.

"I offered the role to the Daughters. The older one merely said, 'Yucky!' and the younger one said, she'd be glad to do it. That's what the White House needs, a going-on-fourteen-year-old Irish matriarch in training."

"Why the foreign visits before the Inauguration?"

"Why not? The president of the United States, despite the constitutional constraints on his office and his own personal weaknesses, can have an enormous impact on the rest of the world. The folks in Moscow and Berlin and Paris and London didn't get to vote, but I want to reassure them that I'm capable enough and that I want to be friends. They're entitled at least to get a look at me. It will be a very important trip."

It would be a great story on the nightly news and the paper's next day headlines saying "**McGurn to Visit Europe and Asia Before Inaugural.**"

On Thursday morning a spokesman for the other side said that after serious consideration, it had been decided that they would not contest the vote in ten states though there was still ample reason to suppose that they had won in all of those states. Asked by the press whether this was a form of concession, the spokesman replied, "It's as close to one as you'll ever get."

The papers were critical of the president-elect the next morning. Editorials screamed about what Jack "needed" to do to build up confidence in him. They didn't like his all-Illini team either. A couple of the more intelligent analysts offered their readers more than to call his victory the greatest upset since Harry Truman.

"President-Elect McGurn knew very well that all the demographic trends were on his side, most notably the great suburban shift to Democratic voting, the increased voter registration among the minorities. So very cleverly he devoted his brief campaign time to those two groups to assure them that first of all he could win and then that he would do a good job. There is no great mystery about why the Wonderful Wizard successfully ventured down the Yellow Brick Road."

A Republican columnist muttered that "Machine Gun Jack McGurn is the most dangerous political demagogue since Huey P. Long of Louisiana."

The European trip was a huge success, despite the complaints of the editorial writers. He flew the proper airlines—Delta to Moscow, Aeroflot to Berlin, Lufthansa to Paris, Air France to London, BA to Dublin, and Aer Lingus (of course) home. He spoke (in Russian) on Russian TV, and said a few words of greeting in German at Berlin. Deirdre greeted the French people in cautious French in her father's name to wild cheers. M. le President de France kissed her hand, at which ceremony she smiled politely. Later she confided to me, "Bishop Blackie, it was extreme gross."

Even the dyspeptic comments of the anchorpersons about a "magical mystery tour," could not overcome the obvious fact that the folks in the countries he visited loved him.

The Asian trip had to be cut short because of the unrest in China. The reaction in Tokyo was polite, the one in Seoul ecstatic.

"He wouldn't let Marianna come on the trip," Deirdre protested on the phone."

"Marianna?"

"Dr. Genovesa . . . He said that since they were not going to China she was needed in Washington."

"Ah."

The Inaugural celebrations were to be low-key, in keeping with mourning in which the McGurn family was still engaged. The President and the Daughters would show up at only one ball, then return for their first night in the White House.

"Creepy place," Granne whispered in my ear right after Sean Cronin had said his prayer.

Then two days before the Inaugural, Suzy Schmidt and Elaine Walsh, volunteer typists during the final stages of the campaign, filed their sexual harassment suit. "Enough dirt," the *Wall Street Journal* pontificated, "to make one want to vomit all through the vertiginous inauguration ceremonies."

Jack flatly denied the charges, as did everyone on the staff.

"We'll have our day in court," he promised, "and we'll win, and we'll collect enough damages to put an end to these dirty tricks permanently."

"With his two daughters watching everything he did," one anonymous staffer said, "he wouldn't have dared to try it."

Then the military leaders in four central Chinese provinces declared their independence of the Beijing government. Leading Republican senators demanded that the new president intervene on the side of the "rebels."

5

"I'm delighted to meet you, Bishop Ryan." Dr. Genovesa enveloped me in a smile which revealed geniality and flawless teeth. "I believe we have some mutual friends."

She smoothed her long hair. Though she looked like Sophia Loren, she spoke with a hopelessly Brooklyn accent, that marvelous dialect which emerged from Irish-speaking immigrants who settled in Brooklyn and which subsequently engulfed Jewish and Italian immigrants.

With mischievous brown eyes and hands that moved in a constant flow of gestures. Italian from Flatbush, I thought. Hold her hands so she couldn't move them and she would not be able to talk.

She shook hands, having with a flick of an eye noted the absence of a ring.

"Jump shooters," I replied.

"Fierce competitors."

"I wonder where they got it," I concluded the exchange.

Dr. Genovesa, not to put a fine edge on the matter, was a knockout. An unadorned dark brown knit dress left no doubt that she had the disciplined posture and the slender waist of a woman athlete and a body that hinted at postwar Italian actresses.

Her facial expression moved along with her hands from one emotion to the next, all more or less with the same message: "What can I tell ya!"

"Marianna," the president interrupted my speculations about his deputy chief of staff, "is helping me with the finishing touches of a statement on China for the press conference."

"In ten minutes," she added. "We're always on time in the McGurn presidency."

"Sit down for a moment, Blackwood," he said, "We're just about finished, aren't we, Marianna?"

He returned to the presidential chair. She leaned over him.

No chemistry at all, I sighed.

I remembered the "family statement" which Sean Patrick read after Communion in place of a eulogy at Ellen's funeral.

"We stand today in silent grief as we face the will of an incomprehensible God, a God who hides His face all too often to please humans. We understand that any God worth the name is necessarily incomprehensible. Yet as a loving parent He understands the pain and bemusement of His children. He sorrows with us; He weeps with us even though we are too frozen by sadness to weep. Ellen, we know, is with God. She has left us but only temporarily, only for a little while. In the meantime she will still be with us in our memories, in our prayers, and in her watchfulness. In the words of the Liturgy, life is changed, not taken away. Ellen is young again, maybe Deirdre's age. We will be young again; we will all laugh again. Until then we will continue to live with the faith she taught us by word and example."

There was not a dry eye in St. Prax's, except the eyes of the governor and his family.

"You don't think it's too strong?" the president's voice stirred me out of my reverie.

"It has to be strong, Mr. President, if men like Senator Bailey are to understand what you mean."

"Right. Good job, Marianna."

"Thank you, Mr. President."

The portrait of General Washington on the wall to the left of the president's desk fell from the wall.

"There he goes again." Jack sighed.

Dr. Genovesa gracefully picked up the painting and returned it to its place. The glass was undamaged.

"You almost get used to him," she said.

Sometimes the childish personalities that generated poltergeist phenomena were boys, more often girls. There was no point in my making that observation.

"By the way, Blackwood, who was Machine Gun Jack McGurn?"

"Everyone knows," I began my prepared speech, "that Machine Gun Jack McGurn was not his real name and he preferred revolvers to machine guns for his score or so of killings, though machine guns were used at the 1929 St. Valentine's Day massacre in which he may have been involved. He came into the world as Vincenzo Gibaldi. Later he called himself on occasion Vincenzo James and Jimmy Vincent. Why he chose an Irish name is not known though his enemy, George 'Bugs' Moran, was in fact Polish. Many of the Outfit members of those days, for reasons we do not know, liked to have aliases, though such phony names never protected them from the guns of their enemies. Even Al Capone sometimes identified himself as Dr. Albert Brown. McGurn was gunned down in the nineteen thirties while his doting boss Al Capone was in Alcatraz, on February 15, perhaps an allusion to the St. Valentine's Day massacre.

"Like his patron Dr. Albert Brown and most of their group, Machine Gun Jack, Lord have mercy on him, was a Republican. Historically, Republicans have always been involved in stealing things, like elections. The Cicero that they ruled was a Republican town. I'm sure Republicans will resent the implications that you might be related to one of them."

The usual playful smile, leprechaun pondering, raced across his face.

"What do you think, Marianna?"

"Absolutely, Mr. President. Right at the very beginning, even before the swimming pool."

"Great! . . . Blackwood, I've asked Dr. Genovesa to assist you while you're here . . . I'm told you have a tendency to get lost."

"Defamation," I murmured.

"Five minutes to the press conference, Mr. President."

"Yes, ma'am."

"I'll take the bishop to the Corner Room."

"Good idea."

"I'll ask Sean Patrick to pass out copies of this draft with the usual caveat that it's the official statement, even if you present it in slightly altered form."

"Showing off my memory."

"The media are in awe of it, Mr. President."

"Then it doesn't take much to awe them."

"Thank you, Mr. President." She left the office.

The president sank into his chair, leaned forward on the desk, face in his hands.

" 'Yes, Mr. President, No, Mr. President, Whatever you say, Mr. President! Thank you, Mr. President.' They say that to convince themselves that I know what I'm doing. I don't have the foggiest."

"I believe that your predecessor, General Washington, thought that it might be a good idea to call him, 'Your High Mightiness'!"

He laughed wryly. "I'm lost, Blackwood. Lost. What the hell am I doing here?"

"Any one of your recent predecessors who was honest and intelligent, which not all have been, would feel the same way."

"I don't know . . ."

"Beautiful woman," I observed.

He looked up.

"Marianna? I guess so . . . There's one element in my psyche that's not operating, Blackwood, almost like it has been removed by surgery."

"Eros?"

"Good name for it. I hope it never comes back. It can get a man in a lot of trouble."

"So I'm told."

"Women hit on me. I hardly notice. They back off. Marianna doesn't."

"She would hardly need to."

"Blackwood, you're incorrigible!"

He rose from his desk, put his arm around my shoulders, and led me out of the Oval Office. Dr. Genovesa was waiting in Ms. Chan's office, sitting on the edge of the administrative assistant's desk and displaying a delightful expanse of nylon-covered athletic leg.

The Corner Office was adjacent to the Press Briefing Room, in the West Colonnade. A tiny room with eight television screens, it was the office of Sean Patrick McGurn. A couple of computers and a line of press association printers lined the wall; the Rose Garden, now brown and barren, watched from the windows on the other side.

Sean Patrick ambled into the office, a relaxed pirate giant.

"Hi, Bishop Blackie! Good to see you! Double Trouble are coming in this afternoon for the weekend! They'll straighten out all the mess here! . . . The copies are passed out, Marianna . . . Shall we begin the countdown?"

They counted slowly from ten down. At four the president of the United States swept by the office, winked, and plunged into the Briefing Room. Sean Patrick lifted a stopwatch.

"Right on time!"

"Bishop, you could watch from the wings, if you want. There's a TV monitor there."

"Astonishingly similar to the one we see on television," I commented, as we slipped into the space just behind the blue curtains.

She looked at me for a moment, as though she might begin to entertain serious doubts about my sanity, then grinned.

"Good afternoon, gentlepersons. The first issue which we must discuss is my swimming problem."

"Ad lib," Marianna whispered next to me as she rolled her vast brown eyes. "We can't stop him!"

"My doctors have told me that my very life depends on my daily swim. As you may not remember, this room once housed the White House swimming pool, which was built for President Roosevelt, Franklin Roosevelt that is. Indeed when they were excavating below here for the pool, they uncovered the remains of a stable from President Washington's time, gutters and all. So actually we are above the gutters and not in them . . . President Nixon, in a misguided attempt to win favor with your predecessors, filled in the pool and created this room. I think that was a mistake. So it would seem not unreasonable to restore the pool."

Groans from the press.

"I'm sure we could find a much more comfortable place for you over in the Old Executive Office Building, which was once the Executive Office Building, and then in happier times, the State, War, Navy Building. I was thinking perhaps of the Indian Treaty Room."

Cries of protest.

"An alternative would be to develop the pool that President Ford caused to be built on the South Lawn. We could put one of those fabric tents over it, pump in hot air, of which there is a surplus in this city, and surround it with a high wall, topped with barbed wire and broken glass. To forestall your question of whether the taxpayers would have to pick up the tab for the John P. McGurn White House Pool, as we might call it, I serve notice that I would pay for it and then take it with me when I leave eight years from now! I'll keep you posted!"

Laughter.

("He's already ordered the material to upgrade the pool.")

"I have come upon some research about my namesake from the Capone era in Chicago, which I know

you're dying to hear. Machine Gun Jack McGurn
was not his real name and he preferred revolvers to
machine guns for his score or so of killings, though
machine guns were used at the 1929 St. Valentine's
Day massacre in which he may have been involved.
He came into the world as Vincenzo Gibaldi. Later
he called himself on occasion Vincenzo James and
Jimmy Vincent. Why he chose an Irish name is not
known though his enemy, George 'Bugs' Moran,
was in fact Polish. Many of the Outfit members of
those days, for reasons we do not know, liked to
have aliases, though such phony names never protected them from the guns of their enemies. Even Al
Capone sometimes identified himself as Dr. Albert
Brown. McGurn was gunned down in the nineteen
thirties while his doting boss Al Capone was in Alcatraz, on February 15, perhaps an allusion to the St.
Valentine's Day massacre.

"Like his patron Dr. Albert Brown and most of
their group, Machine Gun Jack, Lord have mercy on
him, was a Republican. Historically, Republicans
have always been involved in stealing things, like
elections. The Cicero that they ruled was a Republican town. I'm sure Republicans will resent the implications that I might be related to one of them."

("Word for word," she sighed admiringly. "I don't
think I'll ever get used to it.")

Then he launched into his China statement. Without notes, he became the political science lecturer,
making his points clearly and succinctly.

("Does it sound like him?")

("You wrote it?")

("I'm working at capturing the cadences of his
style.")

The position paper was blunt. The calls for intervention in China's civil war were irresponsible. What were we to intervene with? American military personnel? What could be more absurd?

"China has a long history of strong centralization followed by the emergence of regional warlords. Any attempt of outsiders to intervene on either side would deeply offend the Chinese people, who are intensely patriotic. Both sides have atomic weapons, which make it unlikely that either will use them. We sympathize with the Chinese people for this terrible disruption of their lives and hope that peace returns soon. We promise that we will maintain a hands-off policy until peace returns. I ask all responsible Americans to realize that there is nothing we can do about this civil war and nothing we should do."

The journalists were following his lecture on the copies that Sean Patrick had distributed, noting any difference between the text and the lecture.

As he talked, I remember a conversation with Ellen while they were running for governor.

"Everyone thinks I'm the strong one in the family, Blackie. I'm not. He is a very powerful and challenging man. I was afraid of marriage, scared stiff. He overwhelmed me."

"I'm not surprised to hear that."

I was not surprised, however, only after I had heard it.

Marianna Genovesa was engaged in what she thought of as a responsible, loyal, and professional relationship with a snow-covered mountain. She did not realize that the snow covered a volcano deep within which there were unruly, perhaps dangerous infernos that could . . . no, would . . . explode.

Well, she could probably take care of herself.

All hell broke loose, as the president was winding down his lecture.

The podium and the American flag behind it tilted over and hit the floor, lights flickered on and off, television cameras buzzed and whined in protest, recording machines screeched, flash cameras exploded, invisible chains rattled through the room. Someone pounded on the windows of the West Portico.

"Cut it out," I ordered. "This has gone far enough. Stop it. Now."

Reluctantly the energy that had intruded into the Briefing Room departed.

"Republican poltergeists!" the president of the United States cracked. "Or maybe it's a secret weapon we have down in the Situation Room!"

Laugher broke the spell.

"You stopped it," Marianna Genovesa gasped, her face pale, her eyes wide with terror.

Ph.D. from Columbia or not, she was still a superstitious Italian.

"Arguably."

"Are you an exorcist?"

"No. I just don't like silly adolescent behavior."

"Oh . . ."

"It's someone who was a sensitive, troubled adolescent who did this once before and is now, for some reason, doing it again."

"How do they do it?"

"We don't know. Neither do they. They're mischievous but not totally malicious. They grow out of it eventually."

"Boys or girls?"

"Usually girls."

"Do you think it's me?"

"I don't know."

"I'm a little bit psychic sometimes."

The questions began.

"Mr. President, don't you think, given the drain on your time, it would be better if you settled with Suzy Schmidt and Elaine Walsh so you could get beyond it."

"No."

"Why not, sir?"

"I'm a tort lawyer. I know a case I can win when I see one. Settle this one and there'll be another and another and another. We do that to Democratic presidents in this country. It's going to stop. Now."

"Do you mean, sir, that you are planning a countersuit?"

"Maybe." He grinned. "We'll have to wait and see. However, I'm not about to let the Reverend Snodgrass and the Christian Family Union blackmail me."

The Reverend Snodgrass was a tall handsome man who looked like a younger version of Bill Graham mixed with Charlton Heston. He was less than half as intelligent as either of them.

The rest of the questions were about the sexual harassment suits and the harm they were doing to the office of the president.

The president's reply, in one form or another, was consistently, "Blame those who file them and those who publicize them. Don't blame me."

There was not a single question about China.

"Idiots!" Marianna murmured. ". . . Did you hear me say, Bishop Blackie, that I'm psychic sometimes?"

Before I could answer we were back in the Corner Office.

"You see our problem, Blackwood?"

"Nice save, Mr. President."

"Nothing's broken." Sean Patrick, gasping for breath, dashed in. "I've persuaded them that we've been having problems with the electrical currents. A Republican gremlin. That won't satisfy them for long."

"He's getting more public," the president said calmly.

"Bishop Blackie stopped him, Mr. President," Marianna said, her voice trembling. "He just ordered him to stop and he stopped. Only the bishop says it's probably a she. Someone who has regressed to adolescence."

I noted that the deputy chief of staff was talking like a frightened teenage girl.

"Well, we have two adolescent girls," the president said with a wave of his hand. "Thank God, they're not here . . . Blackwood, give me five minutes and I'll see you in the office . . ."

"I can find my way there."

"Bishop Ryan, there is a Dr. Murphy on the phone," Ms. Chan informed.

"Ah," I said, "arguably my sibling."

"Punk, what's Jackie McGurn doing down there? Doesn't he know he's got poltergeist problems?"

Since she had been in high school when the president was in first grade, he would always be Jackie to her, even as POTUS.

"The Cardinal told you where I was?"

She ignored my question.

"What the hell are you going to do about it?"

"Find the source of the manifestations."

"Most likely an adolescent woman. Weak ego strength. Emotionally troubled or an adult who has regressed to adolescence at considerable risk to her mental health."

"I see."

"He's got two daughters."

"You've observed that?"

She ignored my sarcasm.

"They've seemed to me to be cute kids, but they've lost a mother and have been moved around a lot. Prime suspects. They might not even know they're doing it, not fully."

"They are not currently present, however."

"Doesn't matter. We've got data that show that they can disturb the atmosphere and leave psychic vibrations behind. If they were watching that press conference from a distance, they may have been able to trigger it."

"At a distance?"

"There's two cases," my sib responded uneasily, "on record of just that happening. I'd take a good look at those two children. They've been through a lot of stress. Maybe one of them wants their father to pay more attention to them than to the job and the world. It's dangerous stuff. They could mess themselves up for the rest of their lives."

"Indeed . . . Do we know how it works?"

"The theory says strong psychic vibrations. Many of my colleagues don't believe those things are possible, but they don't have any better explanations. We don't know much about it except that it happens."

"Indeed."

"Nothing broken at that press conference, I suppose?"

"Not a thing."

"Figures . . . Jackie was quick to blame the Republicans, wasn't he? Maybe he's right."

"There are no Republicans in this building."

"How do you know?"

True enough.

Now I had three suspects, three women that I did not want to be responsible for the poltergeists.

True to his word, the president joined me in five minutes.

"Well?" he said.

"Before we discuss the playful spirits, I suggest we put in a call to Mike Casey the Cop."

"Why? Does he specialize in poltergeists?"

"It will be necessary, unless I am mistaken, to have some of his agents infiltrate Loyola Law School to prepare for your friends from the Christian Family Union seeking more evidence against you from your years teaching there."

"You think they'll do that?"

"I think it's practically certain. They intend to keep the pressure up."

"What's his phone number?"

"The Reilly Gallery on Oak Street. For Mr. Michael Casey."

"Mrs. Chan, will you make a call to Superintendent Michael Casey at the Reilly Gallery on Oak Street in Chicago. Tell him that it's Bishop Ryan calling from the Oval Office."

He grinned at me, always the imp even if he was also, according to his late wife, an overwhelming lover.

"Mr. Casey on the line, sir."

"Father Ryan," I said modestly.

"Are you really in the Oval Office, Blackie?"

"I believe so, the Rose Garden is right outside the window. No roses in it, however."

"Hi, Mike," the president said, switching on the speaker.

"Mr. President! You should be careful whom you're seen with!"

"I understand, Mike. The man just walked in. . . . He's got an idea for a project in which he thinks you might be able to help. A favor, kind of."

A "favor" is the currency of Chicago politics. You do me a "favor," I owe you one—generally the latter is called a "marker" as in "I'm picking up my marker."

"Name it, Mr. President."

Mike, a former police superintendent and now a painter, also presided over Reliable Security, an agency that provided income for many off-duty cops.

"It seems appropriate, Mike," I said, "to have some of your women agents at Reliable Security don wires and wander around Loyola Law School looking for a person or persons trying to collect information on alleged sexual harassment by the president when he was on the faculty there. You will, of course, inform the Chicago police about this project and gain whatever legal permission you need to carry it out. I'm sure they'll be cooperative."

The president gasped.

So did Mike the Cop.

"I think some of our agents are actually in the law school," he said slowly. "Women cops."

"I take it as axiomatic that the president's enemies

will have a try at more scandal. When we find out who they are in Chicago we will tap their lines, again with appropriate permission, and gather evidence that is sufficient to seek an indictment by a Cook County Grand Jury."

"I don't see any reason why we couldn't do that. It might not work, but it's worth a try . . . Mr. President?"

"As our mutual friend the Cardinal would say, Mike, I'm glad he's on our side."

"Me too, Mr. President."

After we had hung up, the president pondered what we had done.

"I don't think there's anything wrong about it. But it worries me."

"There is nothing at all wrong about it," I insisted, "except that I may be wrong in my guess that they'll try Loyola first. They might go to Springfield, but I suspect that the enemy's agents wouldn't know where it is."

A door swung open and the ineffable Conrad Ward dashed in.

"Mr. President, we had a very successful session over on the Hill. I think we're going to have an excellent liaison with them . . ."

He stopped when he saw me, baffled at my presence in the holy place.

"You remember Bishop Ryan, Conrad?"

For a moment he stared at me like I was a strange form of fauna which had perhaps erupted from the Rose Garden.

"Yes, of course, Bishop Ryan. It's good to see you again. Now I must ask you to leave the Oval Office as I have an important matter to report to the president."

"No," I said firmly.

"I beg your pardon?"

"I said no. I will not leave. I too am having an important discussion with the president."

Jack McGurn waited to see which of us would blink. He should have known.

"Very well, I'll be back later. Thank you, Mr. President."

"That's Conrad." The president shrugged.

I ignored the interruption.

"Now, as to the poltergeist . . ."

"Before I forget, the Daughters are coming in this afternoon for a couple of days. I thought we'd have dinner in the family dining room, which we don't use much. We eat breakfast in the morning in the Solarium up on the third floor while we watch the morning TV programs."

"Ah . . . and where do you eat when the Daughters aren't here?"

"On the fly," he said uncomfortably, "now as to the poltergeists . . ."

"They usually want to get caught because they are both proud of their accomplishments and feel guilty about them. Chances are then that they will give themselves away or simply stop because of the psychic strain."

"That's good." He sighed. "I won't miss him."

"More likely her."

"A woman?"

"Either a teenage woman or one who has reverted temporarily to that state, usually a fragile, sensitive, tense young woman."

"Thank goodness none of those words describes the Daughters." He laughed. "Besides, they weren't around this afternoon."

"Indeed."

"So you sniff around and hope that the woman in question confesses . . ."

"Something like that."

"Dr. Genovesa tells me that you stopped the show this afternoon."

"I assumed that Milord Cronin had reported that I can do that sometimes."

"He did, but I didn't believe him. How do you do it?"

"I talk to her like an angry father and she stops. She's mad at me but she stops."

"So she knows you're here."

"Perhaps. It's hard to know what thoughts run through their heads, even how conscious they are of what they're doing and that they're doing it."

"They grow out of it?"

"Usually. Sometimes they need psychiatric help. Sometimes not. The problem can become very serious when they return to doing it as adults, which may be the situation we are currently facing."

"Good hunting to you, Blackwood," he said, bouncing out of his chair, "I appreciate your help. We don't need more chaos in this madhouse."

No, we certainly didn't.

The family dinner in the family dining room was something less than a success. The room was painted yellow with a lovely French fireplace, shining china and silverware, candles on the table, an oval mirror on the wall, and a fire in the fireplace.

Just in case you didn't notice it, this elegance reminded you that you were in the palace of an imperial capital—not Buckingham Palace or the Escorial perhaps, but in its own way, even more handsome.

In honor of the evening I had actually found a Roman collar. Both the president and the press secretary had changed into business suits. The Daughters, pleading late arrival of their flight, were still wearing the uniform of jeans and sweatshirts, both of which proclaimed in gold on green "Irish!"

They were in a querulous mood, concerned about their father's appearance.

"*Daddy*," Granne began the assault, "you look totally exhausted!"

"You're eating junk food from down in the mess and not running every morning!" Deirdre accused him.

"And you gotta get rid of some of those creeps over in the West Wing!"

"Nerds!"

"Do I get to keep my job?" Sean Patrick asked.

"That depends! Those reporters are extreme bad!"

Through all of this heated conversation, they efficiently destroyed the food, which was excellent, but declined any more than a single glass of wine.

"Where's Marianna?" Deirdre demanded suddenly, as though she had only just noticed the absence of Dr. Genovesa.

"This is a family dinner," the president said with a sigh. "She's not family."

"Bishop Blackie isn't family either!"

"He's an old family friend. Dr. Genovesa is a member of my staff."

"WELL," Granne signed in on cue, "I think she OUGHT to be a member of the family."

"You need a woman in your life, Daddy. Someone has to take care of you in this awful place!"

"I'm not ready to marry, dear, not yet."

"Mom wouldn't approve of that answer," Deirdre glared at him. "And you know it! Doesn't he, Bishop Blackie?"

"As to your mother's position on that question, there can be little doubt. But such matters require time and healing."

They both glared at me.

"*WELL*, Daddy, you could sleep with her and marry her later," Granne said in the tone of voice which indicated that a decision had been reached.

"In the present climate in Washington?"

"You could keep it a secret," she backed off.

"In the White House?"

Silence.

"Bishop Blackie?"

"Affairs of the heart cannot be handled so peremptorily, as I'm sure you both know."

"Well," Deirdre said, retreating temporarily from the field, "Daddy needs a woman."

"Arguably."

"Do you think," Granne looked up from her chocolate fudge sundae, "that Marianna loves our daddy?"

"How could she not!"

General laughter around the table.

The subject turned to the Secret Service, a matter on which the Daughters had very strong opinions, especially about Hal (short of Hallowell) Hitchcock, the Agent-in-Charge.

"He's a creep," Deirdre protested, "and so are all the rest of them. One guy goes to me like if I want to sleep with a boy he won't tell you."

"And you said?"

"I said that he'd tell that supercreep Hallowell and besides the very thought of going to bed with a Notre Dame boy is vomit city."

Sean Patrick guffawed and the president's lips twitched. I gathered that Hal was not popular with this strong-minded first family.

"How do the kids at the Dome react to you?" Sean Patrick asked.

"They're nice except for the Republicans. There's a lot of them down there. I don't think they'll save their souls."

"What do they say?"

"Well, this one bitch goes like aren't you ashamed of all the terrible things your father did to those poor women?"

"And you said?" her father raised an eyebrow.

"I said that the FBI had told me that her father fucks sheep because her mother is a lesbian!"

"You didn't!"

"Yeah, I did and I'm glad I did."

"What did she do?"

"She ran away in tears."

"Was that nice, Deirdre?"

"No, it wasn't nice. I'm sick of being nice. It's yucky!"

"What would your mother say about that?"

"She'd put up her thumb, and say, 'Right on!' "

More laughter around the table, as the Bailey's was served.

"The kids at St. Prax," Granne continued that segment of the conversation, "are totally nice. They adore you, Daddy, and they think I'm cool because I'm your daughter. If anyone at Georgetown Prep tries to pick on me next year I'll tell them that their mother sleeps with Rottweilers because their father is impotent."

"I don't think I want to know any more about your ripostes." The president smothered his laugh. "I'm better off not knowing."

"Did you put up the backboard out by the running track?" Granne asked her brother.

"With a nice little cement court."

The president looked surprised.

"Cool. Marianna will be able to give me another lesson over the weekend."

The Daughters had made their points in the way young women do with their fathers—by combat. They were worried about him and they could take care of themselves—better than he could take care of himself.

The president returned to the Oval Office after supper. Sean Patrick went with him. The Daughters rode the elevator up to the top floor to watch TV in the Solarium. I wandered into the Red Room (in honor of the Cardinal). I collapsed onto the sofa and admired the gueridon (table) in front of me, made in New Orleans by Charles Lanniuer. The room was, as the Daughters would have said, like entirely gorgeous.

First ladies used the Red Room for teas; President Grant withdrew to it with his male guests for coffee and brandy and banned all political talk. He arranged for the secret swearing in of Rutherford B. Hayes who had stolen the 1886 election from Samuel Tilden. The Bushes did not have enough discretion to do something similar.

I pondered the portrait of Dollcy Madison on the wall. She did not seem particularly beautiful. However, I was inclined to believe the written sources rather than the artist.

The Daughters were unquestionably correct in their diagnosis of their father's problem. He needed a woman. South Side Irish Catholic that he was, that meant a wife—at least eventually. Was Marianna Genovesa in love with him?

My answer on the record stood. How could she not be? Nonetheless, she would never take the first step towards such a relationship. Might he?

Next year perhaps. Too late? I hoped not.

And the woman herself? At this point she was a mystery. Had she become frightened when I chased away the brat that was tormenting us? Yet what profit would there be for her in disturbing the president's press conference?

I sighed, so loudly that a Secret Service woman looked in. My friend Wholley.

"Are you all right, Bishop?"

"Irish sigh, Agent Wholley."

"I'm not unfamiliar with them, sir."

"Do you know who's causing the problems around here?"

"You mean the poltergeists, sir?"

"Yes."

"Some teenager, sir."

"The president's daughters?"

She permitted herself a slight smile.

"Those kids? No way. They're extreme cool . . . Good night, sir, sleep well."

"I'll try."

Now I was suspecting Agent Wholley.

A very large black man, looking not unlike P. Diddy, appeared.

"I'm Stefan, sir. I work with Dr. Genovesa."

Also from Brooklyn.

"Fortunate man."

"Yes, SIR . . . Dr. Genovesa asked me to inquire what you might need for tomorrow."

A good night's sleep.

"The personnel files of all the women under thirty-five who work here and a place for me to work."

"Yes, sir. We'll take care of it, sir."

"I'm sure you will."

"Dr. Genovesa asked me to give you this envelope." He grinned broadly and withdrew. It was time for me to go to bed.

"Thank you."

In the Queens' Bedroom I placed a call to Milord Cronin.

"I thought you'd be interested to know that the late Jackie Kennedy is responsible for the name of this room because five queens slept here—the two Elizabeths, Wilhelmina, and Juliana of the Netherlands and Frederika of Greece. That is hardly fair to V.M. Molotov of cocktail fame or to Mr. Churchill . . ."

"What the hell is going on there?"

"It was a haven for secretaries and staff members until Roosevelt (Theodore) built the West Wing and moved administration out of the residence. It was called the Rose Room and Ms. Kennedy changed the name. I shall sleep on Andrew Jackson's bed and wake to a painting of the lovely Fanny Kemble . . ."

"Jack looks like hell," the Cardinal said, obviously uninterested in my reporting.

"He does indeed. It is my impression that he is faced with a fractious and undisciplined junior staff, a hostile and ignorant press, a difficult Congress, a revolution in China, false harassment charges, and two girl children who think, perhaps correctly, that they can run the United States better than he can. In addition he eats very little and, I suspect, sleeps poorly."

"He needs a wife."

"Arguably."

"Is there a candidate for the job?"

"There is one such whom the daughters strongly support."

"Well, he should marry her."

"She may be the cause of the playful spirits."

"That show at the press conference was scary . . . You stop it?"

"Indeed."

"Well, get rid of them, Blackie . . . and tell Jack Ellen would want him to marry again."

"He knows that."

I thereupon prepared to retire to what didn't look like a comfortable bed despite its rose-colored canopy. I peered cautiously into the corridor and across at the Lincoln Bedroom. There appeared to be no spirits abroad.

I then opened the envelope which Dr. Genovesa had sent me. It was an article from the *Wall Street*

Journal, whose reporters were not under the control of the editorial page.

Despite Critics, Low-Key, Light-Touch President Seems to Govern Effectively. Chicago "Outfit" Credited.

"Pretty soon," whispered a veteran Republican observer of the Washington scene, "our right wing is going to wake up to the fact that this guy is remarkably effective. I can't remember a new administration which has settled in so quickly and skillfully. If we're not careful, he's going to own this city."

A few others are whispering the same heretical notions as John McGurn's administration takes charge. "Despite the laughter and the wink of the eye," a prominent Democrat remarked, "these are the most skillful politicians I've seen here in a long time. McGurn's 'Outfit' never wastes time fighting with one another."

"Outfit" is a Chicago nickname for the Mafia.

The White House's style seems to be to ignore the criticism which seethes like a permanent firestorm and to take charge of the government. Already it has pushed its major appointments through Congress in record time, established excellent relations with the Democrats on Capitol Hill, charmed some moderate Republicans, and launched its major legislative initiatives.

The President's staff is almost entirely from Chicago. Chief of Staff Conrad Ward, a liaison with the Hill during the Clinton years, praised for his adroit handling of Congress, is from Baltimore. However, the Deputy Chief of Staff is Chicagoan Thomas Ignatius Horan, who grew up in the same neighborhood as the President and was a student of his at Loyola Law School. His son Sean Patrick is a cool and articulate press spokesman. Communications Director Mae Rosen, White House Consuls "Judge" Ogden Jefferson and "Senator" Jesus Maria Lopez, Secretary Mary Elizabeth Chan, and National Security Advisor Dr. Claire Jones are all native Chicagoans and have been active in Chicago politics for years.

"The Outfit," a junior staff member said, off the record, "seems to be able to read each other's thoughts. Politics seems to be in their blood, maybe in their genes."

Only Dr. Marianna Genovesa, a "temporary" adviser on China policy and an "acting" Deputy Chief of Staff, does not fit in with the Chicago political style.

"Mari is an Italian from Brooklyn," said the junior staffer, "she breathes the same kind of air they do."

The Beltway media are still hostile. However, as the President remarked at a press conference the other day, "my honeymoon with the press was over before it started. Maybe we'll have a second honeymoon in a couple of years. In the meantime I'll have to settle for a love relationship with the people."

He has not been able to mend fences with the Vice President, who, some say, will never forgive him for "stealing" the nomination from her. "Genie's running her own little government in exile over in the Old Executive Office Building," a prominent lobbyist observed. "And no one is paying any attention."

Many in the Beltway hope that President McGurn will be able to temper the fires of partisanship which have burned so fiercely in this city since 1994. An experienced journalist remarked the other day, "This man is so subtle and so clever that maybe it will take the historians to figure out that he cooled off Washington his first year in office."

Indeed! How very interesting. Appearances to the contrary, Jack *had* taken charge. The *Journal* reporter was the first to see beyond the hysteria of his fellow media persons, whose apocalyptic stories had misled even me. That was inexcusable. I should have known that Jack's team had political genes. To understand Chicago politics is to understand all politics.

I turned off the lights and huddled under the covers. The White House creaked and groaned and perhaps even swayed a little. It was, after all, a very old building. I resolved that I must compensate for the sleep deprivation caused by my early departure.

I drifted into the delightful dream world between sleep and wakefulness. Then just as I was about to enter definitively the land of Nod, a presence filtered into the room.

"Get out of here! This instant!" I ordered.

The presence paused, as though its feelings were hurt by my attitude.

"I said get out! I'm not impressed by your cheap tricks! I've seen them all before! GO!"

She didn't want to go. Stubborn brat. She knew she had to go.

Why she knew that escaped me. They always do, however, like the child banished to a "time-out" knows he has to go to the corner.

"NOW!"

Sadly she departed.

Poor thing.

Nine-tenths of the way into sleep I realized that the Daughters were sleeping in the room right above me.

6

Only half-awake, I was consuming my raisin bran, whole wheat toast, bacon, and mushroom omelet the next morning and watching four TV screens in the Solarium on the fourth floor (or third floor, if you wish) when the president and the Daughters bounded in. In their sweat suits, they were soaking wet and happily exhausted, though the president was puffing more than the Daughters. I am rarely able to cope with such enthusiasm before noon.

"Daddy is really out of condition, Bishop Blackie," Deirdre insisted. "He couldn't keep up with us."

"It's raining," I said.

"A fine soft day," the president gasped. "We ran and we played a little basketball on Sean Patrick's new court."

"Marianna was there," Granne said, "so we had a little game. Me and her against them. Naturally we won."

"How fortunate," I said.

"The woman has a wicked elbow." The president sank into the gray couch next to me, rubbing one of his arms.

Pretty clearly no Eros had escaped this morning.

The Daughters set about devouring the food and demanding more. The president sipped a cup of coffee and chewed on a piece of dry toast.

"She also does martial arts," Granne said proudly. "That's why she's in such extreme excellent shape. Daddy better not knock her down again."

The president ignored this sally.

"Anything on the tube this morning?"

"Apparently you had a press conference yesterday in which you threatened the Christian Family Union. Dr. Snodgrass, its executive director, was on with his two victims. They defied you. He promised that there would be more revelations."

He glanced at me.

"That means he doesn't have any more now or he would have disclosed them. So his people are snooping somewhere."

"Like Chicago?"

"If we are fortunate."

"Marianna knocked Daddy down once," Granne said with obvious approval. "He was charging."

"Lie!" the president protested. "The woman is a thug!"

No trace of Eros.

A handsome man with thin hair and a strong jaw knocked on the doorframe of the Solarium.

"Mr. President, I am reluctant to disturb you at breakfast . . ."

"Not at all, Cliff . . . Blackwood, this is Cliff Sommers, the chief usher of the White House, which means he's responsible for everything. Cliff, this is Bishop John Blackwood Ryan."

"Milord," Cliff Sommers nodded respectfully.

Anglican. Very High Church.

"What's happened now, Cliff?" The president

said, pouring himself another cup of coffee. "You like some coffee?"

"No thank you, Mr. President. I'm afraid I have to report that we've had an incident in the China Room."

The Daughters stopped babbling. Though they continued to stuff food into their mouths.

"This morning," Cliff Sommers went on, "we discovered that all the china had been removed from their cabinets, though the cabinets were locked, and thrown on the floor without any concern about breaking them."

"Nothing was broken, I assume," I murmured.

"Of course not, Milord. These little demons never break anything."

"What demons?" Deirdre demanded, her mouth full of omelet.

"I'm afraid," her father explained, "we're having a minor visitation of poltergeists."

"We had that in our dorm at Notre Dame," she said, as if she were in competition. "The proper word, I think, is 'obsession.' "

"Right," said the president. "And what happened?"

"She went away, whoever she was. We all thought it was a hoot . . . I guess it isn't so funny around here."

She went on eating.

"We have tourists this morning, Cliff?"

"Yes, Mr. President.

"Then we'd better get the China Room ready for them, had we not?"

"Yes, Mr. President . . . I can only hope that he doesn't start to do things when the tourists are here."

"She," Deirdre chimed in. "They're almost always women, troubled adolescents with psychic powers. They get over it."

Right.

"You're not doing it are you, Dede?" her sister asked.

Deirdre's eyes lit up, just as her father's did in moments of great merriment.

"What a totally cool idea!"

A half hour later with Stefan's help, I was ensconced in a tiny cubbyhole in the basement of the West Wing, a stack of personnel records in front of me. As Stefan explained, when they could no longer expand the West Wing above ground, they extended the basement underground back towards the White House.

I had previously ambled through the West Wing, so completely inconspicuous and innocuous as to be hardly noticeable. The West Wing was now a place for those who needed to have access to the president every day and their support staff. Or for those whose prestige required them to be in the West Wing.

The West Wing itself was a little more run-down than the set of Mr. Sheen's program. The whole place could use a good coat of paint. Sixteen hundred people worked at the White House, most of them exiled next door to the Old Executive Office Building (once the Executive Office Building and before that the State War Navy Building) and in the horrendously ugly New Executive Office Building. The former, where such important institutions as the Office of Management and Budget and the Office of the Vice President were located, reminded me of a nineteenth-century Jesuit college, except that its high ceilings and empty corridors seemed to go on forever.

In the West Wing, however, swarms of people, most of them young, all of them very serious, and very important, strode purposefully and spoke in intense whispers. Men and women alike wore carefully tailored suits in subdued tones—as important people must. Even a young woman walking to a copier or a young man carrying mail displayed game faces which hinted that the future of the world might depend on his or her work.

The various members of the Outfit were, on the contrary, relaxed, casual, apparently happy. The president wore a business suit, though, I was told, sometimes a Notre Dame blazer. The press spokesman displayed a Connemara sweater. Tommy Horan, it was alleged, didn't own a tie and sometimes appeared in jeans and sweatshirt with a maroon Loyola windbreaker. Jesus Lopez favored loud sports clothes. Ogden Jefferson, as always, was a symphony in brown—shoes, socks, old-fashioned three-piece suit, brown tie with a beige shirt, and a brown homburg which left his bald head only rarely. Mae Rosen carried her King Charles spaniel into her office every day.

Perhaps they were sending a message.

"Strange place from which to run a country," I remarked to Stefan.

"And the world, sir. Dr. Jones and the Situation Room are just around the corner. I'm sure she'll stop by to say hello. She's a Catholic too."

I worked on the personnel records. They were not very helpful. I found three or four young woman whose backgrounds might hint at psychic propensities. I wondered if there were FBI reports hidden somewhere.

Someone knocked on the doorframe. Bishop Blackie's door is always open, right?

A tall black woman with white hair and a young face grinned at me.

"Morning, Bishop," she said, "I'm Claire Jones."

"Fellow Chicagoan and fellow Catholic." I stood up and shook hands with her.

"You got it, Bishop . . .'Bout time we met. Hey, you not wearing no ring."

During our conversation she would shift back and forth from radio standard English to Black American.

"I own one, but my staff is afraid I'll lose it."

"You're here to catch the spirits?"

"Or to persuade them to leave."

"You want to see the Situation Room?"

"Everyone wants to see the Situation Room!"

I put the personnel files in a drawer of my desk. No key to lock it, but that wasn't my problem.

I had seen the Situation Room often enough in movies and TV that the real one was an anticlimax like everything else in the White House and the West Wing. Illuminated maps line the walls, including a large one across from which was the long table where the decisions of war and peace and life and death were made. Several men in military uniforms were monitoring small screens, either computers or television. A couple others were studying teletype output. Still others were poring over documents. Though the artificial light in the ceiling illuminated the room, it still seemed dangerously dark.

"Scary place, huh?"

"Yes."

"Very scary . . . I've only been working here a couple of weeks, but it never gets any less scary. My job is to advise the president on world flashpoints and to prepare a daily security briefing for him. We're watching China very closely as you can imagine."

She pointed to China on the map.

"Also we have a situation in the Indian Ocean . . . A tanker allegedly bound for Bombay has suddenly switched course and is heading towards Southeast Asia. We don't know what it's up to."

"Do we have any idea what the Russians are thinking of doing about China?"

"Pretty much the same thing as us, Mr. Bishop. No way do they want to get caught up in it.

"What's new in China in the last few minutes, Captain?" Claire asked.

A young officer with blond hair turning gray and four stripes on his shoulder board looked up.

"It still looks like the rebels are gearing up for an attack on Beijing. The government there is in chaos. Their world is falling apart. No reports of anyone shooting foreigners yet."

"There's all kinds of spirits in this place, Bishop," she whispered to me. "They're all around us. Can't you feel them?"

I have very slight psychic tendencies that I keep to myself. I listened to the Situation Room. Some low-level vibrations, so low that I would not have ordinarily noticed them.

"I don't think so . . . Who are they?"

"Maybe all the people who got killed by the decisions made here . . . I'm a professor of international law at the University of Chicago, a high-powered academic, Bishop Blackie. Yet I knows when the spirits be around. They be around here . . . Hi there, girl, we'll have another briefing for the boss this afternoon."

"Hi, Claire," Marianna said. "Good morning, Bishop . . . I just wanted to check on China."

She was wearing a loose-fitting navy blue knit dress and carrying a couple of manila folders.

"Anything happen, chile, you be the first to know, won't she, cap'n?"

"Yes, ma'am . . . There's a little evidence of conflict within the power structure in Beijing. Our intercepts indicate they're quarreling with one another."

"No one expected this would happen," Marianna said, glancing at a story coming out on the Teletype.

"Cept'n someone I know who wrote an article that said it would implode all at once and everyone made fun of her."

"Not quite everyone, Claire."

"I smelled you be right, chile, just plain smelled it."

I didn't want to stay in this scary place any longer, whether the spirits were there or not.

"I'd better get back to work," I said. "Thanks for the tour, Dr. Jones."

"You just come back any time, hon. If there be a big crowd here, it means someone be thinking of blowing up the world."

"May I have a word with you, Bishop?" Marianna said, as we left the spirits behind.

"Sure . . . Little basketball this morning, huh?"

"I'll feel it all next week . . . I didn't mean to knock Kerryman down. He charged into me."

"Macho?"

"Not really. Just clumsy and out of condition, poor man. I did help him up."

"Unnecessarily gracious. He did charge you!"

She laughed.

"I hope Sean Patrick gets that swimming pool open soon."

"Ah?"

"Hal Hitchcock is the only one against it. He doesn't think it appropriate that everyone on the staff can use it, especially in the summer, when the cover is rolled back. Thinks it will be like a country club or a resort."

"Everyone?"

"It will be reserved at certain hours for the president and his family. Then it will be open to everyone. The man is an egalitarian."

We entered my office.

"Is this the best Stefan could do for you? Not even another chair. Just a minute."

She placed her two files on my desk and left. I noted that they were her personnel file and the FBI report on her.

"The people you interview," she said as she dragged a straight-backed chair into the office, "will need to sit somewhere."

"I won't drag anyone in here. I'll just wander around the building looking helpless . . . What's going to happen in China?"

She sat down on the chair and shrugged. No matter how plainly she dressed it was impossible to hide her elegance.

"We might be lucky. The rebels might capture Beijing soon and disperse or eliminate the party leaders. They'll try to restore some kind of tranquility and will need our help or at least our forbearance. There'll still be some confusion and chaos as the rebel leaders work out what they want to do."

"How did you know they were going to implode?"

"Someone once argued that the socialist leaders in Russia made the mistake of letting their people know the truth during the nineteen eighties. The Chinese tried to avoid that mistake, though the truth got around on the net and in other ways. They made a worse mistake. They hid the truth from themselves. Now they're paralyzed with surprise and fear, as well they might be . . . those are my files. You told Stefan under thirty-five. My thirty-fifth birthday was last month, so he excluded me. I thought you should see my files."

The tiny age lines on her face made her even more lovely.

"Even the FBI file?"

"I admitted to you yesterday that I was psychic. I thought you should see the whole story."

This woman, I decided, would surely be the first lady and soon at that. It would be an unmitigated blessing for the country. But what did I know!

"Tell me about the experiences."

"My parents and I were very close. They married late in life and I was the only child. They were both professors at Columbia. We lived in an apartment on Flatbush because that was our neighborhood. Most people think it's only Jewish but there are lots of us around too. My parents were civilized, sophisticated people, interested in many things, including Chinese art, which probably is why I chose China as my field. I was in my last year in graduate school, teaching a class in late afternoon. I glanced out the window and saw a jet explode in the air above us. I screamed. None of the kids saw it. I laughed and said that things like that happened to me. Later I found that an NYPD police car crashed into their car in a chase after drug suspects. There was an explosion and they both died instantly."

Tears appeared in her deep brown eyes.

"Terrible," I said.

"Other things happen occasionally, not very often. I kind of collapse the way I did yesterday when I sense something is about to happen. I knew our little friends would begin to play their silly games before they did."

"First time here?"

"I think so. If there were other, what should I call them, hints, I hardly noticed them . . . So I should legitimately be considered a suspect."

"Arguably."

"I went into therapy after my parents died. It's in the FBI files. The therapist was a big help. I knew that life had to go on."

"You told the therapist about the jet?"

She nodded.

"He said he didn't believe in such things and that was that. I didn't argue. It didn't seem worth arguing about."

"You wouldn't pick a team in an office basketball pool on such hints?"

"No way." She laughed, revealing her glistening white teeth.

"I thought not."

She stood up.

"So you'd better look through my files carefully. I

may be doing all of this, though I can't imagine why. I go to church every week, by the way, in case you were wondering."

"I assumed as much."

"Good luck, Bishop Blackie. We have to stop these silly little twits before they do more harm."

"You suspect the Daughters?"

"Oh my, no! I didn't mean to imply that. They're not silly little twits. They're impressive young women!"

"Patently."

After she left, I glanced through her files. The FBI had been very thorough. There was nothing in their record that could be used against her. I sighed with relief. We didn't need a vulnerable first lady.

Might she be responsible, nonetheless, for "the silly little twits"?

Whatever my biases in favor of her, I ought not to exclude that possibility.

My old friend Mae Rosen drifted in and parked in the available chair. Mae is the dean of Chicago media mavens and has on occasion managed to keep me out of trouble with the press.

"Is this the best they can do for you, Blackie? You need an image makeover!"

"Better that I not be seen at all."

"Wherever you go there's trouble. I've never seen it to fail."

"That's a correlation, not a cause. How's Barry?"

I was referring to her King Charles spaniel, a Jewish dog with an Irish name.

She produced a lined, yellow legal pad.

"He likes it here in the Beltway . . . Now what do we do about these ghosts?"

"What we always do, usually. We tell the whole truth. And we follow the Boss's lead from yesterday, we blame the Republicans. These are natural phenomena which science is not yet able to explain fully. They are usually traced to troubled young people with some psychic propensities who eventually grow out of them. While they make a lot of noise and create considerable confusion, they never break anything or harm anyone. Thus they have apparently done nothing here when the tourists are coming through—check with someone to make sure of that. We are confident that they will stop. We note incidentally that they happen when the Daughters are not here."

"So they're not doing it?"

"Who knows what those imps might do! Surely it is not to their advantage to do so. However, and we don't want to tell the media this, my good sister, Dr. Mary Kathleen Ryan Murphy, tells me that the imps can leave vibrations behind to operate when they're not present."

"No, we don't want to tell them that . . . We don't want to tell them anything if we don't have to. So you better get on with your work."

"Patently."

I selected five young women from the files for further investigation. There was something about each of them, as much in their photographs as in their records, which suggested that they might be troubled.

I gathered up the files and navigated my way upstairs, being careful not to drop them as is my wont. In fact I dropped them only three times.

I asked a number of passing folk where Dr. Genovesa's office was. I didn't quite find it, but I did blunder into Ms. Chan's office.

"Bishop Blackie, you look lost!"

"Defamation! I know where Dr. Genovesa's office is, only I don't know how to get there."

"It's right around the corner here, right next to Mr. Horan's."

The admirable Tommy was staring out the window at the South Lawn.

"These people are recommending assassination, Marianna. That's treason."

"I know it is, Tommy. Kerryman doesn't want to go after them."

"I keep telling him that there are a lot of crazies out there in the country who need only a spark to seize their fifteen minutes of immortality. He thinks he's immortal, doesn't he, Blackie?"

I have always found it difficulty to maintain my wonted invisibility in the presence of the remarkable Tommy Horan.

"More accurately, one might say that much of his motivation to live was lost in the cold waters of Lake Michigan a year ago . . . Incidentally you could make a better case against them on the grounds that they are advocating the violent overthrow of the government."

"He wants to wait till those who are talking assassination become so obnoxious that the public demands action against them," Tommy observed. "I wonder how many assassination attempts he thinks will create such a demand."

"Attempts he'd better survive," Marianna said gloomily. "And Hal Hitchcock is not the swiftest Agent-in-Charge either."

"I agree, he has to go. The boss doesn't want to make any waves with them. What do you think we should do, Bishop?"

"Pray," I said.

"For what?"

"For Kerryman."

"You've got those files, Bishop," Marianna said to me.

"I do." I put them on her desk.

"I hope you can stop this stuff, Bishop." Tommy sighed. "We have enough trouble as it is without spooks."

He ambled off, still deep in thought.

Marianna pointed at a small, very small, coffee table.

"Coffee?"

"I avoid it."

"Tea?"

"That would be unnecessarily gracious."

"Caffeine-free?"

"Surely not."

"You didn't realize how bad it is, did you, Bishop Blackie?" she said as she poured the tea.

"I was not taking the hatred seriously."

"We have to. Some of the most reputable people in the country, Republicans, of course, are hinting at measures that might involve the violent overthrow of the government. They want to regain control of Congress in the next election. They don't really want anyone to kill Kerryman, but they want to keep the flame of faith burning in their loyal followers."

"Some of them wouldn't mind if he were killed."

"Then they'd have that horror—Genie—ranting, screaming crazy woman, to deal with," she said with noticeable asperity. "What do you have here?"

"Five women to whom I'd like to talk. I won't summon them to my dungeon; I'll kind of amble around and meet them. They won't know I'm investigating them."

She nodded.

"Let's see who they are . . . You don't have me among them?"

"I've already talked to you."

"Germaine Connelly . . . Native American girl from New Mexico. Assistant to Ogden Jefferson, special counsel to the president. Nice kid, pretty, probably knows all kinds of Apache spells. Could be a medicine woman. She tells me that her Apache name is 'Travels By Night.' I think she's putting me on. BA from Las Cruces. Sort of mysterious."

"Ah."

"Rita Suarez . . . Do you know who she is?"

"Alas, no."

"She's the daughter of the vice president by the first of her three marriages. Blond, blue eyes, usually wide-open. Twenty-three. As nice as Genie is a raging bitch."

"Any signs of psychic propensities?"

"Takes one to know one, huh? None that I've noticed. She's a straightforward, uncomplicated kid. Everyone likes her. Most don't even know who her mother is. Kerryman knows but he forgets, deliberately I suspect."

"Ah."

"Jane Effingham . . . All these women are attractive, Bishop Blackie . . ."

"Call me Blackie."

"Not Ishmael?"

"As in Black Bart or the Black Prince or Boston Blackie."

"Or the Black Sox?"

"I am a Cub fan, it is a matter of faith."

"This one is about my age. Strawberry blond from upstate New York. Old family, old money. Really bright. A little brittle. She works for Conrad, kind of research scholar. SUNY Buffalo."

"She likes Conrad?"

"No one likes Conrad. May be a lesbian, but they say that of everyone who isn't sleeping with someone, me included."

"Absurdity."

"Francesa Jackson. African-American. Chicagoan. Middle twenties. Works for Jesus Lopez, administrative assistant. Kind of tough but very competent. Chip on her shoulder maybe. Adores Kerryman."

"Doesn't everyone?"

She glanced at me quickly.

"Arguably, to use your word. And finally Luisa Peña—Mexican-American from Tucson. Stenographer in the bull pen. One of our witnesses against those two bimbos. Effervescent, excitable, loads of fun. She'll want to talk to you about devotion to Guadelupe. Like I say, all attractive, all stable, all loyal."

"Even *la señorita*?"

"More so than most of us. I don't think she gets along too well with her mother . . . How did you choose these five, Bishop, uh, Blackie."

"Their eyes."

She rearranged the files, deftly putting them in whatever was their appropriate order.

"What do you see in their eyes?"

I hesitated.

"Fear, pain."

"You don't see that in mine?"

"Not at all. Vitality perhaps, sensitivity surely. No pain."

"I hope you're right . . . You're obviously stabbing in the dark, but what else can you do? Would you like some cookies? What kind?"

"Oatmeal raisin, if you have any."

"My favorite!"

She dashed out and returned with a large plate. Apparently the good Stefan was not expected to perform such services.

"One more question. Do you think that your colleague Dr. Jones might make wax statues in her apartment?"

She burst out laughing and refilled my teacup so I could dunk the cookies into the tea, one of the great venial sins of all human history.

"Claire? She's Catholic, Blackie. Not voodoo."

"Many Haitians would claim both."

"She's famous all over the world for her work in international law, a brilliant woman. I don't even think she's Haitian."

"Yet she sees the spirits everywhere."

Marianna Genovesa hesitated.

"I know. She scares me every time I go down there. I don't think she's making it up . . . Quite a White House we have here, isn't it?"

"We know what Kerryman needs, don't we, Marianna?"

Her facial muscles tightened.

"Don't look at me, Blackie. I'm not a candidate."

"I did not mean to imply that you were."

Actually I did mean it.

"I could not possibly hit on that poor man. He has enough worries. Some of the other women hit on him. He doesn't like it, and I don't blame him."

"Indeed."

"Besides, I don't think I'm really the wife and mother type. You saw in the FBI files about my two love affairs. I was a fool in both of them. The first guy left me because he didn't like my grief when my parents died. The second was a broker who turned out to be connected. I'm not inclined to risk a third strike."

"Connected" in the parlance that she and I both understood meant linked to the Mob.

"It could be a home run!"

A dusky rose color flooded her face.

"I'm not going to hit on the poor man," she insisted firmly.

"I'm not suggesting you should."

"Oh."

"Indeed."

"You're suggesting that I wait till he hits on me . . ."

"Arguably."

"I'll decide about that when and if it happens . . . Now go find our poltergeists, Bishop Blackie, and stop filling my head with silly ideas."

I withdrew, pleased with myself. I had raised a question of considerable importance and got an acceptable answer.

She had, of course, thought about her response should the president "hit" on her, which was not a good word to describe the kind of approach Jack McGurn would take.

7

I wandered aimlessly through the West Wing as though I were lost, an act that was easy to carry on because I was lost. A young blond woman took pity on me.

"Hi, Bishop, are you lost?" she asked brightly.

"I believe I am in the District of Columbia. Arguably I am somewhere in the precincts of the White House, and, if I remember the TV program properly, I am in the West Wing. So patently I'm not lost."

She laughed happily.

"I'm Rita Suarez," she said, "and they hired me to write, especially for Hispanics."

I looked at her eyes. They were as bright and as merry as she was. No sadness there.

"And the president uses what you write for him?"

"I do two kinds of things. I prepare memos that might interest him on things he might say. I pass them up the chain through Marianna, uh, Dr. Genovesa and I don't know what happens to them. The president always sends a nice note back, so I know he reads them."

"And the other thing?"

"Sometimes they ask me to draft speeches. That's really scary because some of the words I put on paper, he might actually use in talking to the people. I did a talk for a graduation at a Cuban school in Florida. He used a lot of what I wrote. I was terrified, but I guess it went okay because he sent me a nice personal note which I couldn't read very well because he has terrible handwriting."

"You must have been relieved."

"Was I ever! I had a big head for a couple of days, then I came back down to earth . . . I'm going down to the mess for a bite. Could I buy you lunch, Bishop?"

"My mother, God be good to her, told me never to say no to a free meal."

The White House mess was a high-class version of a college cafeteria. Its customers were stuffing themselves with food and talking nervously about the events of the morning. She ordered a Diet Coke and french fries, a certifiably teenage meal. I settled for linguine à pesto, which would compare favorably with anything I could have found in Liguria. There was no red wine available. No drinking in the White House mess three-quarters of a century after the repeal of the Prohibition Amendment.

"Thank you very much, Ms. Suarez," I said. "I don't have one of those magic cards."

"I'm sure the president would give you one if you asked. The poor dear man has so much on his mind."

Starstruck, obviously.

A thin, wasted-looking man with hollow eyes and a widow's peak of sandy hair, stopped by our table.

"Good afternoon, Bishop," he said as though he had a hard time forming his words. "I hope all is well."

"The linguine is excellent," I replied guardedly.

The man was a cop and a mean cop. My hostess looked away.

"I'm Hallowell Hitchcock, the Agent-in-Charge of the Secret Service detail here."

He was the one "who had to go." Small wonder. Holdover from the last administration?

"I must commend Agents Chick and Wholley, who collected me at Ronald Reagan Washington National Airport with commendable efficiency."

He nodded, as if he were displeased at the praise of his subordinates.

"We try to do our best," he said, and slipped away.

"He's a mean man," Rita Suarez whispered to me. "Everyone is afraid of him. They say that he and Mr. Ward don't get along at all."

"Why doesn't that surprise me?"

"They also say that you're here to get rid of the ghosts. Are you an exorcist?"

In those wide, eager eyes there was no room for fear or pain or so it seemed to me.

"I'm afraid not, Rita. I'm the pastor at the Cathedral in Chicago. I grew up in the same neighborhood as the McGurn family. Sometimes I help the Cardinal with little mysteries like these playful spirits."

Trial balloon.

No reaction.

"Isn't Sean Patrick totally gorgeous? Everyone around here is in love with him."

"I would imagine . . . What do you think about the playful spirits?"

"I think it's all silly. I haven't seen any of these

things happen. Some electrical currents or something like that . . ."

Not a subject she wanted to touch.

Nothing like fear in her eyes, however.

If she were the playful one, she probably knew that I was her nemesis. Did she want to tell me about what she was doing to escape from it or was she determined to fool me?

The playful ones were very clever indeed, in their own self-defeating way.

Stefan walked by us, nodded, and rolled his eyes.

"Hi, Stefan," she said brightly.

"Hi, Rita, how's it going?"

"Working hard, naturally."

They both laughed as though they had some secret joke.

"Isn't he cute, Bishop? I tell him to just pretend to be the bad nigger rap singer and he laughs. But it's all an act."

"I don't imagine Dr. Genovesa would be amused by such an act."

"She hardly ever gets mad. I can't stand her, she's so good. I think she ought to marry the president, don't you?"

"Does everyone think that?"

"Lots of us do! Wouldn't she make a great first lady! They'd be a handsome couple, wouldn't they? I know the Daughters are all for it. He looks so lonely and sad."

"He has a lot to worry about, Rita," I said. "A wife might just add to his worries."

"Maybe you're right." She sighed. "Anyway, I have to get back to work. I'm doing another memo for the president. It's so exciting to work here and send memos to the president."

I rode the elevator up to the second floor, as I was now calling it because that's what everyone else called it.

Not once did she mention that her mother was the vice president. Did she live at the vice presidential home over at the Naval Observatory? Why would a young woman so ebullient about everything else keep that important datum secret? Did she assume I knew it?

One more suspect. Yet could anyone think that Jack McGurn would leave office and Genie would succeed? He was in good health, popular with the people, and organizing what would be a memorable presidency.

Unless someone killed him, as Tommy Horan and Marianna Genovesa thought someone might.

I retired to my room—which was impeccably clean—and decided that it was time to give my overworked eyes a bit of a rest. The problem was, I thought, that I had too many suspects—and no real evidence, not that there could be real evidence in such a case.

I fell asleep trying to remember whether I had seen any fear in Rita Suarez's eyes.

I woke up with a start. Three o'clock. My power nap had lasted too long. Where was I? I looked around, oh, yes, the Rose Room.

An imperious voice told me that it was time to take a walk. I listened closely. The command came again. It was inside my head. I rose from bed, attired myself properly—with the Roman collar for some reason I did not know—and prepared to take my leave of the room.

Bring your camera, the voice insisted.

I knew who it was, of course. Small wonder that her guardian spirit watched over the White House.

I walked through the West Wing, greeted the guards at the gate, who replied, "Good Afternoon, Bishop," and walked out onto Pennsylvania Avenue, now closed to traffic. A group of protesters, for animal rights I think, were marching up and down with what I took to be little enthusiasm.

I strolled across Lafayette Park, noting that there were as yet no signs of buds on the cherry trees and up Sixteenth Street as far as I Street. Then I turned around and walked back, fearful that if I left Sixteenth Street I might end up in Baltimore.

At the end of Sixteenth, across from Lafayette Park, in front of the Hay-Adams Hotel, I pointed my tiny Ixmus M-1 at the North Portico of the White House, framed perfectly by the bare trees and glowing in the late-afternoon sunlight.

I heard a noise to my left. A large, ugly Ford van had turned the corner and stopped in the middle of the street, right next to me. As I watched, the back door of the van fell open. A long tube emerged from the inside and two young men pointed it at the White House.

Automatically I pushed the button on the top of the camera—and kept pushing.

One young man held the tube steady, the other popped something in the front of it. The first one pulled a trigger. A projectile burst from the pipe, sizzled its way across the park, barely cleared the fence and roared into the North Portico where it exploded. Flames erupted. Sirens roared.

The back door of the van slammed shut and the van leaped forward, swerving through the traffic on Sixteenth Street. I finished the roll with several shots of the van's escape.

I found a used Bears ticket and a pencil stub in my pocket and wrote "1998 Ford van black. Two young men in jeans, both apparently white, license number Maryland 134251. Rocket launcher."

8

I was halfway across Lafayette Park before cops of every variety swarmed around the White House. One fellow threatened me with a billy club, but I evaded him and approached the fence in front of the West Wing. Three massive retired linebacker types in Park District Police uniforms converged on me, then backed off when they saw my Roman collar and my green security talisman. My friend at the gate waved them off.

"He's a guest of the president," he shouted. "Leave him alone."

They retired from the scene with ill grace.

I noted a group of men in bomb removal clothes clustering around the North Portico, one of whose colonnades was black.

You won't find anything, I advised them silently.

Others were spraying the portico and the lawn in front of it with some magic liquid, which presumably was to retard the fire that wasn't burning.

Inside the West Wing chaos ruled. A Secret Service person, noting my talisman and my collar, waved me in. I headed for the Oval Office, which seemed to be the center of chaos. Inside it people were screaming at one another, phones were ringing, Secret Service folk were posturing with drawn weapons which I assumed were Uzis. Conrad Ward and Hal Hitchock were swearing at one another. Ward was bent over in his chair, visibly shaken. He seemed to be trembling.

Tommy Horan and Ms. Chan were working telephones. The Daughters, arms around each other, were huddling in a corner, looking more angry than frightened. The president appeared on a television monitor.

"Quiet, everyone!" Marianna Genovesa ordered. "Conrad, Hal, we've had enough of your bad language, can it!"

"Sorry, Marianna." Conrad sighed and collapsed farther into a chair.

"I want to report to the American people," the ashen president spoke, "that an explosion rocked the White House this afternoon, apparently at or near the North Portico"—he glanced at his watch—"about twelve minutes ago. As best as we can tell no one was killed or injured and only minor damage was done to the White House itself, broken windows and some damage to the portico. However, old Jimmy Hoban built this place to last and the structural integrity of the portico does not seem to have been weakened.

"It is possible that the explosion was a rocket-powered grenade which was fired from the other side of Lafayette Park. It is most fortunate that the rocket, if such it were, did not hit the fence on Pennsylvania Avenue. It would have killed or maimed many of the pedestrians out there."

He didn't say protesters. Remarkable restraint.

"Our various intelligence agencies tell us that there is no preliminary evidence that this attack was carried out by a foreign power and that there are no troop movements anywhere that would suggest that the attack was part of a larger threat to this country . . ."

I found Marianna in the chaos, watching a TV monitor intently.

I pulled on her sleeve.

"Just a minute, Blackie."

"License number . . ."

"Hmn . . . Oh my!"

"Pictures," I proffered the camera, observing with considerable relief that I had closed the lens cover, the sort of thing Blackie Ryan might not have done in a crisis situation.

"Hal," she shouted, "will you get this information out to all police units? . . . Stefan, get these pictures developed—enlargements. Now!"

Clutching his Uzi the way a child would clutch her blankie, Hal glanced at my precious Bears stub.

"What's the source of this information?"

"The bishop," she nodded at me.

"Where did you get it?" he demanded.

"In front of the Hay-Adams."

"Hal," Marianna shouted, "will you stop being a tight-assed idiot and get these pictures out."

"Don't you order me around, bitch," he snarled at her. "I am the Agent-in-Charge of the Secret Service detail."

"Not for long!"

"What were you doing there?" he demanded of me.

"Taking a walk."

"How convenient."

"Hal, for the love of heaven, get this stuff out on the lines."

"I can take no responsibility for doing that."

Marianna glanced around the melee, looking for help.

"Deirdre, honey."

"Yes, ma'am."

She was ready to ride to Concord, bring word to General Grant, take the message for Garcia.

"Would you run down to the Press Office and tell Sean Patrick to give this to the president before he leaves the podium?"

"Yes, ma'am!"

As Gale Sayers used to wend his way through masses of the hated foe, Deirdre weaved through the throng and out the door of the Oval Office. The message would get to Garcia. Chase music in the background.

The president was answering a question about whether he suspected Arab terrorists.

"At this point I think we should all suspend judgment on the source of the attack. We have no evidence yet to accuse anyone."

"How soon will you evacuate the White House?"

"Eight years from now when my term is up."

"The Secret Service is reporting that the decision has been made to evacuate the White House, Mr. President."

"They can if they want. I'm not leaving. Anyone here who wants to leave is free to do so. I'm not leaving."

Deirdre appeared at the podium, gave her father my Bears stub, and whispered rapidly to him. He

frowned and asked her a question. Her answer was
one word. He nodded.

"Temporary deputy press secretary," he said with
a grin. "Gotta keep the job in the family."

The press cheered for Deirdre as she left the stage.
She waved.

"It seems that we have some information. I hope
that all the relevant police agencies have their pencils
ready. He struggled with my handwriting. '1998
Ford van black. Two young men in jeans, both apparently white, license number Maryland 134251.
Rocket launcher.'

"I repeat the license number Maryland 134251.
Perhaps we can pick them up before they abandon
the van. However, we *will* find them eventually, one
way or another . . . I think that this suggests that we
may be dealing with local terrorists."

"Mr. President, so you think that the Secret Service and the Park Service Police have failed to protect you adequately?"

"I have complete confidence in both. Naturally
we will review this incident like all such incidents to
see how we can do a better job. However, if someone
wants badly enough to fire a rocket at the White
House and if the rocket launchers are available in
mail order catalogs as they are, there's not much
we can do to stop them."

"Could you not, sir, build a high wall around the
White House?"

"Then they might fire mortars over the walls . . .
No, I think this edifice is too much like a fortress as
it is. I will not be party to making it more of a fortress. The president ought not to be isolated from his
people."

Next to me, Marianna gasped. At the phone Tommy Horan looked up and rolled his eyes.

"A couple of geeks were harassing Sean Patrick," Deirdre reported breathlessly, "so I just went out and gave it to him. He wanted to know who it was from— as if anyone else would have a Bears ticket from October in his pocket!"

She giggled and hugged me.

"A year ago October."

"Am I concerned for my personal safety? Anyone who runs for this office would be criminally naïve if he didn't think that his life expectancy would decline dramatically, especially in the current fevered style of political discourse in this country. I'd be more concerned for the safety of my family than for my own safety. I have to realize that if someone out there really wants to kill me, they probably can."

Marianna groaned. Tommy shook his head in dismay.

"It's true," Deirdre said solemnly.

"Sir, are you blaming this attack on the Republicans in Congress?"

"I'm merely saying that it would be a much happier country if the tone of political controversy was a bit lower."

"Sir, are you aware of the jets overhead?"

The president listened.

"They ought not to be in our airspace. Let me go and get rid of them."

There was not much spring in the president's step when he came into the Oval Office.

"Prime Minister Blair on the phone," Tommy Horan told him.

"Tell him just a minute . . . Conrad, did you call

the chairman of the Joint Chiefs and tell him to stand
down from DEFCON 2?"

Slumped in a chair by the windows, Conrad
looked up, apparently bewildered.

"Yes, Mr. President. He said he could not assume
responsibility for that. I ordered him to."

"I see . . . Call him back and tell him that if he
doesn't get those jets out of our airspace and call off
the alert within five minutes, I'll replace him. And,
Hal, for the love God, put your guns away."

"I won't be responsible, Mr. President . . ."

"I said put away the guns and get out of my office."

The other agents, including Agent Wholley even
grimmer than usual, promptly holstered their weapons and departed.

"I got pictures," Stefan appeared.

"I gotta talk to the prime minister . . . Tony, sorry
to keep you waiting. A lot of people around here
don't seem to want to do what they're told . . .
Thank you very much for your concern . . . The
Daughters are fine, looking like they're ready to
launch a counterattack . . . Best bet now are local en-
trepreneurs, extreme Republicans . . . We'll get them,
but it won't change anything . . . Third-level alert?
I've ordered them to stand down. They tell me that
they won't take responsibility, which is a fancy way
of saying they won't obey orders . . . You have the
same problem too . . . I've been trying to get through
to Vladimir Vladmirovich . . . haven't made it yet . . .
My best to your family too . . . We'll keep you informed."

"Let's look at the pictures," he came over to his
desk, where Stefan had spread out my handiwork.

The enlargements were striking—a second-by-second picture of the launching of the rocket grenade, its flight across the park and the lawn, and its impact at the base of the colonnade.

"Just missed the fence," the president mused. "Those protesters are lucky to be alive."

"Bishop Blackie got the license number right, Daddy," Granne informed him.

"These are enlargements of the faces of the alleged perps, Mr. President."

"Blond, white, and all-American . . . Well done, Blackie."

He didn't ask what I was doing out there at just the right time. Nor was I about to tell him that his wife had made me take a walk.

"There are two sets, Mr. President," Stefan said proudly.

"Good. Sean Patrick, you go out and show them, with the help of your charming assistants. Yes, Granne, I said plural. Get Hal back in here."

The Agent-in-Charge returned, prim and defiant.

"Yes, sir," he snapped.

"Hal, you get this set out to all the agencies."

"I can't take responsibility for circulating those photographs," Hal insisted, "unless I can verify the source."

"Hal, do it now. That's a direct order. If you choose not to obey, I will dismiss you from your office."

"The Marines will be landing shortly, Mr. President," Conrad Ward said glumly, still hunched over in his chair, head still in his hands.

"Marines!"

"President Putin on the line, Mr. President."

"Vladimir Vladmirovich," the president began and then, in what I suspected was very poor Russian, thanked the Russian for his concern, assured him that there had been no casualties, and that the Daughters were well and feisty, and that almost certainly it was a domestic plot. Then his face became pained, doubtless as Putin raised the question of the security alert. The English words "stand down" were repeated several times. Then there was an affectionate and sentimental farewell. Whenever Jack McGurn went into Russian, Ellen had often said, he turned as sentimental as a real Russian.

"Without the vodka!"

He hung up slowly.

"Marianna, call Bill down at Foggy Bottom and tell him we're sure that there's no Arab involvement and he should tell the relevant Arabs that we regard the rumors that there were to be both false and bigoted."

"Yes, Mr. President."

"Marines, Conrad?"

The chief of staff was a hollow man. He knew he had blown his job by falling to pieces at a time of crisis. He did not look up.

"There's a contingency plan that, if there is ever an attack on the White House, a special company of Marines will be lifted by helicopter from Quantico up here."

"Why didn't I know about this?"

"I didn't think it worth bothering you about."

"Great! Everyone will think there's a coup d'etat going on . . . Sean Patrick, you and your two charming assistants go down to the Briefing Room and show them these pictures. Ask that all law enforcement agencies look for these two perpetuators. Tell them I'll be back shortly. They'll want to know who took the pictures. Tell them that it was a tourist who happened to be walking along Sixteenth Street with a camera in his hand . . . Right, Blackwood?"

"Where's Sixteenth Street?"

"Yes, Mr. President," Granne replied without a trace of a giggle.

"Secretary of state, Mr. President."

"Yes, Bill, I know about the security alert and the jets in the air over us. Did you know that the Marines are going to land here in a few minutes? Yeah, I know, no one fired a rocket at the White House during your term. Did they refuse to obey you too? How did you deal with it? Okay. I'll try that."

"Mr. President, the vice president is on the phone. She says she's about to leave for the White House."

Jack closed his eyes and shook his head.

"Genie, we don't need the two of us in one place if there is another attack. Please stay where you are . . . I understand you want to help and I appreciate it. However, right now your personal safety is of utmost importance . . . No, Genie, it's just not a good idea. Thank you for understanding . . ."

None of the staff said a word or even gave a sign of reaction.

Patently the vice president was a problem.

Cliff Sommers, the chief usher appeared, somewhat hesitantly.

"What's the bad news, Cliff?"

On the TV monitor, Sean Patrick was at the podium while his charming assistants, poised and serious, displayed the photos.

My photos. Well, their mother's photos.

Clever idea using the Daughters. It said that the White House social system was still intact.

"Not too bad, Mr. President. The White House architect thinks that the Colonnade is structurally intact. There's a lot of glass on the floors inside and a fair amount on the lawn.

"We are scheduled for a tour tomorrow, are we not?"

"Yes, Mr. President."

"Then we'll do the tour. Activate all our military aides and have them here for the tour in full uniform. That will create the impression that the United States of America is still functioning efficiently."

"Yes, Mr. President."

"Fix up the windows in the Queens' Bedroom first. I don't want Bishop Ryan cutting his feet on glass or freezing to death tonight."

"Yes, Mr. President."

"Marianna, the chairman of the Joint Chiefs, if you please."

"Yes, Mr. President."

"Admiral, I want to hear only two words from you—'yes' and 'sir.' I now give you a direct order. If you do not obey it, I will dismiss you from office and appoint a successor who will obey. I will have you up for a court-martial on every possible charge tomorrow. Is that understood? Good. Now within five minutes, under the same penalties I have mentioned, I want the military to stand down from the unauthorized security alert and I want all those jets out of White House airspace, is that clear? Also I want the Marines out of here tomorrow, is that clear? Are you prepared to obey my direct orders, Admiral?"

Just enough silence for the man at the other end of the line to snap, "Yes, sir!"

"Good, see to it then!"

Just like Sean Cronin.

"What do I have to do next?" he asked.

"Tell the people about the Marines."

"I better do that before they land. Ms. Chan, a cabinet meeting immediately. Congressional leaders tomorrow morning."

"Yes, Mr. President."

He arrived at the Briefing Room just as the Daughters had vacated it, the two looking extraordinarily pleased with themselves.

"I've just been informed that the Washington police," he began, "have recovered the van from which the rocket was fired, on a side street in the northwest side of Washington. They found several more rockets and another rocket launcher. They are looking for fingerprints.

"We ask everyone in America to watch carefully for the young men whose pictures you've just seen. Do not try to apprehend them yourselves. They may very well be dangerous. Inform your local police.

"The Marines will land shortly. Apparently there is a contingency plan which indicates that when there is an attack on the White House a company of specially trained Marines will be flown in by helicopter. The Marines are always welcome. I regret that we do not have the Marine Band to welcome them.

"I also wish to announce that the jets which were patrolling the airspace above the White House have been recalled. Moreover, American armed forces around the world have been ordered to stand down from a heightened state of alert. Finally, we will have the broken glass swept away and the windows replaced by tomorrow morning. So the regular Saturday tour will occur. I have spoken with Prime Minister Blair and President Putin, both of whom were very much concerned about my safety and that of my family and the whole White House staff."

Many questions.

"Mr. President, are you absolutely certain there was no involvement of a foreign power in this attack?"

"Not absolutely certain, but there is no indication that the assault was anything but domestic terrorism."

"Sir, do you have any comment on Representative Dillingham's comment?"

"I am not familiar with the congressman's comment."

"He said that the attack was little more than a childish prank in protest against the current occupant of the White House."

"Ah, that sounds like the congressman . . . Well, if one of Jimmy Hoban's colonnades had not intervened, the missile could have penetrated into the crosshalls of the White House and killed or maimed anyone present there."

"Like your daughters, Mr. President?"

"Like anyone who works there."

"Mr. President, do you believe that this attack was aimed at you personally?"

"I don't know."

"You don't think it might be a manifestation of the rage of decent Americans against you and your administration?"

"Decent people don't try to kill other people."

Back in the Oval Office, he glanced around at the crowd that was thinner than it had been.

"Where are the Daughters?"

"Arguably in the Corner Office, facilitating the work of the press secretary."

"Blackwood!" he said, noting my presence for the first time. "Great pictures! I don't want to know which of your instincts sent you out there . . ."

"No, you don't want to know."

No way.

"What about Congressman Dillingham!"

"By his own admission, a devout Christian."

"Yeah . . . All right, I need to see Mae, Claire, Jesus, Ogden, Tommy, Marianna, and of course you, Blackwood. Now!"

"Yes, Mr. President!"

The Oval Office cleared, the small group he had convened filed in.

"Sit down, everyone," the president invited them. "I think we all need a drink. Mae, Ogden, you're not Catholic, but I never knew either of you to refuse a sipeen of the crayture."

He removed from the recesses of his desk a bottle of Jameson's Twelve Year Special Reserve, now almost thirty years old.

"Marianna, what's the weather like tomorrow?"

"Like today, maybe a little warmer."

"Why don't you see whether we can get the Marine Band to do a concert on the front lawn tomorrow morning. There'll be a lot of curious people coming to look at the wounded White House. We might provide a little entertainment for them."

"Yes, Mr. President."

He found a cabinet of Waterford tumblers and

distributed them to all of us. Then he made the rounds and poured each of us a drink with a heavy hand. In my case the hand was, appropriately, even heavier.

"Gentlepersons," he said as he sank in the chair behind his desk, "to our continued survival."

A modest enough proposal.

"Blackwood, will you say Mass for us tomorrow afternoon? In the Blue Room, maybe . . ."

"Where Grover Cleveland was married . . ."

Not an appropriate comment, but hardly unintentional.

"Though," I continued, "Alice Blue Gown was married in the East Room."

"Tommy, you still an altar boy?"

"Perpetually, Mr. President."

"You'll get all the stuff for Bishop Ryan?"

"Sure."

I would call the Cathedral and request an immediate translation to D.C. of such full pontifical robes and appropriate jewelry as could be found.

We sipped a little more of our Jameson's.

Outside the windows, I noted a group of helicopters settling on the South Lawn. The Marines had landed. They poured out of the copters in khaki-and-blue uniforms with red trim and white hats, like they were on dress parade. I had expected fatigues, boots, and grenades at their belts. As I watched, they formed up in ranks, weapons on their shoulders. Three men strode towards the West Wing.

"All right," POTUS said, "Conrad is going to take over our liaison with Congress at his own request. Tommy will become chief of staff. Marianna will be the sole deputy chief of staff . . ."

"Might I suggest that we all hide our drinks," I interjected. "The Marines have landed and even at this moment are at the gates."

The president leaped to his feet and threw open the door from the Oval Office to the Rose Garden.

"Mr. President," a handsome colonel with several rows of ribbons and a square face said. "The Marines have landed, sir."

He saluted crisply.

"And the situation is well in hand!"

"Yes, SIR!"

"You and your men are most welcome, Colonel. The whole nation will be reassured that for the next twenty-four hours the Marines will be protecting the White House. Don't worry about the Rose Garden. There are no roses in it yet."

I caught Marianna's eye. She struggled to squelch a giggle. She would have to learn that when an Irishman like Jack McGurn is laying it on thick, he really lays it on thick.

"Yes, SIR . . . Now if you permit, we will deploy our personnel inside the White House, according to orders, SIR."

"I think we can change those orders, Colonel. There is no danger inside. I need the Marines to reassure people outside that the situation is well in hand. Your men are trained to direct traffic, if necessary?"

"Marines can do anything, SIR!"

"Very good, deploy half of your persons in Lafayette Park to direct traffic quickly through the area and protect Pennsylvania Avenue. Let the protesters continue to protest if they're not as scared as they should be. Create the impression of friendly but firm professionals."

"That's what Marines are, SIR! Friendly but firm professionals!"

"Deploy the rest around the fence on the South Lawn. Advise them to be considerate of the feelings of the Park Service Police and the Secret Service, both of whom are quite nervous at the present. Nonetheless, the Marines are in charge."

"I understand, Sir."

"Are their weapons loaded?"

"Yes, SIR!"

"Good. They are only to fire if fired upon, but then they should return fire immediately."

"Yes, SIR!"

"Thank you, Colonel . . ."

"MacIntosh, Sir. Major Thomas. Captain Saunders."

The major was black. The captain was a woman. All very correct.

George Washington fell from the wall. The American flagpole behind the president swayed. He held it in place. Dr. Genovesa gracefully scooped up the first president and returned him to his place.

"Get out of here," I whispered, "you nasty little bitch!"

"What was that, sir!" asked the disconcerted Colonel MacIntosh.

"General Washington periodically expresses his opinion, Colonel. I'm sure he's celebrating the landing of the Marines."

"Yes, SIR."

"Colonel MacIntosh, this lovely woman is Dr. Genovesa, my deputy chief of staff. She will act as liaison with the United States Marines."

"Ma'am." Formal bow.

Marianna, her face a lovely rose, shook hands with the colonel, the captain, and the major. They all beamed, as she enveloped them in her magic smile.

"Welcome to the Oval Office," she said as if she owned it.

Colonel MacIntosh saluted again, as did the other two Marines. They marched out across the fallow Rose Garden.

"Thank you, Mr. President," she said evenly.

"You have to understand, Marianna, that this scene was originally enacted in the Manila Hotel in 1936 with General Douglas MacArthur coming down the staircase with Greta Garbo on his arm."

"I see, sir . . . Mr. President, might I ask a question?"

"Certainly!"

"Do you prepare these little scenes beforehand or do you make them up as you go along?"

Aha, I told myself, the ice is cracking just a little.

"They're all prepared beforehand," he said. "Naturally."

Jesus Lopez laughed. "They're all based on some movie he may have seen twenty years ago."

We had recovered our drinks. He would not dare fill the tumblers again in the present laid-back mood of his staff.

"Claire, what effect will this little interlude have on the rest of the world?"

"Good thing the bourses aren't open till Monday. The world gasped, Mr. President. It's just beginning to breathe again. I don't think you realize how important you are and how popular."

"Maybe it's a good thing I don't . . . What's happening in China?"

"New troop formations are approaching Beijing. Best guess is that they're loyal to the hardest of the hard-liners. There might be a bloody purge of those who want to avoid civil war. Maybe street fighting in a day or two."

"Then what?"

"The CIA guess that it will be summer before the various rebel groups get their acts together. While that's happening the hard-liners in Beijing will sweep through the countryside, killing everyone they encounter as they did in Tiananmen Square and brutally reasserting their authority."

"You concur?" the president asked.

"Girl, she be saying CIA forgets about cell phones and Internet. She say rebels get their act together in week, two most. War over by summer, new government, maybe not much better. Girl she be right usually."

"No guarantees, Mr. President," Marianna said modestly. "Only guesses. That's all any of us can do about China."

"We have to go with the good guessers . . . You want to get back downstairs, Claire?"

"Yes, Mr. President. As quickly as I can. Need you, I yell."

"You'd better come to the cabinet meeting."

"Yes, Mr. President," she said without much enthusiasm.

"Now I want to talk to you about Congressman

Dillingham . . . Jesus, Ogden, did that comment of his break any laws?"

Ogden Jefferson, a man with the face and physique of an African-American Abraham Lincoln, drew himself to his full height.

"There are laws, Mr. President, against murder, against inciting to murder, against murder of a president or inciting to murder a president and there are laws against advocating the violent overthrow of the government. Ole Jeremiah Dillingham has come pretty close to breaking those laws. You could probably make a case in court on the basis of a summary of his statements that he is advocating minimally the violent overthrow of the government. Thing is you'd only want to make that case when you're sure you'd win. I don't think you can be that sure. Then a lot of what he says is under congressional immunity."

"I agree with Ogden," Jesus added. "There is a lot of stuff in the Christian newsletters that is incendiary and against which you could make a good case. You have to be wary of charges of violating freedom of speech and freedom of the press. Yet the things that are being said, even in places like the *Wall Street Journal*, taken together, constitute a pretty bad pattern. Most people don't think you're a degenerate. They like you, as the polls show. They are not aware yet of how prevalent this other stuff is."

"Maybe the first thing to do," Mae Rosen interjected, "is kind of an educational campaign to bring the depth and viciousness of this campaign to public attention. You could get friendly congressmen and clergy to denounce them."

"Perhaps," Marianna offered, "you could serve warning that you consider this stuff dangerous to the country and that if it does not stop you will have to consider taking action."

"All right, we'll begin with what Mae suggested. I'll hold off on the warning. Okay, everyone?"

"We can use Congressman Dillingham's comments as a start," Tommy proposed. "Get our counterattack out first thing Monday morning."

"The point is," the president, said thoughtfully, "that they believe that the election of any Democrat is in and of itself illegitimate. First they tried to impeach one, then they stole the election from another, now they want to kill a third. We have a long history of extreme partisanship in this country. This, however, is something new."

"And very serious," Ogden said. "Very, very serious."

"It's the mix of political reactions and religious fundamentalism," Marianna observed. "Congressman Dillingham is both. Somehow the elite media don't see how dangerous they are. Most Republicans don't want to see the president dead."

"The *Wall Street Journal* wouldn't mind," Jesus Lopez suggested.

"We're agreed then," the president summed up. "We'll begin to talk about them and make some preparations for further steps if we have to."

Ms. Chan buzzed him.

"I think my cabinet is here. Tommy, you'd better come with me. You too, Claire. Marianna would you mind taking care of all the things I asked you to and have forgotten."

"Certainly, Mr. President . . . One compliment goes a long way . . ."

More laughter from the group.

A touch of flirtation?

One hoped so.

"Supper upstairs in the Solarium, Blackwood," the president shouted after me. In the corridor between the Oval Office and the Cabinet Room, the Daughters were getting an autograph from the secretary of state.

I went up to my room, where the window had already been replaced, and glanced out on the darkening North Lawn. The Marines were very much in evidence. The crowd in Lafayette Park seemed friendly. Marianna was out on the lawn talking to some Marines.

I dialed headquarters on my cell phone.

"What the hell is going on?" Sean Cronin began our conversation the way he always did. Its premise was that somehow I was responsible for the attack on the White House. Or at least hadn't prevented it.

"We repelled the attack, the Marines have landed, and the situation is well in hand."

"Who were the attackers?"

"Republicans."

"I assumed that . . . I also assume that those were your pictures."

"Arguably."

"I don't want to know how you knew it was coming."

"Neither did the president."

"Good thing you didn't leave the cap on the lens, as you have done before."

"Defamation!"

There had never been a chance of that.

"Any progress on the poltergeists?"

"A little. It was interrupted this afternoon as you may have noted."

"And the bimbos?"

"I have alerted the wise Mike Casey the Cop to the possibility that Republican elves might be sniffing around Loyola in search of more false charges."

Pause.

"Very clever, Blackwood, very clever. Well, see to it."

The rules of the game prescribe that I am not given time to respond to such injunctions.

The phone rang again.

"Mr. Casey, Bishop."

"Blackie, some hints that you might be right in your suspicions."

Patently.

"Ah?"

"My people have learned that there is a couple which has been sniffing around Loyola, very discreetly seeking dirt on the president. They are apparently acting slowly as though they have all the time in the world."

"They must proceed very carefully."

"My people haven't got any names yet, but it's Friday night . . ."

"I seem to have remembered that."

"And they know a couple of bars at which our friends hang out."

"Excellent!"

"The trick will be to establish contact with them, then to assess their sophistication and determination. It would appear that they have had little success so far. Jack, after all, was very popular at the law school."

"We invite them into the trap and let them talk
. . . Your personnel are solid, I presume?"

"Rock solid."

Naturally.

I would not tell the president until further progress
was made.

I looked out the window again. Marianna was still
talking to the Marines, who were now wearing off-
white windbreakers over their uniforms.

Then to my astonishment, there appeared in Lafayette Park, the president of the United States, his
daughters trailing after him, accompanied by a couple of Secret Service people, among them Agent
Wholley, and a half squad of Marines.

I turned on the disgracefully small television that
was out of place in the Rose Room, as I preferred
as a name to the Queens' Bedroom.

"The president has just emerged from the West
Wing and is walking out on Pennsylvania Avenue,"
the anchorperson described the obvious for us. "He
is crossing the street to greet the crowd in Lafayette
Park . . . Mollie, you're down there, what's it like?"

"It's amazing, Jennifer. The president is walking
among the crowd, shaking hands with them and
thanking them for their support. It is a very friendly
crowd. His charming daughters, who apparently followed him out here without bothering to ask permission, are doing the same thing. The Marines are
holding back the crowd, keeping them under control."

"Is this not very dangerous, Mollie?"

"Or very brave, Jennifer. The crowd, however, is
friendly. I believe there's a public address hook up
now. The president is about to say a few words."

"The United States Marines told me the crowd was very friendly, a typical Marine understatement, and wanted to see me. So I thought I would come out and say hello.

"So hello everyone!"

"Hello!"

"Thank you! My daughters joined me without exactly asking permission, but that's the way with young people these days."

(He extended his arms around both the Daughters.)

"It's been a long hard day. We've all survived. I'm grateful to the Marines that they dropped in to visit us. Thank you, Marines!

"And I'm grateful to all of you who came out on this lovely evening to tell me that the people of the United States are still on my side. That means more to me than I could possibly tell you!

"So thank you very much!"

His little entourage slipped back into the safety of the West Wing gate.

No sign of Marianna Genovesa in the whole interlude.

What film?

Jimmy Stewart landing in Paris in *The Spirit of St. Louis.*

9

"Conrad goes," Deirdre said firmly. "Immediately. He's rancid."

New teenage word.

"And Hopalong Hal," her sister added. "I hate him."

The four members of the McGurn family and I were demolishing a tasty sea bass dinner in the Solarium.

All four TVs were on but the volume was low.

"I have already anticipated your wishes," the president replied. "Mr. Ward will head up our office of congressional relations, which he has already started and where he wants to work."

"Cool!"

"Mr. Thomas Horan will now become chief of staff. Dr. Marianna Genovesa will continue as deputy chief of staff."

"We're saving this news for next week," Sean Patrick told his sisters. "Too much already this week and we don't want to look like Conrad was dumped because he lost his cool under fire."

"That could happen to anyone," the president said soothingly.

"It won't ever happen to Tommy."

"Or Marianna. Will it, Bishop Blackie?"

"Patently."

"Moreover, I told the secretary of the treasury that if he did not get Hopalong out by Monday morning, I would personally throw him off the balcony up here."

"Righteous."

"Blackwood, what can a man do about daughters that are deliberately disobedient?"

Cries of outrage from the Daughters.

"You didn't tell us not to follow you out!"

"Anyway, those cute Marines said it was safe, didn't they?"

"It is an interesting question, Mr. President, and I must respond from the secure perspective of one who doesn't have any daughters. However, I suspect the original mistake was having them in the first place. After that the whole algorithm is locked in."

"See!"

The phone rang.

"Sean Patrick . . . Yes, Marianna . . . That's cool. I'd better let you talk to himself.

"They've got tentative IDs on the perps," Sean Patrick said as he handed the phone to his father.

"Marianna! Solid IDs? . . . From local cops? . . . FBI warrants? . . . That should be good enough . . . Where? . . . Ohio? In Dillingham's district! Go ahead with it . . . You want Sean Patrick to come down? Okay. He'll be right there . . . Thank you, Marianna."

He hung up the phone after a moment.

"You better go down there, Sean. You know how camera shy she is. Be cautious about the announcement. Tentative identification. Not certain. FBI warrants. Don't mention the congressman."

"Got it!"

Off he went.

Well, if I were as totally gorgeous as she is," Granne informed us, "I wouldn't be camera shy."

"I didn't notice either of you being camera shy today," her father observed.

"Daddy!"

We turned up the volume on the bank of televisions on the opposite wall. The waiters cleared away the remnants of the meal and asked about dessert. I was the only one who accepted chocolate ice cream—in lieu of the rum raisin that I prefer.

Sean Patrick's flaming red hair and beard appeared simultaneously on all four screens.

"We have tentative IDs on the gunmen," he said casually. "I insist that they are still tentative. The information is from the police chief in Boonstown, Ohio, who recognized the gunmen from the photographs as two young men who had been in trouble there. He identifies them as Mark Hannah, that's with a final 'h' and Steve Andersen, that's s-e-n. The FBI has issued arrest warrants for these two suspects. I don't think we can take any questions at this time."

"Good," the president said.

"Either one of us could do it better," Deirdre muttered.

"Deirdre!"

"All right, all right! He is pretty good!"

CNN had an earlier interview with Congressman Dillingham. He affected the image of the old-time rural politician or perhaps rural preacher—flowing white hair, black suit with a vest, string tie. I remembered that southern Ohio was the land of the Buckeyes, not the football team, but the rural folk clad in butternut clothes, who had supported the Confederacy.

"I am completely opposed to violence," the congressman began. "He who takes the sword will perish by the sword as the Book says. Yet I can understand completely the anger of good Christian men and women about the degeneracy [he pronounced it like it was two words] in high places in our land today. Fact is, we have a de-generate president today. Fact is, he associates with known degenerates. Fact is he discriminates in favor of de-generates in the government. Fact is this angers a lot of good Christians. Fact is that people are gonna keep shooting at this man until he does the decent thing and steps down. He has no right to be president, no de-generate does."

The Daughters screamed imprecations at the CNN screen that I will not repeat.

"You're predicting more attacks on the White House, Congressman?"

"God will not be mocked, the flames of hell are burning around our executive mansion. The president cannot escape them."

Not notably upset about these predictions, the president smiled contentedly.

"Perfect target." He sighed.

"You or him?"

"I'm not worried, Blackwood."

"You should be worried, Daddy. That man is evil."

"He would tell you, darling, that he's a Christian."

The phone rang again.

"Yes, Mae, I saw it. Wonderful, huh? NBC wants one of us to go on with him on Sunday morning? Is that a good idea? Well, I suppose it is. Who should we send? Marianna? I'm not so sure about that. You want to ask her? No, you don't. You want me to ask her. I'd rather not. All right, if you say so."

He hung up.

"Hooray!" yelped the younger daughter.

"She'll cream him!" cried the elder daughter.

"Blackwood?"

"I'm not going to ask her."

"What do you think?"

"Either Dr. Genovesa or no one."

He nodded thoughtfully.

"You're right of course."

Silence.

Reluctantly he dialed a number.

"Marianna? Jack . . . You saw Dillingham? . . . I agree he was fabulous for our side . . . Uh, we have a chance to put up someone from our side on NBC on Sunday morning . . . Volunteer duty of course . . . You'd love to? . . . Why doesn't that surprise me! . . . Thank you very much . . . Yes, Bishop Ryan is here . . . I'm sure he'll pray for you . . . Again thank you very much!"

The Daughters high-fived each other.

"Remarkable woman," I observed, trying to sound like an Irish-American Polonius.

"Indeed. I'll be afraid to watch."

"Patently she will destroy that Buckeye Grendel."

"Oh, yes, Blackwood. The Archbishop of Washington is coming for lunch on Sunday . . ."

"For what purpose?"

"To lay down the law to me about homosexuality and abortion."

"Indeed!"

"He invited himself."

"Patently."

"You'll join us?"

"What was it that the virtuous Dr. Genovesa said? I'd love to."

"Any hints about how to deal with him?"

"First of all, he is not, despite what you think, deaf. He simply ignores what he does not want to hear. Secondly, he is not blind. He simply does not want to see women because that would require that he acknowledge their presence."

"We want to come!" Deirdre.

"I don't think that would be a good idea. Would it, Blackwood?"

A poltergeist took possession of me.

"I think it would be an excellent idea."

It would be an interesting Sunday. Dr. Genovesa's appearance on television would be a turning point. The nation would find out about her, an intelligent and beautiful woman who worked for the president. They would wonder . . . So too might the president.

From the point of view of those who hoped that he would move not so much out of grief as out of paralysis, this could be a very interesting event. In any case, the discovery by the nation that such a fascinating woman was on his staff would win him points too.

In the "Molotov Room," as I thought of it at the moment, I said my prayers on my knees and prayed for all involved. They would need my prayers in the next couple of days. I also prayed for the ghost player. She needed my prayers too, poor little thing.

I was wakened from deep sleep by the sound of the television and the flicking on and off of the lights in the room. At first I had no idea where I was, why the television was on, and why the lights were flicking on and off. Slowly it dawned on me that I was in the Molotov Room at the White House and that, after a day of not being the center of attention, the merry prankster was back.

I permitted myself to be very angry.

"Get out of here, you silly little bitch. I have no time for you. Run away to your cave with all the other freaks!"

The noises stopped. Sadness, deep, yearning sadness like a child who has just lost all her Christmas presents. I felt sorry for her. She was a nuisance, just a poor lonely little creature seeking attention. However, one cannot yield to such sentiments when dealing with ghost players.

"I don't care if you feel sad. That's your problem. Stop messing around with this house. Now get out of here. Now! Scat!"

She hurried away.

"Come back and turn off the lights and the television."

They both went out. I had the impression that the departing ghost player was running down the corridor. I opened the door. No one in sight. The little witch was fond of me. That was intolerable. I would pray for her at Mass. That might offend her. Good.

It took me a long time to sleep. The next thing of which I was conscious was a very large band which, with considerable fervor, was playing John Philip Sousa's *"Semper Fidelis"* just outside my window. Dr. Genovesa had delivered the Marine Band as promised.

I peeked out the window, a glorious false spring

day with bright sunlight. The Marines were fully in charge of Pennsylvania Avenue and Lafayette Park, controlling the scene with a combination of efficiency and charm. The crowd in the park was in good humor, a little festival provided for the American people by the McGurn administration.

In the Solarium, while consuming my usual modest breakfast, I discovered that the press had mixed reactions to the assault of the day before. The *Washington Post* lamented the president's cowardice. Why had he not taken the opportunity to denounce the right-wing extremists who were responsible for the attack? Did he need another Muir Federal Building explosion to take action?

That we had found out late in the evening, perhaps after the *Post* had gone to press, who the attackers were, had not bothered the *Post*'s pontificators in residence.

The *New York Times* for its part lamented the shallow braggadocio of the presidential response, his frivolous pretense that the first attack on the White House since the British burned it was not a serious matter. Moreover risking himself and his children to serious harm during his silly walk through Lafayette Park revealed once again the lack of gravity in his person and his administration and confirmed once again that he had been an inadequate choice for president.

The Daughters would raise the roof at the suggestion that they were children.

Heads the editorial writers won, tails the president lost.

Meantime CNN was on with an overnight poll showing that 78 percent of those polled approved of how the president had handled the crisis and 15 percent had no opinion.

These findings were displayed on the screen with pictures of the Marines in the Park and the Marine Band playing "From the Halls of Montezuma."

Jack McGurn and his crowd were not yet experienced enough and perhaps not clever enough or cynical enough to turn the attack on the White House into a public relations victory. Yet they had done so, more by chance than by deliberate plot.

Typical shallow Chicago Irish Catholics, no solid principles, no clearly thought-out policies, only pragmatic and instinctual responses.

The next pictures were of the two "alleged perps" being taken into the Boonstown jail. Punks, shabby losers, probably high school dropouts. But they had earned their fifteen minutes of glory—they had fired a rocket-propelled grenade at the White House.

Then the ineffable Congressman Dillingham appeared on the monitor.

"I protest against the administration's diabolic witch-hunt against these two young men. They're good, clean living, all-American boys. I deplore all violence. Yet I can understand why upright, God-fearing American Christians would be upset about the deterioration of American life. We have a servant of Satan sitting in the White House. He must be stopped from selling the soul of our country to Satan like he has sold his own soul."

"How do you know that the president has sold his soul, Congressman?"

"Why else would he order all the offices of government to hire de-generates? Pretty soon the whole country will be run by de-generates!"

The congressman, elected in the Gingrich revolution, had been reelected this time by only a few hundred votes. I suspected that by now even the conservatives in southeastern Ohio had had enough of him. He had no influence in Congress. The media ran to him whenever they were looking for a hot copy quote. Unfailingly he provided it. Then he would be cited in the Christian newsletters that appeared across the country every week. "Congressman says president has sold his soul."

Daft, without influence within the Beltway (as this manic segment of our society liked to call itself), he was still a voice heard all over the country. Dangerous? More than somewhat.

I would indeed pray for the virtuous Marianna as she entered her gladiatorial combat with this Buckeye Grendel. I had, however, no doubt about the outcome. Defeated or not, his voice would still be heard across the land.

The next CNN shot was live from the North Portico. The president was showing a group of congresspersons the damage to the colonnade.

"The rocket, as we now know," he was saying, "was fired from the north side of Lafayette Park, from which you can get a clear shot at the White House if you are of a mind to. If the trees in the park were in bloom, the grenade would have surely exploded in one of them, probably causing injury and even death to anyone walking through the park, like that women with the buggy over there."

The camera instantly picked up the woman with a buggy.

She surely was not a plant, but the president doubtless had one of his eyes on the park.

"It barely cleared the fence on the North Lawn. If it had exploded there, it might have hurt scores of tourists on Pennsylvania Avenue."

"Protesters," sneered a congressman, obviously a Republican.

"American citizens, exercising their right of freedom of speech," the president corrected him. "... Finally it collided with this rock-hard pillar of Jimmy Hoban's, the Irishman who built the place. It broke a lot of windows, which have been repaired for this morning's tour. Little damage, no casualties, thanks be to God ... Did you know that when they redid the East Façade a few years ago they found marks of the fire the English lighted. Maybe two centuries from now they'll rediscover the explosion marks on the colonnade."

"What if the shooter had moved the launcher a few inches to the right?" the majority leader asked.

"It could have easily crashed into the lobby of the White House and exploded there, killing or maiming anyone in the general vicinity."

"You think then that the appropriate charge against the perpetrators," the Speaker of the House asked, "is attempted murder?"

"I'll leave that to the Justice Department ..."

"Mr. President," a handsome fellow with a New England twang, a Serious Republican perhaps, asked, "what do you think can be done to prevent a similar attack in the future?"

"We can easily prevent a copycat shot from the same place by controlling the traffic at the north end of the Park. I don't know how in our society we can do any more than take the usual security precautions and pray."

"That seems a little weak, sir."

"Does it, Congressman? Look at this mail-order catalog. You can buy a rocket launcher of the model used for $145.00. It is allegedly fixed so that it can't launch rockets but as we all know those 'fixes' can be unfixed. As long as you and your friends in the National Rifle Association block meaningful gun control, there will be such attacks. And as long as the right wing of your own party suggests that I have sold my soul to the devil, there will be such attacks."

Properly rebuked, the congressman retreated.

"Do you feel your life is in constant danger, Mr. President?"

"As I said yesterday, any person who seeks this office knows that risks go up enormously. A president has to take his chances. It would be a bit easier, I should think, if the passion of partisanship would diminish somewhat, if there were less of a conviction that no Democratic president has a claim on legitimacy. However, I have no control over such matters."

"Aren't you making yourself a bit of a hero, sir?"

"Just an Irish fatalist, Congressman."

Another PR victory for our side. We had made our points with the help of the opposition. How could anyone be so dumb as to say such things in front of a television camera? Perhaps you had to be from a district where people expected you to say such things.

I decided to drift down to the West Wing.

My friend Agent Wholley, expressionless as always, opened the door for me.

"Good morning, Agent Wholley."

"Good morning, Bishop Ryan ... You're really

saying Mass in the Blue Room this afternoon?"

"Yes, Agent Wholley, I am."

"Secret Service personnel permitted?"

"Required."

"It counts for Sunday?"

A pious, old-fashioned Catholic!

"Certainly."

"I can come?"

"You'll be most welcome."

"Thank you, sir."

The West Wing was relatively quiet. On Saturdays, even after attacks on the White House, men and women in the McGurn presidency obviously felt free to stay home. Not much chance of interviewing people today, not that I had much confidence that my interviews would uncover anything about my sad young friend, whoever she was.

As I wandered through the building, I encountered Ms. Genovesa, in jeans and sweatshirt (with the White House in white on dark blue). The sweatshirt revealed only the barest hint of belly, unlike those that the Daughters affected.

"Good morning, Bishop Blackie," she said somewhat flustered. "I'm going home to dress before Mass."

"Ah."

"I told the Daughters they had to, so I must myself."

"*Buona fortuna* in the fight with Grendel tomorrow."

"I'm not worried yet about him, more worried about what I should wear. The Daughters say a white dress. I think it would make me look like a trollop."

"Hardly."

It might make her look more like Cleopatra.

"Mae says black with a touch of white at the neck. No jewels of course."

"Just like the vice president!"

She laughed.

"I guess I'm not the Rodeo Drive type. Flatbush Avenue."

"Does not the president permit his top staff a day off?"

"Stefan and I are putting together a dossier of material in which the president's life is indirectly threatened. Chilling."

I wandered down to the Corner Office.

"No charming assistants today?"

"They're still abed. Collapsed after yesterday."

"I assume that they will be furious to learn that they are now officially children?"

"I hope I'm not around when they read it . . . Incidentally your robes have arrived from Chicago. I had to fight Hopalong to get them cleared. He didn't understand what that stuff was all for. It took a call to the secretary of the treasury at home to make him let it through."

"The secretary then understands the problem."

"If he didn't already . . . I had one of the ushers hang it in your room."

"Excellent. Now if I can figure out how to put all that stuff on . . ."

I returned to the residence and sought refuge in the Green Room and sat on the uncomfortable couch in front of which was a table boasting a coffee urn which belonged to John and Abigail Adams and two candlesticks purchased by James Monroe and sold to his friend James Madison to defray the expenses of negotiating the Louisiana Purchase. John Quincy Adams and his wife Louisa stared down at me with which I thought to be faint disapproval.

Couldn't blame them.

Thomas Jefferson's dining room, James Madison's office, James Monroe's card room, Mrs. Theodore Roosevelt's receiving room, the embalming room for poor Willie Lincoln (who died of typhoid fever) and the place from which the Kennedy children watched a requiem Mass for their father.

Too much history.

A woman, pretty, very dark skin, with a Native American jacket and a plain gray skirt, knocked at the door.

"May I come in, Bishop?"

"Certainly," I stood up, "Travels By Night, I presume. But you're not Apache, as I was told. Patently your jacket is Yaqui."

"Paschua Yaqui, Bishop, seven-eighths that is. They think it is the same as Apache. Since the Apache are high status I don't argue."

She sat down on the chair next to the couch, both pieces of furniture, in addition to being outstandingly uncomfortable, date to 1790.

"Germaine Connelly is music to my Irish ears," I said. "However, Travels By Night is much more mysterious."

"I'm not exactly a medicine woman, Bishop. Maybe a little bit sometimes to help people. Not serious work. Actually they sent me to find you to see what kind of altar you want for Mass tonight."

"Standard issue—table, white cloth, two candles,

crucifix, hosts, chalice, wine, and water. Mr. Horan will be the acolyte."

"Reader?"

"Hadn't thought of it . . . Would you like to do it?"

"Love to . . . If you think we Yaqui are real Catholics. Not everyone is sure of that, you know."

"Do you think you're real Catholics?"

"Sure, kind of anyway, we do some other things, but they don't seem to us to be against Catholicism."

"I'm not going to second-guess God, Germaine."

"Maybe one of our altar hangings, it's perfectly Catholic."

"This administration is firmly in favor of multiculturalism."

"Tell me about it!"

There was nothing about this young woman that suggested she was any way "mysterious," as I had been told she was.

"We have to pray real hard," she went on, "for Marianna that she can defeat that evil man tomorrow."

"You think there's a doubt?"

"No, still it never hurts to pray, does it?"

"Patently."

"It will be good to have a Mass in this house, Bishop. There's a lot of bad medicine here, real bad."

All right, now she was mysterious.

"Bad medicine, Travels By Night?"

She nodded solemnly. "Awful medicine, evil medicine."

"You mean the poltergeist?"

"Poor little thing. She doesn't come around me. She's afraid of my kind of medicine."

"You can't make her go away?"

"I'm not an exorcist, Bishop. Neither are you, of course. You have lots of good medicine. White man's medicine. Maybe Irish medicine like my great-grandfather."

"Ah."

"She lives a little off the bad medicine here, I think. She really does suffer a lot."

"You don't talk to her?"

"I try but she's afraid of me. Believes that I'll make her admit what she's doing. I can't do that. I wish I could."

"Usually those who play with spirits suffer a lot, especially if they're doing it when they're adults."

She nodded solemnly.

"Ogden doesn't believe in spirits at all. Most Black people do and are afraid of them. We Yaqui are not afraid of spirits. Most spirits are good. They protect you from the bad ones. Sometimes, when Ogden has gone home for the night I light little candles in his office to get rid of the bad spirits in the West Wing. Sometimes I think it helps a little."

Claire Jones thought there were evil spirits around the West Wing too.

"Against the bad medicine?"

She nodded solemnly again.

"I don't know where it comes from, Bishop. Not these people anyway. Maybe from a long time ago. We have to keep the president alive, so he can rid us of it. He's just like my great-grandfather, who used to fight off bad medicine with a laugh . . . Well, see you at Mass! If you have any new ideas about what you want, Sean Patrick will know where to find me."

Will he now? Was there an involvement here?

None of your business, Blackie Ryan.

I wandered back to my room and discovered that my episcopal vestments had been scattered about with reckless disregard for my limited abilities to put order in them. As I entered the room my St. Brigid pectoral cross, made for me by my cousin Catherine Collins Curran, rose from the floor, flew across the room, narrowly missed my head, then flew out into the corridor and smashed viciously against the closed door of the Lincoln Bedroom. My crosier followed, slashing through the air like a javelin.

"You ought to be ashamed of yourself. Go back to hell where you belong and don't bother me again."

The ruckus stopped. I sensed that the playful ghost felt she had been insulted. Her feelings were hurt. She was just playing. She went away sadly.

"I can't help you until you're ready to grow up," I informed her.

There was no reply. There never is. If you know who the source is, then you can deal with her directly. However, the playful ghost is mute.

Why? I don't know. No one knows because no one understands the dynamics of the process by which a troubled teen, desperate for attention and affection, creates psychic energies with such enormous power. Nor, I reflected as I walked across the corridor to retrieve my badges of office, did anyone understand why invariably they do not or perhaps cannot cause any physical harm to persons or property. There was no damage to either the cross or the crosier and no marks on the door to the Lincoln Bedroom.

"Little brat," I muttered.

I felt her scurrying off. She had waited to make sure I noted that she could smash things around and still do no damage.

I remembered another playful spirit, who created a huge snowball without leaving any footprints on the new-fallen snow and heaved it with enormous force against a picture window. Which did not break. There were two suspensions of physical laws in that incident—the snowball seeming to make itself and the undamaged window. Was it all an illusion?

The trickster was perhaps a good illusionist, but she had scooped the snow from the lawn. I know because I went out to make sure. And this one had actually messed up my vestments and scattered them all about the room. I wasn't imagining that. Or was I?

About the existence of the playful spirit phenomenon there was no doubt. That troubled teens were correlated with the phenomenon seemed obvious enough. Yet how they did it was pure mystery. After young persons broke out of the grip of the condition, they were not willing to talk about it much or even admit that they were responsible, though they knew they were.

"I knew I was doing it," a girl had said to me. "I hated it and I loved it and I didn't hurt anyone so I didn't do anything wrong did I? When I was doing it, I don't know how I did it, I just did it."

"You just wanted to scare the others?"

"I was so angry at them. I really did scare them, didn't I?"

"You did."

"I'm sorry."

"I know you are. You won't do it again?"

"Oh, no. It was so terrible!"

All of which told me very little except perhaps that the experience was worse for the raging playful spirit than for her victims.

Some clerics of my acquaintance insist that little devils are unleashed that cooperate with the playful spirit and then slip back into hell or whatever when the interlude is over.

I doubt this explanation, especially because exorcism usually doesn't work with these kids, only makes them more angry. Yet if by "devils" they mean latent psychic powers in the kids, they're probably right but they have not advanced our knowledge of the subject.

The playful spirit was the ultimate of a teenage show-off.

Later the Daughters awaited me in the Red Room, where I was to vest. They were both, they informed me, extraordinary ministers of the Eucharist and could they please exercise their ministry at this Eucharist.

"Sure . . . What about poor Sean Patrick?"

"Oh, he's doing the incense. We'll carry the candles too . . . Didn't Travels By Night fix things up nice?"

I acknowledged that she had.

"What about her? Is she a medicine woman?"

"Sure, why not?"

"Only good medicine."

"She's sweet on Sean Patrick, isn't that cute?"

"And what does he say about that?"

"Not much."

"Boys don't."

"But we know that he likes her. The way he looks at her."

"Like he wants to take her clothes off, but all very respectfully."

"It would be extreme cool to have a medicine woman for a sister-in-law."

Playful spirits in the technical sense the Daughters probably weren't. Yet dangerous young women they were. Given time they would have complete control of the White House and the West Wing. Small wonder their father had decreed that they had to go back to school on Sunday, "after Marianna's TV Show," as they called it.

The Blue Room is the oval room of the first floor of the White House, above the oval diplomatic Reception Room on the ground floor and beneath the Yellow Room on the second floor (and the oval Solarium on the third floor). The White House is filled with ovals because Jimmy Hoban liked the idea of an oval design for the South Portico. The Oval Office, over in the West Wing, does not fit into that rather square and businesslike addendum but presidents become obsessed with ovals.

Larger than both the Green Room and the Red Room that flank it, the Blue Room in size and in its blue and gilt Empire elegance dominates the central part of the first floor. The Red Room is truly red and the Green Room truly dark green, but the Blue Room is only pale blue. However, the view of the South Lawn through the colonnade of the portico was a good backdrop for Mass. I was led in by a thurifer (Sean Patrick), a cross bearer (Tommy Horan), and two woman acolytes in white dresses.

(I dared not ask where the Daughters had found such dresses.)

Since we lacked a choir and an organ, we recited in English, the Church's ancient celebratory chant *"Te Deum Laudamus"* while a CD played it in Latin in the background.

I was in full regalia, zuchetto, mitre, crosier—the works. I disposed of the latter two as quickly as I could, retaining the skullcap because the Daughters thought it was extreme cool.

"We're here to celebrate and to give thanks," I informed the congregation which flowed out into the corridor and into the Green and Red Rooms. "We thankfully celebrate that we survived and are alive and well, no small accomplishment considering what the possibilities were yesterday. We also celebrate the United States Marines who brightened the evening and the morning for us and are now about to leave. We celebrate the loyalty and friendship among us that is now stronger than ever. We celebrate our resilient Republic, of which this storied building is a symbol. We celebrate the storied Jimmy Hoban who built this house to endure and all the men and women who through the years added to its beauty and dignity.

"We pray that just as James Monroe, who is greatly responsible for the elegance of this room, presided over an Era of Good Feeling in our country, so might our present incumbent be able to begin a new era of good feeling. President Monroe ruled after an era of bitter partisanship in the land. For many reasons, which need not detain us, terrible partisanship has torn at the fabric of our land for the last decade and a half. It is time for it to end, that is to settle down to the ordinary healthy partisanship that is essential for our Republic.

"Surely the incumbent in his campaign, free of attack ads and dirty tricks and dense with happy laughter, is doing his part. We pray that he may continue to do so, undaunted by the onslaughts of his enemies. We pray too that his good example may spread across the land and that we stop shouting angrily at each other and questioning each other's good faith.

"In today's Gospel of Thanksgiving we note that only one leper came back to thank Jesus. We pointed out to God what he patently already knows: that we are here to give thanks and that we hope to continue to give thanks. May God continue to bless and protect us and to grant us in these difficult times the gifts of life and love and laughter."

The congregation seemed satisfied. The Daughters nodded their approval just as their mother used to after she had heard a homily, a thought that made my eyes sting.

10

We sat in the Oval Office; Tommy, the first family, and the virtually invisible auxiliary bishop, waiting for the eleven o'clock Sunday Washington interview program. Most people in America, excluding college professors, did not watch it. However, most important folk inside the Beltway did. Reputations could be made or broken during a half hour confrontation with the talking heads. We feared not for our intrepid heroine. Rather, as the president remarked, it was something like waiting for a Bulls championship game in the old days.

The interviewers can be identified by the names AAF (Aggressive and Abrasive Female), GEM (Genial Empty Male), and SAM (Snide Angry Male).

Congressman Dillingham wore his usual costume. Marianna wore a black dress and white scarf (as planned) and a small gold pin. Her lustrous black hair framed her lovely face, from which it was difficult to remove one's eyes. She was an empress, waiting on the throne for the amusement to begin.

AAF: Dr. Genovese, you're supposed to be an expert on China, are you not?

Marianna: It's Genovesa and there are no experts on China. I'm a political scientist whose specialization is the history of Chinese politics.

She smoothed her hair.

AAF: Well if you're so smart, how come you didn't anticipate the present civil war in China?

Marianna (faint smile of amusement): I beg your pardon?

AAF: Why didn't you predict what is happening over there now?

Marianna: Responsible scholarship tries to understand rather than predict. However, I did write two articles last year predicting the present situation, one in *Foreign Policy* and the other in the *International Journal of Political Science*. I've brought copies along and I can give them to you after the program.

AAF: Well, why didn't you warn the president about what was coming?

Marianna: I did give the articles to the president and he did read them. Dr. Claire Jones concurred with my analysis. So the administration was prepared for the implosion of the Socialist regime.

AAF: Why didn't the president do something about it?

Marianna: He did issue a statement last week on our China policy. At the press conference your colleagues did not seem interested in it.

SAM: Dr. Genovese . . .

Marianna: Do you think you could try to get the name right? It ends with an A.

SAM (sarcastically): Thank you for the correction, Dr. Genovesa . . . I presume you read the *New York Times* editorial yesterday.

Marianna: Yes.

SAM: You are aware then that the *Times* criticized the president for foolish braggadocio in his response to the rocket attack on the White House and in particular criticized him for walking in Lafayette Park the night of the attack. Do you have any comments?

Marianna: The United States Marines reported that the crowd was friendly and wanted to see and talk to the president. He thought it appropriate to accept the invitation.

SAM: Was that not a political act more suitable for a campaign than for a sitting president?

Marianna: Irish politicians, sir, don't think in those terms. There were people out there who wanted to see him live and he responded to them.

SAM: He could have been killed.

Marianna: He can be killed almost anytime, sir, if someone wants badly enough to do so.

SAM: And he endangered the lives of his daughters!

Marianna: Sadly, their lives are always in danger too. They know it. They will never hide.

GEM: Does it surprise you, Dr. Genovesa . . . See I got it right . . .

Marianna: Thank you. I realize all Italian names sound alike.

GEM (flustered): Does it surprise you that the country's most important paper is constantly critical of the president?

Marianna: Yes it does. The policies he stands for—environment, gay rights, taxes, campaign reform, more intelligent foreign policies—are the ones that the *Times* editorial board also supports. However, they declared war on him immediately after he was elected and have been unremitting since then. They just don't like him.

GEM: Would you want to guess at the reason?

Marianna: I don't think there's any doubt. He's an Irish Catholic from Chicago.

GEM: You're accusing the *Times* of religious and ethnic prejudice.

Marianna: Their editorial board, yes, of course.

GEM: Don't you think the sex scandal has something to do with it?

Marianna: What sex scandal?

GEM: The charges made by those two women who were on his campaign staff.

Marianna: What the editorial board of the *Times* knows and what everyone who was on the campaign knows, including the reporters, and what every serious reporter in Washington knows is that those charges are frivolous. Yet the media persist in reporting them as though they are serious. Thus when he released his statement on China at the press conference last week all the questions were about sex. The elite media in this country are competing with the supermarket tabloids, for whom no low road is too low to take.

AAF: Congressman Dillingham, are not the two young men who have been arrested for firing a rocket at the White House on Friday from your district in Ohio?

Dil: Yes . . .

AAF: Didn't they in fact work for your reelection campaign?

Dil: Yes they did. I don't approve of violence. As I always say there's no appeal from the ballot to the bullet. I honestly believe that they are innocent of the charges. I firmly believe that they are being framed by the de-generate clique which is running the White House these days. I can understand why clean-living, red-blooded American Christians feel called upon to rise up and smite this conspiracy of de-generates and its de-generate leader.

AAF: You approve of that, Congressman?

Dil: I said I understand it. I will smite my enemies, says the Lord of Hosts!

AAF: Do you think that Dr. Genovesa here is a degenerate?

Dil: Course she is. You can tell by looking at her that she's one of the lesbos . . .

Marianna (laughing): It's the white scarf, I knew I shouldn't have worn it.

Dil (prosecutor): Tell me, young woman, are you one of those lesbos that Machine Gun Jack has working for him over in that Babylon?

Marianna: My own sexual orientation, sir, is my own business. I know of no lesbians working for the president, but there may well be some. We have rejected discrimination on the basis of sexual orientation.

Dil: God will not be mocked. Revenge is Mine, saith the Lord, I will repay.

Marianna: I think Jesus said let him who is without sin throw the first stone. And the Jewish scriptures say judge not that you might not be judged.

Dil: You're no Christian, woman. You have no right to quote scriptures.

Marianna: I am, sir. I'm a churchgoing Roman Catholic.

Dil (mumbles): Catholics aren't Christian.

Marianna: Catholic voters in your district will be interested to hear that.

SAM: Do you believe, Congressman, that there will be more attempts on the life of the President?

Dil: Sure there will. The country has to be puri-
fied. It must return to the good old American, God-
fearing way of life.

SAM: Is there room for Jews in that way of life?

Dil: Most Jews down my way are God-fearing too.
They're people of the Book. Up here in Washington
and New York there are a lot of de-generate Jews
too.

Marianna: No room for Catholics?

Dil: Not unless you repent of your idolatry.

GEM (trying to cool things off): What do you
expect to happen in China, Dr. Genovesa?

Marianna: I said earlier that there are no experts
on China. It has an ancient, rich, complex culture
that is not like ours. They are a proud, patriotic people. They feel they have been exploited by the West.
In the worst case, there will be a reversion to rule
by regional warlords, a long period of conflict, and
probably a deterioration of the economy with attendant suffering for Chinese people and for the rest of
the world which is heavily engaged economically
with China. The best case is that the present conflict
will be resolved shortly.

GEM: What do you think?

Marianna: I lean tentatively in the hopeful direction.

GEM: Will China then become more democratic?

Marianna: Please God. I wouldn't count on it.
Moreover, if it does, it will be a Chinese-style democracy, not one like ours.

Dil: Don't you mention God, you evil woman. His
name becomes filth in your filthy mouth! You're a
trollop! You're the president's mistress, one of his
concubines.

Marianna (completely unfazed): Congressman, I am not the president's mistress. He has neither mistress nor concubine, as everyone who works at the White House knows. The Irish generally do not lean in the direction of mistresses or concubines, probably because they know they're not very good at it. I note, however, that you have changed your judgment from being a lesbian to being a whore.

GEM: Do you think the president will remarry or become sexually involved?

Marianna: I don't know. Moreover, if he does, it's his business and no one else's. The president has a right to a private life. What everyone in the media knows—and probably even the editorial writers and columnists—is that the president is a man with a broken heart. The love of his life, a woman whom he worshipped from second grade on, died a tragic death in the waters of Lake Michigan. He and his family have dedicated his presidency to her memory. That shows the kind of man he is. I have never known him to be anything other than sensitive, thoughtful, and respectful to us women on his staff.

AAF: Does that mean he'll live without sex for the rest of his life?

Marianna: Possibly. The Irish are rather good at celibacy, particularly their men.

(Laughter, some of it embarrassed, in the Oval Office.)

Dil: Remember what I say: God will not be mocked!

Marianna: I can quote the Bible too—scribes and Pharisees are whitened sepulchres, all white and shiny on the outside and within filled with dead men's bones.

(Interview Ends.)

We applauded enthusiastically.

"Roses, Daddy," Deirdre ordered.

"What, hon?"

"A dozen, no two dozen for her office. Now. That's what a sensitive, thoughtful, and respectful man does. She'll come back here."

"Sean Patrick . . ."

"Yeah, I'll see to it! She was sensational!"

"Three dozen!" his father said.

The flowers came a few moments before they returned from the station. The Oval Office and surrounding rooms were filled by people who had come to work on Sunday morning to cheer for her.

Agents Wholley and Chick brought Marianna and Mae (and Barry) through the Rose Garden door. Everyone cheered. A couple of Ivy League guys began the Columbia fight song.

I didn't know they had one.

The president embraced her, though he did not kiss her.

I heard a sigh of protest next to me.

Granne.

"Well done, Marianna," the president said. "We're all proud of you!"

"It didn't seem fair," she responded. "He's just a poor old man who's more than a little senile. They set him up."

"They thought they might be setting you up too," Tommy told her. "They'll know better the next time."

"Mr. President," she exclaimed, when she glanced into her own office. "Roses! Thank you very much!"

"That's what a sensitive, thoughtful, and respectful man does," the president replied.

"Vomit city!" Deirdre complained.

Gradually the celebrators drifted away from the Oval Office. Agents Chick and Wholley were conveying the gloomy Daughters to the airport for a return to school. Only Mae, Tommy, Marianna, and I remained. And Barry snuggled in the president's lap.

"You should have a dog, Mr. President," Mae informed him. "I'm sure Nuala Anne and Dermot could find you a great white Irish wolfhound. It would make a great picture—president and his wolfhound Rory gaze out on the South Lawn."

"Wolfhound Rory and his president gaze out on the South Lawn," the president laughed. "They own you."

"It might aid the reputed ease we Irish have with celibacy."

It was very wicked of me to say that in the circumstances.

Everyone laughed anyway.

Mae and Barry went home to their apartment. The Daughters were hustled off to the airport, grumbling that they didn't want to go back to school. Marianna went to her office to "catch up" on some of her work before lunch with the Archbishop of Washington.

The phone rang.

"For you Blackwood."

"Is that the woman?" His Eminence the Lord Cardinal of Chicago asked.

"Arguably!"

"Wow!"

"If you say so."

"Tell Jack he's a fool if he lets her get away."

"I won't."

"I figured you wouldn't. Now get those poltergeists."

"We're working on it."

"See to it."

"Milord Cronin calling to express his approval of Dr. Genovesa's work."

"Hmm . . ." The president was involved in heavy thinking.

"How are you doing in the search for the poltergeists?" he asked me.

"The very question that troubled His Eminence."

"Any clues?"

"Sometimes I think I see it all, then it fades away like an elevator door closing. One of these days it won't close and I'll know."

I often use that metaphor to describe the odd process in which I finally recognize something I've known for a long time.

"Do you think it is political, Blackwood?" he said, pouring me a small splash of Jameson's.

"I'm inclined to think so. Anything that involves a president is political."

"Republicans?"

"Arguably. We know they'll stop at nothing. Yet not mainstream Republicans like all those semi-Democratic senators from New England. And not the fundamentalists either. They're scared of the devil."

"You think the devil is involved?"

"More likely a human with devilish intent."

"Someone manipulating this poor young woman . . . If it's a woman?"

"Arguably."

"What do you think of that Apache kid who works for Ogden?"

"Yaqui."

"Aren't they the same?"

"You'd be in deep trouble in Arizona if you make that mistake out there."

"What's her name again . . . Germaine . . ."

"Connelly."

"She doesn't look like a Connelly."

"Great-grandfather. Big medicine man from Ireland. He laughed at evil spirits. A lot of Irish filtered into the Gadsen Purchase from Mexico."

"They call her 'Travels By Night.' That sounds spooky. Sean Patrick is kind of sweet on her. Nothing wrong with that. Daughters say she's a medicine woman."

"So they tell me too. However, they assure me that she does only good medicine."

"You have any idea what that is?"

"Herbs and prayers most likely."

"She seems like a good kid . . . Wouldn't she and Sean Patrick make a striking pair?"

"Arguably."

"I wonder, though, if she might be, uh, involved in this stuff."

"Perhaps," I said. "It's not impossible. There is much depth to her. Not all of it is necessarily happy."

"Yep," he drained his glass. "Can't you imagine the president of the United States saying to his Irish Viking son, 'Sean Patrick, I don't want you dating that . . . Yaqui . . . kid they call Travels By Night be-

cause I think she might be a witch.' At his age in life
that would look like an endorsement."

"It would not play with the minority vote."

"Well, we have to have lunch with the Archbishop
of Washington in a few minutes. I'm glad I asked
her to stay. I suppose he saw her on TV earlier."

"Not a chance."

Tommy Horan and his deputy joined us waiting
in the lobby at the door of the North Portico. The
archbishop arrived in a long Mercedes. He and another priest stepped out. Harry Sanchez, a nice
young Latino auxiliary not altogether the swiftest
bishop in a hierarchy notably unmarked by swift
people.

"If any of you kiss his ring, I will never speak to
you again," I warned everyone.

"You're most welcome to the White House, Your
Excellency," the president of the United States
reached out his hand. The archbishop extended his
ring. Jack McGurn grasped his hand and shook it.

The archbishop was in fact younger than I am,
one of the bright young lights of the American
Church, *Time* had called him. The trouble was that
the light had grown pretty dim. He looked twenty
years older than I, tall, gaunt with thin gray hair, a
lean and hungry face, pale blue eyes that seemed
perpetually unfocused behind rimless glasses. He de-
fined the word "vague." He seemed puzzled always
about what to say, where to step, how to act. The
image was completed by a dry cough, which could
indicate the advance of TB, but was merely a nervous tic. How dumb was he? Milord Cronin on the
subject; "Dumber than most people think he is."

Rumor had it that the newest Nuncio, as I may

have mentioned, not one of Cardinal Cronin's favorite people, had noticed the dim light at their first meeting and remarked to one of his staff that the archbishop might make a good chaplain for a convent of elderly nuns.

This is the kind of man the Vatican assigns to the capital of the world's only superpower, on the grounds that he is "sound" on doctrine.

"Your Excellency, may I present my good friend Bishop John B. Ryan, who is visiting us this weekend."

He extended a limp hand in my direction.

"Surely not a Roman Catholic bishop?"

Neither Tommy nor Marianna snickered.

"Auxiliary to Milord Cronin, Cardinal Prince of Chicago."

"Strange, I can't remember you from any of the meetings of the hierarchy."

"I'm usually there, Your Grace, running errands for Cardinal Cronin. However, I'm one of those people blessed with the grace of invisibility."

"Hi, Harry," I said to the auxiliary.

"Hi, Blackie, good to see you again."

"I also wish to present my chief of staff, Thomas Horan, and his deputy, Dr. Marianna Genovesa."

"Of course."

As I had predicted, he acted as if he did not see Marianna. Thank God we had dispatched the Daughters back to the shores of Lake Michigan.

The president led the way, the local hierarchy on either side of him.

"May I congratulate you, John," the archbishop said, "on your escape from injury in the deplorable attack on the White House. I did notice the marks on the pillar. Will it have to be replaced?"

"The White House architect will test for structural soundness tomorrow. If it seems stable, we'll paint it over with the special White House whitewash and it will be as good as new."

"Whitewash is always useful around here," I remarked to dead silence.

"Is he real, Bishop Blackie?" Marianna whispered to me.

"No, he is an illusion. Leave him to me."

"But . . ."

"I said, leave him to me. Don't argue with what a bishop tells you to do."

"Yes, Bishop," she said with a phony tone of docility.

The luncheon, cold salmon salad with a magical dressing accompanied by a very pleasant Rhine wine, was excellent. However, our guests ate very little of it. The archbishop toyed with the salad, picking at it like a bird with anorexia. Harry seemed afraid to eat any more than his boss did. The president tried without success to make small talk. Tommy, Marianna, and I made up for the others' lack of appetite.

Purgatory of the old variety would have been an improvement.

Our guests waved off lemon ice, as did the president. Following my lead, the members of the presidential staff devoured large chunks of it.

"It's a very wicked world we live in, John," the archbishop remarked as he delicately sipped a cup of decaf. "Sometimes I fear there are only a few devout Catholics left in the country. The deterioration of our culture is tragic. You must find it very difficult to govern under such circumstances."

"The presidency is never an easy task, Archbishop. It may be a little more difficult in this time of intense and bitter partisanship. However, as a political scientist, I tend to be skeptical about overarching trends. Doubtless in some ways, things are getting worse and in other ways they are getting better. High school students continue to shoot one another and will until we get more effective gun control. On the other hand, more and more teenagers volunteer to help others, as my elder daughter did in Honduras after her freshman year at Notre Dame. I don't say these two cancel each other out. They don't. They merely indicate opposing trends. There are more volunteers than shooters, thank God."

"The amount of sexual degeneracy in the nation is appalling."

"You didn't happen to see the debate this morning on television between Dr. Genovesa and Congressman Dillingham?"

"I'm afraid not," he said as if he were not quite sure who Dr. Genovesa was.

"There was considerable discussion of degeneracy on it."

"I firmly believe, John, that the Catholic Church's mission in this terrible secularist, materialist, pansexual culture, is to take a firm stand for historic values against a hostile society. Don't you agree?"

"I think that it's always been the Church's task to stand in a position over the culture in which it finds itself and at the same time discern carefully what might be good in that culture—as St. Gregory did when he instructed St. Augustine of Canterbury on how to respond to the religious ceremonies of the Angles."

If the archbishop knew who Saints Augustine and Gregory were, he did not seem to recognize them.

"It is your task, I think you will agree, as the best-known Catholic layman in America to be a model for all Catholics, at all time."

"If you mean those sexual harassment charges, Archbishop," the deputy chief of staff could no longer contain herself, "they are patently false."

The archbishop seemed surprised at the sound of her voice. He ignored it.

"Thus I feel that it is appropriate for me to call upon you as a member of this Archdiocese to take the lead in stamping out the horror of abortion. It is your sacred duty to do so."

"I have said during the campaign"—the president was frowning, the Irish temper which always lurked deep within his charm, beginning to stir—"and I will say again that, if a law for forbidding third trimester abortions is put on my desk, as a Catholic I will sign it. I also expect the Supreme Court will declare the law unconstitutional as it did the previous law."

"Then you must bend all your efforts to appoint judges who will reverse *Roe v. Wade*. I charge you to do that as your solemn duty."

"Abortion will certainly be one of the issues I would consider in appointing judges. However, I must tell you in all candor, Archbishop, that the temper of the land today makes it most unlikely that *Roe v. Wade* will ever be overturned. If it is, then laws permitting abortion already exist in most states. My opinion is that the Church would be much wiser to try to reeducate its own flock on this issue than to attempt to impose its moral judgments on the whole country."

"Moreover," the archbishop went on doggedly, "I must also ask you in the name of traditional Catholic morality to revoke your scandalous rule requiring the hiring of sodomites in government office. I can tell you that Rome is shocked by this rule."

"There seems to be some misunderstanding." The president's lips tightened. "My order only forbids discrimination against them. They are Americans like everyone else. They have the right to employment just like everyone else. The Church itself teaches that homosexuality is not a condition that anyone freely chooses. If they don't freely choose it, how can we deprive them of rights that are inherent in human nature?"

"I believe that I am on firm ground in conveying to you that the Vatican wishes you to take these actions."

"Let's stop right there," I said coldly. "The president is not a member of your Archdiocese. His permanent home is in the city of Chicago and in the Archdiocese of Chicago. Such orders from Rome, should they exist, ought to come from Cardinal Cronin. Secondly, you are attempting to do what anti-Catholics said forty years ago we would do—elect a Catholic President and Rome will tell him what to do. Patently that did not happen. If this is a new policy that you present today, then the Vatican is doing grave harm to Catholicism in this country. Thirdly, should that be the Vatican's intent, then President McGurn will have no choice but to resign as president with attendant disastrous effects on ecumenism in this country. Finally, I don't believe that you speak for the Pope at all. Rather, I think you're cloaking your own personal feelings in the legitimacy of the Vatican. Before the day is over, I will inquire of Milord Cronin whether there is any new demand of the Holy See which you are conveying to us. Until then I advise the president to defy you. Indeed I would suggest that he throw you out of this house because you are trying to interpose yourself between the president and his oath of office."

Jack McGurn barely concealed his smile.

Harry looked worried.

Tommy Horan's frosty eyes twinkled.

Marianna Genovesa enveloped me in her most admiring smile.

The archbishop acted as if he hadn't heard a word.

The president repeated the substance of my position.

The archbishop nodded sadly.

"I fear I must conclude our conversation with the promise, John, that I will pray for you. I believe that your immortal soul is in danger of hellfire. Come, Harry, we've done all we can."

Tommy showed them to the door.

I picked up the phone and asked the switchboard to call Holy Name Cathedral in Chicago.

"Holy Name Cathedral!" the Megan-on-duty announced brightly.

We hire the Megans because they add extreme brightness to the rectory.

"Father Ryan, Megan. Might I talk to the Cardinal."

"I think he's napping, Bishop Blackie. He has had to work extra hard today because you're not here."

"Poor dear man. Nonetheless, this is important."

"Cronin."

"I apologize for interrupting your well-earned rest," I said. "I think I told you that we were to have lunch today with the Archbishop of Washington."

"I sympathized with you. What more could I do?"

I repeated, almost word for word, the archbishop's message.

"Where are you, Blackwood?" His voice was controlled, ominous, dangerous.

"In the White House."

"I know THAT. Where in the White House?"

"Family dining room."

"Who is with you?"

"POTUS aka Kerryman, Tommy, Dr. Genovesa."

The president turned on the speakerphone.

"Dr. Genovesa," now he was once more Sean Cronin, practiced charmer of women, "I want to congratulate you on your marvelous performance on television. You deftly dispatched those fakers and delivered some nice jabs at the Irish punks you knew in Brooklyn, to say nothing of those who surround you presently. Very well done!"

Marianna blushed and smiled. Even on the phone the Cronin voice was magic.

"Now, to the subject at hand. I will be in touch with some of my friends in Rome first thing in the morning. I will insist that they tell that jerk to stop harassing you. I will warn of the consequences if this demarche should become public knowledge. I will tell them that you are under my jurisdiction—which as Blackwood would say together with the fare will get me a ride on your friend Rich Daley's subway.

Nevertheless the Romans think it means something and that, unless they can promise me that he'll leave you alone, I will denounce him in public."

Gulp again.

"Thanks, Sean."

"No problem, Jack . . . I presume Blackwood told him off?"

"With his usual competence."

"Splendid. Dr. Genovesa, a pleasure to talk to you. I hope to meet you soon. Tommy, my best to Sheila, saint that she is. Blackwood, get rid of those poltergeists."

"Remarkable," I said. "Would that all our problems could be resolved that simply. I'm sorry, Mr. President, that you had to put up with that gobshite."

"What's a gobshite?" Marianna asked.

"Irish phrase," Tommy explained, "for a gob of shite. If you weren't present, the Cardinal would have used it."

Arguably.

Marianna collected her roses and went home to her apartment. Tommy went home to the long-suffering Sheila. I walked with the president along the Rose Garden to the Oval Office.

"I got some work to clear up, Blackwood. Supper up in the Solarium at 7:00? I'll bring the rest of this bottle along." The President picked up the bottle of Jameson's. "Shame to waste it."

I agreed that it would indeed be a shame to waste it.

I reflected on my way up to the second floor that perhaps POTUS could use a nice, dignified Irish wolfhound, regardless of what such a pooch would do to Mrs. Kennedy's Rose Garden.

The phone was ringing in my room. Mike Casey.

"Blackie, is Jack McGurn in love with that woman?"

"Alas, no."

"He's crazy."

"The precise opinion Milord Cronin expressed earlier."

"Grief?"

"Perhaps too much to be healthy. But what do I know?"

"Does she love him?"

"What do you think, Mike?"

"How could she not?"

"She will not, nonetheless, make the first move. Not ever, ever, ever."

"God will have to take over."

"God and hormones."

"We have some good news for you, Blackie. It's been straightforward so far. My people established contact with our subjects at a Rush Street bar. In your parish, I would add."

"We have ceded Rush Street and Division Street to the Diocese of Pago Pago."

"They chatted about a lot of things, then the subjects said they were doing some secret investigation into President McGurn. Really, one of mine said. I now play a tape for you.

The voices were blurred, one man three women.

"Trying to figure out whether he did anything around Loyola when he was there. Some evidence that he did."

"Be pretty hard to dig up something like that by now. He hasn't been around here for three years."

"Yeah, we've found that out."

"The information might be available. It would cost."

"That's no problem."

"Cost a lot."

"No problem either. Look, here's the point, we know he's a habitual molester. Our job is to get him out of the White House, which we're pretty close to doing now. He'll settle the suits and then he'll have to resign. No one goes to trial. All we're doing is looking for testimony that will support what we already know about him."

"Cost a lot."

"Like I say, that's no problem."

"What do you think, Blackie?"

"Are the two subjects true believers?"

"My people think they're enthusiasts who love the secret agent game and half believe it's all true."

"Dumb and dangerous."

"Precisely."

"They're called Carrie and Drew."

"Sound like Southerners?"

"Yeah. Anyway, they gave my kids a phone number. Give us a ring sort of thing. Well, we got a tap on the line this morning. There's a call to a Reverend Rhea Snodgrass this morning."

"Christian Family Union!"

"Right. Listen to this part of the tape."

A woman's voice talking to Rhea.

"I think we got two fish last night, Rhea."

"Good work."

"Kind of disgusting women, cynical. Eager for money. Ready to say almost anything."

"You don't believe them?"

"Does that matter?"

"Not in a war against evil like we're waging. You know that."

"Right."

"You think you can get them to say the things we need?"

"For the right amount of money these two will say anything."

"How much money?"

"I don't know for sure. A lot."

"It will probably be worth it. You find out what it will cost and I'll clear it with Mr. Sleidel."

"Okay. These two will be easier to deal with than the two we have already. They won't have any moral scruples about making stuff up."

"That's good."

"We almost had to write the affidavits for Suzy and Elaine. I think these two have been around long enough to do it for themselves."

"Good work."

"What do you think, Mike. Is there a case there?"

"Beginnings of one. My girls, who are fanatical Democrats by the way, are going to have to be careful. The idea is that the Chicago police arrest these two, play the tapes for them, and offer them a plea with the state's attorney if they'll do evidence against Snodgrass and Sleidel. We can convene a Grand Jury overnight if we have to."

"Seamy kind of stuff, isn't it?"

"My kids haven't told any lies and won't."

"I understand that."

"Standard police practice. Only way the good guys can fight back."

"Okay. Keep me posted."

"Probably not a good idea to tell Jack yet. We don't want to get his hopes up too high."

"Good idea."

I sat in the Churchill Room for a few minutes, pondering the issues as a quiet night spread over

Pennsylvania Avenue. When would the next attack come?

Mike was right. This was the only defense we had.

There was still no sign of the player spirit when I left. Might it have been one of the Daughters after all?

The president and I ate roast beef with an intriguing French sauce, drank some (but not all!) of a nice California Merlot, chatted about the old days in the neighborhood, and watched CNN which replayed every half hour, snippets of Marianna's tour de force, accompanied by snippets on her background, emphasizing her role as an all-American point guard on the Columbia Lions.

So that's what they were called.

"There are certainly a lot of eccentrics in the neighborhood, aren't there, Blackwood?"

"More than a random distribution would account for."

"I think I might have been headed in that direction . . . absentminded, quirky professor."

"Not an impossible outcome, though add the adjective 'well-loved.' "

"I suppose you think I'm crazy, Blackwood, for not pursuing that woman."

"I take seriously her generalization that the Irish are not good at concubines and mistresses but good at celibacy."

"You know who it was aimed at?"

"I felt she was quite explicit about it."

"You thought it was a sexual challenge?"

"One could put that interpretation on her remarks. Fortunately, they were delivered with enough wit as to be relatively harmless, unless one wanted to make something else of them."

"As the Daughters tell me repeatedly, she is intelligent, beautiful, charming, and funny."

"Arguably also sexy."

"And she would be content to take care of me for the rest of my life."

"That too."

He sighed.

"As you know, Blackwood, men sometimes undress attractive women in their imaginations. If they're civilized they do it discreetly so as not to embarrass those involved."

"Reactions of the sort necessary to sustain the species in existence and are not meant to cause any harm, nor to offend a potentially jealous spouse."

"When Ellen was alive, I did that on occasions. If she caught it, she'd make fun of me."

"Secure in her own position."

"She said that one woman was more than enough for me to contend with."

"Patently."

"In those days, a woman like Marianna would occasion delightful fantasies. Now that I no longer have a wife this side of paradise, she stirs no reactions in me at all—other than disgust that I can't react to her."

"Ah."

"I don't think I show that disgust, do I?"

"Not to me surely. There is, however, no way a mere male can judge a woman's reaction to rejection. On the other hand, her remarks on the television this morning suggest that if she does know your disgust, she is not offended by it."

"The country now has a romance with which to entertain itself."

"There are worse entertainments."

"They'll demand a happy ending to their damn love story."

"Arguably . . . that's the way the groundlings are."

"They'll blame me."

"Has not the good doctor given you a dispensation?"

"A broken heart?"

"The truth."

"Yeah. A whole broken organism . . . The thought of touching her repels me . . . Or being touched by her."

"One could make a case that the hug when she returned this afternoon was unnecessarily proper."

He chuckled.

"What does God think of me?"

"He loves you as His dearly beloved child, the way you love Sean Patrick and the Daughters."

"Maybe I need a therapist . . . president of the United States, fabled Kerryman, goes to a shrink because he's psychically impotent. Prescribes Viagra."

"More likely prescribes time and patience."

"Suppose she's no longer interested?"

"One could hardly interpret this morning's event as a sign of everlasting love, but one could read it as proof of amused patience."

He simply sighed and poured himself another glass of Merlot.

11

The next morning when I stumbled into the Solarium for my breakfast, I observed with some surprise that Sean Patrick was on all four screens. Something big was up.

He began reading from a prepared text:

"From beginning to end, the *USA Today* story about the Mass Bishop Ryan said Saturday in the Blue Room is wrong. Bishop Ryan is not an exorcist but an old friend of the president's family. The prayer at the beginning was not in Latin. It was an English translation of an ancient Catholic hymn the *"Te Deum Laudamus."* It is not a hymn of exorcism but rather a hymn of celebration and thanksgiving, which Catholics sing at times of great events, such as the survival of a president from attempted assassination. We have copies of it here for you. The president asked Bishop Ryan to say Mass on Saturday to celebrate and give thanks that no one was injured in the White House by the rocket which hit us on Friday. My sisters did not consecrate the Eucharist with Bishop Ryan, but distributed it in their role of extraordinary ministers for which they have been trained and mandated in our home parish in Chicago. The incense in the thurible I was carrying represents our prayers of gratitude ascending to God and are not an attempt to smoke the devil out of the White House. The hymn we sang at the end was not an African-American spiritual for casting out demons. It was 'Lord of the Dance,' a poem by Sidney Carter sung to the Shaker tune of 'Simple Gifts.' I believe 'Lord of the Dance' has been sung often in virtually every Christian church in America.

"There was no exorcism in the White House on Saturday. We do not plan one. There will not be one. The White House is not possessed by the Devil, much less by my mother's good spirit as *USA* cruelly suggested.

"It is hard to believe that such offensive ignorance could have been accidental. We assume that *USA Today* will want to issue a correction. Until such time, we are barring *USA Today* reporters from the White House. We will issue shortly a statement on the poltergeist phenomenon which is occurring here. I will now play Bishop Ryan's homily on a videotape, which we made of the Eucharist in the Blue Room and which we believe is a historic first. You will note that there is no mention of hellfire or the devil or possession as *USA Today* has claimed."

While the tiresome little auxiliary bishop, looking absurd in his miter and crosier, droned on in his dry, Midwestern voice, I searched for *USA Today* among the morning papers. The headline said "Exorcism Mass at White House!"

Heaven forgive me for it, but I laughed.

Then I picked up the *Wall Street Journal.* Its editorial was headed "Near Miss at White House." Like Congressman Dillingham it deplored violence but suggested that many Americans might lament that the rocket missed. It also carried an op-ed article by

a priest from Georgetown explaining that Thomas
Aquinas had approved in rare circumstances tyran-
nicide. "Thus," the good Jesuit concluded, "Catholic
theology would not have considered the murder of
Hitler or Stalin or other modern tyrants to be sinful."

Sweethearts.

Questions for Sean Patrick:

"Sean, do you have any comment on the statement of the Washington Chancery this morning that
no permission had been given for an exorcism Mass
at the White House and that such Masses may only
be offered with approval of the local bishop."

"I would have hoped that the Chancery would
have checked with the White House before issuing
its statement. We would have told them that there
was no exorcism here. We have delivered to them
by hand a copy of the videotape, which is a recording of the entire liturgy, and suggested that they
might want to make a correction."

"Aren't you being too hard on the working journalists from *USA Today?*"

"We are not blaming the beat reporters for the
story. Presumably they would have checked the
facts. Just now, however, we would rather have writers from the supermarket tabloids in this building
than anyone from *USA Today.*"

Oh, my. We're playing hardball.

The Solarium phone rang.

"Cardinal Cronin, sir."

"Naturally."

"Blackwood, I'm proud of you. Sensational homily! Here's the text of my statement . . ."

"There is no need to make a statement."

He ignored me as he often does when he's made up his mind.

"Bishop Ryan is one of the finest priests in America and, as his homily at the *Te Deum Mass* at the White House shows, one of the best homilists in the country. I deplore the lies told about him. I also deplore the absurd statement from the Washington Chancery. The archbishop there is new on the job. Perhaps with more experience, he'll show greater restraint."

"You can't say those things!" I protested. "Cardinals don't say things like that about other bishops."

"This one just has!" he said proudly.

Mostly Sean Cronin disliked other bishops and hated some of them.

"You've said it already!"

"I wrote it as soon as I saw the headline because I knew the media would be after me. You should see it any moment now."

"Ah."

"Now get rid of those goofy poltergeists. See to it."

He hung up.

Then he appeared on CNN, in front of the Chicago Chancery office building. I noted that it was snowing. He was wearing a neatly fitting overcoat and a white silk scarf which still revealed the tiny red piping around his Roman collar. Naturally he held the statement in his right hand, which displayed his massive ring of office.

It was imprudent of him to issue such a statement. Nonetheless, if the Chicago Irish have any virtue (as the *Times* did not think they have) it is loyalty. You are loyal to your own.

I felt properly grateful.

I sighed loudly and prepared to descend to the Oval Office, where plans would be under way for an explanation of poltergeists.

I stopped in the White House mess to collect a large cup of black tea and three donuts, which would have to serve as my breakfast. I encountered the virtuous Claire Jones also in search of nourishment.

"Hey, Mr. Preacher man, you made it plain yesterday."

"One tries."

"And those creeps from *USA Today* gave it great publicity."

That was true. Doubtless Mae Rosen and Sean Patrick McGurn had rejoiced in the opportunity.

"I say to myself, maybe it will scare them bad spirits away. Didn't though."

"Ah?"

"She throw all the copies of the *Times* and the *Post* which are delivered here every morning into the Dumpster in back. Everyone going crazy find out what they say. She let *USA Today* get through."

For a brief moment I saw the solution to the puzzle, then the elevator door slammed shut.

"What's happening in China?"

"Street fighting in Beijing. Artillery outside of town. Jet flights over the city. This is all internal to the loyalist regime."

"Who's winning?"

"Right now, no one."

I climbed back up the stairs and walked down the corridor to the Oval Office.

Some well-meaning but frivolous young women cheered.

"Great work, Bishop!" Ms. Chan said as she waved me through.

I walked into the Oval Office and encountered the president, his chief of staff, his deputy chief of staff, and the ineffable Mae Rosen.

"Guess what, Blackie?" the last named asked.

I thought I knew what, but I forbore to answer.

"Your sister Mary Kate is flying down here to help with the poltergeist problem."

I sighed loudly.

"Patently there are not enough strong women on the premises, so we need another one."

"We talked with her on her way to O'Hare," Marianna informed me. "She likes the statement Sean Patrick is going to read in a few minutes."

"That approval is of the same merit as an infallibility seal from the Pope."

"She sounds like a cool lady."

"Few will dispute that and none twice."

"She has a high regard for you, though she refers to you as Punk."

Tommy Horan intervened with an ethnic explanation.

"We Irish have the habit of using affectionate nicknames that to other people might sound like insults."

"I'll keep that in mind," Marianna said softly.

"In point of fact," I said, "that one, which also appears in such cognate forms as Uncle Punk refers not only to my being the last born but to a family suspicion that I am so different from the rest of the family that I might be a changeling. That is a replacement baby slipped in by the fairie who had stolen the real Ryan child."

"Are they serious?" Mae asked.

"The Irish, and you might note this too, Dr. Genovesa, never say what they mean and never mean what they say. Presumably it is not necessary for me to grant my nihil obstat to the statement on poltergeists."

"You heard what she did this morning?" the president asked.

"Protected you and your staff from the papers of record?"

"And assured that we would read the MacPaper first."

Again the elevator door opened and slammed shut.

The president gave me a two-paragraph statement on poltergeists.

"The poltergeist (German for playful spirit) syndrome is a recognized psychological problem that normally occurs in troubled adolescents, most frequently young women. It usually responds to patient psychotherapeutic treatment accompanied by appropriate use of tranquilizers. It rarely recurs later in life, but should it recur it may present a much more serious challenge to the ego strength of the victim. Those who are most likely to suffer from the syndrome tend to be quiet, somewhat sullen persons with passive aggressive tendencies. Generally they are seeking attention and affection though there is reason to think that some of their behavior is intended to be punitive. The syndrome is marked by occasional and sometimes frequent physical disturbances in the environment such as objects apparently flinging themselves across the room, disturbances in electrical currents, slamming doors, knocking on the walls. No explanation is yet available to account for these phenomena. Surprisingly, no other person is hurt by these phenomena and no property damaged. Eventually the manifestations cease. Attempts at exorcism seem to be counterproductive.

"Some occurrences have been noted in the White House since the beginning of this administration, most notably at the president's press briefing on China. You will remember that none of your equipment was damaged that day. Similarly the other night all the china in the China Room was slammed to the floor, yet none of it was broken. A couple of times every day, the poltergeist knocks the picture of President Washington off the wall in the Oval Office. The president remarked the other day that the problem was with Republican poltergeists. He intended only to suggest that the poltergeist was not a Democrat. I'll answer a few questions now, but we will have an expert this afternoon who has worked with such cases."

"So what do I know?" I asked. "The good Dr. Ryan vetted this statement for accuracy?"

"Is she Dr. Ryan or Dr. Murphy?" Dr. Genovesa asked.

"Depends on her mood. I wouldn't worry, Dr. Genovesa. I predict with great confidence that you and she will bond . . . Against the rest of us."

Uneasy laughter. Sean Patrick left for the Press Briefing Room.

We watched on the TV monitors.

"I have a preliminary statement on the White House's first poltergeist phenomenon . . . that we know about. The McGurn administration offers you another historic first. I will read the statement and then answer a few questions. We will have an expert here after lunch."

After the statement, there were indeed questions.

"Sean, you don't seem very worried about all this stuff."

"At first it's kind of scary, then it's annoying, then it's boring."

"What reason do you have to exclude diabolic possession?"

"The fact that this is a reasonably well-known psychiatric problem."

"Sean, I don't mean to be offensive, but you do . . ."

"Have a couple of adolescent sisters. Funny, I've noticed that. However, neither of them have been on the premises during some of the phenomena."

"You're telling us that there are no dangers to the president from these poltergeists?"

"None at all; he is in much more danger from the editorial page of the *Wall Street Journal* this morning, hinting that it might be all right in Catholic moral theology to kill him."

"Oops," the president said.

"Strong point for our side," Mae Rosen argued.

"Good for Sean Patrick," Tommy Horan said, showing a rare display of emotion.

I finished my last donut and regretted that I had not brought four.

"Dr. Ryan is expected at one?" the president asked, glancing at his watch. "Where should we feed her?"

"Family dining room?" Marianna asked.

"Solarium?" Mae Rosen suggested.

"White House mess," I said. "It will make a great

story for her children and grandchildren. She has the family weakness for stories."

"She'll be staying the night, Bishop," Marianna informed me. "Her husband will join her later in the day."

"The long-suffering Joe Murphy, a living saint."

"She said that she had to be able to tell her kids that she stayed in the Lincoln Bedroom."

"Doubtless, which her poor sibling was barred from."

"She seems very fond of you."

"Doubtless."

Well, you can't expect an Italian from Flatbush Avenue to understand the dynamics of sibling relationships in Irish families.

Say anything bad about Blackie Ryan in the presence of his sister and she might kill you.

"It might be wise, unless she humiliates us all this afternoon, to do a major spread in the family dining room."

"By all means," said the president.

"One more matter. All present should realize that madam my sister was in high school when the president was in first grade. That means she is incapable of calling him anything but 'Jackie,' as in 'cute little Jackie McGurn.' "

General laughter.

"I would expect nothing less," the president said.

I departed from the Oval Office to make my morning patrol of the corridors and of the bull pen, where many of the support staff were pounding away on computers. I was hopeful that I might encounter Jane Effingham, Francesca Jackson, and Luisa Peña. None of them, however, ventured to introduce themselves to me. That could prove nothing or something. I half expected that the player would seek me out. Sometimes they do, but then sometimes they don't. It is extremely difficult to sense the mental state of someone caught in the poltergeist situation. They want help and they don't want help. They want to be applauded. They don't want to be suspected. They crave attention. They hate attention.

I thought I had picked out Luisa Peña in the bull pen, a beaming young woman who seem to be humming to herself as she worked.

I encountered Barry scurrying down the corridor. He had escaped from his cage in Mae's office and was patently lost. In the condition of the McGurn White House a wandering dog would hardly be noticed. I captured him easily enough because he knew me as a friend and ally, though in truth most dogs would jump into the arms of anyone with a friendly face.

"Good dog." The president petted him and Barry licked his fingers.

"Mae is with Marianna," he said.

"You really should have an Irish wolfhound," I informed the president.

"We had a very old black Lab. Got him when Granne was born. He was Ellen's dog. Died a couple of weeks after she did."

Right. Nonetheless, I would talk to the good Nuala on return and arrange an offer of a male, white Irish wolfhound for the White House, a well-trained puppy.

I retired to my room and called Mike Casey who reported that there seemed to be a problem about funds. His agents had been instructed to ask for twenty-five thousand down for "expenses" and the same again if they actually were called upon to testify. Drew thought that was a bit steep. It would have to be cleared with higher-ups in the "investigation."

"The more they ask for, the more they will be respected. Sleidel has tons of money."

"I think you're right, Blackie. If they offer them less, my young women will turn them down flat."

"They can claim that they don't want to be another Paula Jones or Monica Lewinsky."

"Right!"

12

"Dr. Murphy's car is approaching the White House."
It was agent Chick in his role as Acting Agent-in-
Charge.

"I trust the red carpet is ready."

No response to that.

Someone, doubtless the matriarchal Dr. Genovesa,
thought that the silly little bishop ought to be there
to greet his big sister.

I descended to the diplomatic reception room.

"Just in time," said the Ligurian matriarch.

Chatting volubly with the normally taciturn Agent
Wholley, the valiant Mary Kathleen emerged from
the limo clad in an unbuttoned bone trench coat,
blue blazer, white blouse, beige skirt, appropriately
short and with a compact flight bag flung over her
shoulder—the model of the professional, very attractive grandmother, discreetly designer garbed.

Batten down the hatches, folks, the good witch of
the South Wind is arriving.

"Punk." She embraced me enthusiastically. "You
were extreme cool on the tube this morning. Caught
it at the Admirals Club. The kids all called me on
my cell phone. Why don't we see you dressed up
like that more often? Joe's flying in later. We're staying in the Lincoln Bedroom. Big turn-on. Hi, Mary

Kate Murphy. Hey, kid, that was a marvelous show yesterday. Poor old man was set up. Those idiots deserved all you gave them. I liked the Brooklyn accent too."

"Mari Genovesa," the deputy chief of staff replied with a broad grin. "Welcome to the White House. We're delighted you're here."

Irish matriarch encounters Ligurian matriarch. Instant bonding as predicted.

I do not want to portray madam my sister as merely a mindless flitterer, an irresistible torrent of South Side Irish babble. In her game face with a patient on the couch, she is, I am told, one very tough, indeed implacable therapist, particularly with male patients who have the mistaken notion that her good looks mean she's a pushover for their neurotic defenses.

Long ago she had propositioned the long-suffering Bostonian Joe Murphy during a psychiatric clerkship at Little Company of Mary Hospital when he was about to expel her—with ample reason—from the program for disrespect and insubordination. He had never escaped.

We conducted her to the Lincoln Bedroom and sitting room.

"Extreme." She sighed. "Abe really sleep here?"

"During the war, clerks and telegraphers worked at this end of the floor. The president and the first lady used the same bedroom at the other end, same as today."

"No first lady today . . . I liked your comment about the broken heart on the tube yesterday, Mari. Very perceptive."

"Will he get over it?"

The valiant doctor shrugged.

"Maybe, probably, I'm not sure. Wouldn't bet on it. Like you said a celibate routine and a broken heart can become a protective cocoon, especially when you have the genial shanty Irish mask to hide behind."

Marianna hadn't said that at all.

My good sibling put her travel bag on a table and removed a manila file.

"My articles on the subject and my curriculum vitae. You can make copies if you want."

"Yes we will . . . You travel light."

"Don't need much for an overnight with your husband in the Lincoln Bedroom . . . So long as the husband shows up."

One might safely assume there was no form of nightdress in the bag.

"Who needs a nightgown in a hotel," I had heard her remark once to a daughter, "when there's a towel in the bathroom?"

In the oval office she kissed the president with some gusto.

"Jackie, you look like hell. You're not taking care of yourself. You ought to see a doctor."

"We thought we'd have a bite of lunch before your briefing," the president managed to gasp. "Big dinner tonight after Joe gets here."

"Great idea. Like Roman wine, he doesn't travel very well."

We then adjourned downstairs to the White House mess—the president, Sean Patrick, Mari (as she now must be called), Wonder Woman, and the aforementioned supernumerary bishop. We all supplied ourselves with salads and yogurt. Well, I had a Swissburger and chocolate ice cream. I do not gain weight when I eat nor lose it during Lent when I fast.

"Hi, Sean Patrick, you look great, more than I can say for your dad. Any cute young women around here to take your mind off your job?"

The perceptive will observe that there was a swift jab at his father and a compliment to Mari in that party.

"I am told," the president said with a mock sigh, "that he is sweet but not yet extreme sweet on an Apache medicine woman called Travels By Night."

"Yaqui," I said.

"Hey, great! We medicine women have to stick together. I bet she's totally cute."

"My sisters," said the furiously blushing but not unhappy Sean Patrick, "talk too much. People tell me she's cute, so I guess she is."

"And the Daughters?" She turned to the president.

"More disrespectful of their poor old father than ever. I'm always happy to see them drive up and even happier to see them leave."

Dr. Genovesa opened her mouth as if to defend the Daughters and thought better of it.

"Hi, Mary Kate." Tommy Horan kissed her and joined us at the table.

"How are Sheila and the kids?" she asked.

"Miss the neighborhood and the parish, but you know Sheila, adjust to anything and end up loving it."

"What's up, Tommy?" the President asked.

"Some Republican senators are talking about filibustering the Supreme Court Amendment."

"Do they have the votes?"

"Conrad says he doesn't think so. We'll have to wait to see how it plays out."

"Might be necessary to lean on some of them a little."

"Conrad will let us know. He's as happy as a clam over there."

"Now about this statement." Mary Kate had assumed her game face #1.

Class came to order.

"As I understand it, this has been distributed to the media goons this morning and I'm to comment on it?"

"Not quite, Dr. Murphy. You can never count on the press to read anything you give them. Some will, of course, but others are averse to work. Besides, the television people will need clips for the nightly news. We need a collection of clips that make the point that this is a psychiatric problem not a supernatural one."

"Psychiatric it is, but there's a lot about it that we can't explain. I think we can say that a number of different ways."

"You have no idea how they do it?" Mari asked tentatively, in awe of the great woman.

"Not much. I am increasingly persuaded that there is a dimension of the human organism and indeed of all creation that we do not understand and will not explore because old-fashioned science says it can't happen. Troubled teenage girls simply can't do the things these poor kids do and that's that. I don't believe most of the psychic stuff. I believe the poltergeist thing because I've seen it and I've watched kids get over it. They don't even know how they do it . . . Supernatural? . . . Not exactly, but very mysterious."

"So," the president observed, "we have to convey the idea that it is not a serious problem though it is a little strange."

"Serious enough for the person causing it, especially since she's probably not a teen anymore. Might spend the rest of her life in an institution."

Just to remind us that she was still around, the player seized Mary Kate's decaf cup and hurled it across the room, where it smashed against the wall and fell with a loud bang on a table at which two young women were sitting. They both screamed, then went back to chewing on their coleslaw sandwiches.

"I'll get your coffee back," Sean Patrick said helpfully.

"Get out of here, you little bitch," Mary Kate barked harshly. "Crawl back into your wormhole and leave us alone. We'll talk about you as much as we want."

I sensed the player slipping away, head downcast.

"That gets rid of them. It also makes them realize that we're not frightened and certainly not impressed."

"Do they hear what you say?"

"The energy vibration might. The source? Who knows!"

Sean Patrick returned with the coffee cup, nothing spilled of course, in one hand and Travels By Night in the other.

"I told Germaine, Dr. Murphy, what you said about medicine women sticking together and she asked if she could meet you. This is Germaine Connelly."

No way this shy Yaqui child would have said that. Sean Patrick had asked her if she wanted to meet the great medicine woman.

"I majored in psychology at New Mexico/Las Cruces," she said demurely. "I hope someday that I can be a real medicine woman."

For a very brief moment of silence, Mary Kate peered into the eyes and presumably into the soul of the Yaqui child.

"I'm sure you're already a real medicine woman, Germaine. It won't hurt to go to more school. But you read souls."

"Thank you, Dr. Murphy. So do you."

"Take good care of this big lug of ours."

"He is a sweet lug." She slipped her hand out of Sean Patrick's and, face scarlet, returned to her table.

"Well," my sister observed, "I might tell you, Sean Patrick, not to let that one get away. But I don't think I have to."

The press secretary's face turned redder than usual.

"Anyway"—game face back on—"I agree, Jackie. I have to keep the right balance—unusual phenomenon, we've had experience with it, can't quite explain all the details, no one's going to get hurt, not supernatural, it will go away. Right?"

"Arguably quantum theory could account for it." I spoke for the first time. "It is improbably alleged that every atom in the universe has immediate access to every other atom . . ."

"That's even scarier, Punk!"

My valiant sister wanted to go to her room to

rearrange her face. Mari said she would accompany her. The president and his son left for their respective offices. I meandered down the main corridor of the West Wing by the bullpen. I had become part of the scenery and was again invisible. In this instance that was not an asset.

I did notice Jane Effingham staring at me. She would be the first target tomorrow when I could settle down to do my work.

Later in the Corner Room, my sibling was waiting somewhat nervously for the briefing to begin.

"Do I look all right, Punk?"

"Devastating."

"She's a wonderful young woman."

"Travels By Night?"

"Her too, but I meant Mari. She must scare the hell out of Jackie. By the way, our little playmate unpacked my bag for me and threw my things all round the Lincoln Suite. It was a little embarrassing when Mari saw how little in the way of clothes I brought."

"I believe you once said that you didn't need much in a hotel room because there were always towels in the bathroom."

She colored faintly.

"Well, here's Sean Patrick. Wish me luck."

I watched the show on the TV screen in the Corner Room.

"We have invited Dr. Mary Kathleen Ryan Murphy, who is an expert on these matters, to comment on our statement about the poltergeist phenomena in the White House."

My valiant sibling put on game face #2, the clinical expert lecturing to professional colleagues.

"You can call me Dr. Ryan or Dr. Murphy or Mary Kate [charming smile] which is my real name. I am a clinical professor of psychiatry at the Northwestern University Medical Center and a professorial lecturer in the same discipline at the University of Chicago. I think that Sean Patrick has passed out my curriculum vitae and copies of my three articles on the poltergeist phenomenon. I don't think there are any experts on this strange and rare syndrome. I've treated a half dozen cases and written a couple of articles on the subject.

"I have good news and bad news. The good news is that these phenomena eventually stop and that no one gets hurt, except sometimes the person responsible, and no property is broken or even spilled. The bad news is that we have very little understanding of why it happens or how it works.

"I have recently heard a theory that links such displays to quantum dynamics, if every atom in the cosmos has immediate access to every other atom—an idea which I find scary—then perhaps an explanation might be found in that fact.

"We do know that psychotherapeutic treatment is successful in most cases. A combination of powerful tranquilizers plus sensitive and very firm counseling helps the client to escape from the syndrome and become a relatively normal teenager. Sometimes it doesn't work but the young person improves anyway, at least to the extent of stopping the poundings and the knockings and the rattling and such like. The fact that therapy works argues in my judgment to the conclusion that the poltergeist syndrome is a natural phenomenon, though one we do not fully understand.

"I can assure you that while the phenomena are scary at first and ultimately boring, there is no reason to attribute them to any supernatural force. The White House is not haunted. It is not possessed by the Devil. It is rather being pestered, in a spectacular way, by a troubled young person, desperately craving attention. I worry especially about her—the players are usually young women—because this is probably her second time around, a dangerous regression to early adolescent behavior. It may well be that someone who knows her past experiences is pressuring her to create the impression that the White House is haunted for purposes of their own. That, of course, remains to be seen.

"Finally, does the young person responsible for the poltergeist know that she's getting national attention? I suspect she does and is both delighted by it and profoundly frightened by it."

"Dr. Murphy, does not the president have adolescent daughters?"

"He does indeed. They are not in the White House at the moment, yet the playful spirit took my coffee cup down in the Mess and heaved it across the room with tremendous force, smashing it against the wall. The cup was not broken, nor was any of my coffee spilled. The Daughters, whom I've known all their lives, strike me as young women with strongly integrated personalities and not likely candidates for this syndrome. If they want attention, they tend to get it the way my children got it—by shouting at their parents and lecturing them!"

"Mary Kate, do you think Ellen McGurn might return from the dead?"

"I don't feel particularly qualified to comment on

contact-with-the-dead experiences, though I know they are widely reported. However, having known Ellen Marie Fitzgerald since she was a two-year-old toddling down Longwood Drive in our neighborhood, I can assure you she would not bother with such trivialities as flying coffee cups if she wanted to make a point. Tornado, firestorm, Potomac flood? She might do those things if she could, but she would not throw the contents of my flight bag all over the Lincoln Bedroom."

Ah, I thought to myself, we're doing splendidly. Naturally.

"Mary Kate, are you Bishop Ryan's sister?"

"He's my brother."

"Sorry about that. Is he an exorcist?"

Expression of astonishment on her face.

"My brother an exorcist? Hardly! He is a man of many talents, including the most remarkable common sense in any man I know with the exception of my husband. Sometimes He wouldn't mess with that stuff. I'd disown him if he did."

"Nice compliment," Mae Rosen whispered to me, as the good dog Barry jumped into my lap and snuggled up.

"You didn't listen to it carefully enough."

"What do you recommend that the president do about this infestation . . ."

"Clinically we call it an obsession, but I'm sorry for being a pedant . . . I'd say that his reaction should be one of extreme cool. He should get on with the business of governing the country until our little friend gives up."

"Do you think, Dr. Murphy, that all of this is aimed at him?"

Thoughtful pause.

"I wouldn't be surprised if it were. He's the guy, you know."

"Do you believe in the Devil, Dr. Murphy, like all Christians do?"

"I'm a Catholic Christian and I believe in evil. Anyone who reads the morning papers or watches the evening news knows that the world abounds with evil. I don't see any reason why evil needs to be personified."

"You've known the president all his life, haven't you, Dr. Murphy?"

"More or less. I remember him as an obnoxious if charming little punk hanging around the parish. Now he's stopped being obnoxious, I'm told."

"Do you believe the stories of his sexually harassing campaign workers?"

She laughed loudly.

"I'd rather believe that the Pope is a secret Mormon. It's an absurd idea."

"Thank you, Dr. Murphy," Sean Patrick ended the conference.

"Home run," Mae Rosen informed me.

"For the literate or intelligent segment of the population. The Fundies will believe that the Devil has taken over the White House."

Mary Kate entered the Corner Room and collapsed into the chair that I had quickly vacated.

"That was more fun than I thought it would be!"

"Home run," Mae Rosen repeated.

Barry, who had been sleeping in my lap, opened his eyes.

He was shifted from my lap to his traveling cage. What would he do if a massive hound were introduced into the West Wing? Probably role over on his back every time he saw him.

"The president says drinks for everyone in the Roosevelt Room!" Sean Patrick put down the phone.

"I hope you made a tape. My husband will want to critique it."

"First time in the marriage he would do that," I murmured.

A brand new bottle of Jameson's awaited us in the Roosevelt Room.

Mari proffered a bottle of high-price Barolo.

"In case anyone wants a civilized drink," she said.

"Northern Italian wine," I commented.

"There is no southern Italian wine."

I opted for the Jameson's. Mae and Marianna, however, settled for the Barolo.

"The other Dr. Murphy is here, Mr. President," Ms. Chan announced.

Joe Murphy, a man with curly white hair, whimsical eyes, and a face marked irrevocably by a lifetime of smiles, swept his bride up in his arms, into which she collapsed with practiced ease—a new image of my sibling for those who had not seen the act a thousand times.

"I hear you were sensational," he said, "blew the demons all the way back to hell."

She clung to him for support.

" 'Bout time you showed up."

"Good afternoon, Mr. President," Joe said, releasing his grip on his subservient wife.

"First things first," said the president.

The clinging was part of the act too. Not that it was not a genuine aspect of their complex and patently satisfying relationship.

He accepted a glass of wine. He's from Boston, you see.

Sean Patrick appeared.

"CNN is playing it straight," he said. "So are the early local news programs in New York and here. Leaving open the possibility of the supernatural but emphasizing the natural explanation. I don't think they want to mess with the supernatural either."

"What we've done, Mr. President," Tommy Horan suggested, "is isolated the infection. Okay, a poltergeist obsession is another historic first for the Executive Mansion, but it is a rather trivial event, nothing much to be excited about. It's tonight's news and tomorrow morning's. Then it's back page. We beat the tabloids to it and we knocked out *USA Today*."

"Unless our little friend manages to pull off something really spectacular in public," I commented.

"I have a hunch she won't try that," Mary Kate surmised. "She's already had opportunities to do that and has not."

"Nonetheless," I insisted, "we must find out who she is, if only to save her from herself."

"Then do it quickly," Mary Kathleen urged.

The dinner in the family room was elegant as such things seem always to be in the White House, glistening tableware, delicious roast beef, an irresistible Oregon Cabernet, witty conversation. Marianna Genovesa was surrounded by South Side Irish (after all his years in the neighborhood Joe Murphy was functionally South Side Irish, save for the funny way he talked). She held her own to say the least. She also was amused by us.

"Do you have any Irish like this crowd in Flatbush?" I asked her once, throwing a little spice into the discussion.

"The Flatbush Irish don't talk funny like you do, but they are almost as noisy."

Nice hit.

Later in the sitting room of the V.M. Molotov suite, Joe, Mary Kate, and I shared a bottle of Bailey's that I had liberated from the liquor cabinet in the Oval Office.

"That woman must drive Jackie crazy," my sister offered.

"She'd drive almost any man crazy," her husband replied, playing out another of their scenarios.

"You'll have enough trouble tonight with just one woman."

"Maybe."

"What I mean," she continued, "is that she is almost the perfect match for him, save for the funny way she talks. And she has the kind of boobs that drive men crazy. Besides, she's available, ready, and willing to become his and on whatever terms he wants, though she's pretty confident about what they'd be."

"She is not obviously available," I suggested.

"Doesn't have to be, Punk. All she has to do is to be around, be competent and pleasant and to fight with him and win some of the time. Most men in Jackie's position would succumb almost immediately."

"But he won't?"

"Can't. Right, Dr. Murphy?"

I filled their Waterford tumblers again.

"No more, Punk. I have a busy night ahead of me."

"You're right again, Dr. Murphy," Joe replied to her question. "He'd love to carry her off. But he can't."

"No testosterone?"

"Maybe less than usual"—my sister dismissed this suggestion with a wave of her hand—"but that's not the problem. In a nutshell he is tormented by wanting to want her but unable to want her."

"Ah," I said.

"If a man has a long and loving and satisfying sexual relationship with a woman and he suddenly loses her, he is likely to suffer from a long period of sexual aridity in which desire not so much dries up as does the ability to activate desire. The processes, the dynamics, the rhetoric of desire are denied him. The body of an attractive woman—and, Punk, it is precisely the body in the most basic physiological sense—is a reproof, an intolerable challenge, a source of raw terror."

"It doesn't happen all the time, does it?"

"Only to the good guys and then only to some of them," Joe replied. "If Mari should ever put a move on him, he'd fall apart."

"I doubt that she will without some encouragement."

"I think she knows that instinctively," Mary Kate said. "She'll wait around patiently for a while, then probably disengage, with great sadness. The strain on her is considerable, as you may imagine, even though she bears it gracefully as she does all things."

"What is to be done? Therapy?"

"Probably wouldn't work." My sister waved her hand again. "The problem is not a body problem though it permeates his body. It's a head problem, but not the kind of head problem that people like the good Dr. Murphy here can cope with. Maybe I should say it's a spiritual problem, though probably not the kind of spiritual problem that a priest would be much good at."

"Jackie needs to believe," her husband explained, "that life is worth living, that a woman, in this case the woman, is worth pursuing, that he is permitting himself to dry up and wither, for all his presidential charm."

"He must make a vast movement of his soul, Punk. A huge leap into the dark all around him."

"Patently," I agreed. "Will he?"

Silence.

"Joe?" his wife asked.

"I wouldn't bet on it."

"Neither would I. Poor Mari put her finger on it. The Irish are good at celibacy, at becoming dried-up old bachelors probably because of the famine and probably because of a cultural fear of women. Think of that funny poem by what's his name . . . you know, the Midnight Court?"

"Brian Merryman."

"Right. Finally in the present situation it comes to this: after a wonderful relationship with a fine woman and having it destroyed, your friend POTUS in his heart of hearts is terrified at the prospect of falling under the power of another woman, however satisfactory a bedmate she might be. To belong to Mari might be bad enough. What if you lose her too?"

"Ah."

"Not a very bright prospect."

"I'm afraid not," Joe Murphy agreed. "Grace is

going to have to blow him over . . . And, now Dr. Murphy." He took his wife's hand and drew her to her feet. "We must abed. We have a busy day ahead of us tomorrow."

"And possibly a busy night too."

"As your brother would say, arguably."

I watched them walk across the corridor into the Lincoln Bedroom and close the door.

At the other end of the corridor Jack McGurn would be very well aware what would be going on. Poor dear man.

I reached for the bottle of Bailey's. One more splasheen wouldn't hurt. It was torn from my hands and hurled against the portrait of Fanny Kemble. Neither Fanny nor, more importantly at the time, the Bailey's were damaged.

"Get out of here, you worthless brat," I ordered. "And leave those lovers across the way alone or I won't bother to help you out of the hell you've created for yourself."

And to which someone else has pushed you.

13

I was sauntering down the main corridor of the West Wing the next morning hoping to stir up a conversation with one of my suspects. Again my habitual invisibility had set in. I was once more the little man who wasn't there again today. Even the inestimable Dr. Genovesa sped by me.

"Good morning, Dr. Genovesa," I murmured.

She stopped in surprised, looked around to see where the voice was coming from, and spotted me, apparently under my rock.

"Bishop Blackie! Sorry. I was preoccupied. You have to be that way around here half the time or no one thinks you're working . . . Your sister and her husband are wonderful people . . ."

She was wearing a tailored blue suit, not light blue exactly but lighter than navy blue. No matter how much she tried to underplay her good looks, nothing worked.

"Arguably." I sighed.

"And they worship you."

Not very likely.

"What reaction in the media this morning?"

"Not too bad. Back-page stuff, which is where our little friend belongs."

"Ah, we have demythologized her."

"Our response to *USA Today* was well received, but that's because everyone else hates *USA Today*. We're still trying to figure out who their source is. Probably won't. There's always someone dissatisfied and disloyal in the White House, no matter who's in office."

"Not just to Irish Catholics from Chicago."

"And the *Times* editorial wondered if there was a connection between Catholic superstition and the poltergeist. It also suggested that medieval mummery in the White House might be a violation of the separation of church and state."

"They used the word 'mummery'?"

"The president called the publisher and reamed him. I was in the Oval Office with Tommy when he made the call. I think he scared the publisher, who admitted that it was an unfortunate editorial. I suspect that he doesn't quite have his editorial board under control."

"They once carried an editorial which compared Easter unfavorably to Passover, a comparison which overlooked the fact that they are patently the same festival."

"Much of what looks like anti-Catholicism over there is just ignorance, Bishop Blackie."

"Perhaps . . . On another matter, did we hire Rita Suarez as a favor to the vice president?"

"Hardly. She applied for the job. Her memos on the Latino situation were brilliant. We only found out that she was Genie's daughter by her first husband when she filled out her employment form. The president said we could hardly discriminate against her because her mother is so unpleasant. She's a

sweet kid ... You don't think she might have been
USA Today's source?"

"Not necessarily. I was merely curious."

More suspicious of her than before? Not really.
How could I be suspicious of anyone?

"Mary Kate and Joe both thought the president
looked terrible. Do you think so too?"

"Oh yes."

"He's under enormous pressure. His budget resolution has already passed. The Social Security reform is moving through Congress. The gays and
labor and the environmentalists are happy that he
has restored Clinton's rules and made some new
ones. He's getting along fine with foreign leaders. Yet
he's constantly being beaten up by the media, the
Religious Right is calling for his impeachment and
indirectly for his assassination, the local Catholic
Church doesn't like him, there's these sexual harassment charges, and the China haters in Congress are
all over him, and the White House is obsessed by
our poltergeist brat—she knocked down President
Washington five times in ten minutes this morning."

"And he has a broken heart."

"I shouldn't have said that."

"Yes, you should. It's true ... What's happening
in China?"

"All is confusion today. The battles in the streets
of Beijing seem to have stopped without either side
winning. The rebel leaders are trying, without too
much success, to complete their occupation of Shanghai. There's fierce fighting along the Yellow River.
So far neither side is killing foreigners, which usually
happens when China splits up."

"And when that happens?"

"We try to get our people out or at least into safe areas. It won't be easy."

Before I had come down from the Churchill Bedroom, I had talked to Mike the Cop. There was still trouble about the details of the agreement between his agents and Snodgrass and Sleidel. There was also the problem of persuading the intermediaries to admit they didn't care whether what was said about the president was true or not. If those words were said and the money was handed over, the cops would promptly arrest them. I had to assume that there was a video camera somewhere that would record this exchange.

"Bishop Ryan, I should like to say something to you. Would you like to sit down?"

Jane Effingham, a strawberry blond in her middle thirties who would have been pretty save that her narrow face was severe and her eyes were stern. Her plain gray blouse and her long black skirt hinted that the nineteen sixties were still among us.

"I don't believe in any religion," she said when I had ensconced myself in a chair in her tiny cube. "In my opinion life is merely a brief interlude between two kinds of emptiness. Religion tries to hide this harsh reality from us, but fails. It often merely reinforces bigotry and prejudice ... Having said these things I was most impressed by your Mass on Saturday and by your sister's presentation yesterday. In my part of New York there are not many Catholics. Those I knew growing up did not impress me. You Chicago Irish are different ..."

"Despite the medieval mummery?"

"The *Times* has become another form of religion, a cult in its own right."

"Patently."

"When I was growing up we had poltergeists down the street, an Italian worker's family. I found it all vulgar and offensive. The child, a classmate of mine in junior high school, was clearly troubled. There were eight or nine children in her family. She was neglected, passive, unhappy. The stories about her tricks scared all of us. We were afraid to make fun of her. My father said that she needed a psychiatrist but the Church would not permit its members to see a psychiatrist. The parish priest finally came over to bless her. She terrified him with the things that she threw at him and cries of pain that wracked their house. He ran away and came back a couple of days later with an exorcist. The poor child went mad during the ceremony and had to be removed to an asylum. The family moved away shortly thereafter. We never heard of them again."

"Tragic . . . Too many people saw *The Exorcist*, I fear."

"I have gone home only occasionally since I graduated from college and almost never since I finished my Ph.D. I no longer ask about the poor child. I hope she recovered . . ."

"Often they just grow out of it."

"Yes, that's what your sister said. The human organism is not without its strengths, is it? I suppose you would say that's the way God made us."

"Through the miracle of the evolutionary process."

Her eyes flashed. She had not expected such a devious answer.

"I will never forget them carrying the poor child out of the house. She was screaming, rocks were smashing against the windows, her mother was drenching her with holy water, her father was cursing the priests, the other children were wailing . . . It was horrid."

Her hands were clenched, her jaw tight as she recalled the memory.

"Abominable," I said, mentally denouncing all the idiot priests in the country who went about doing stupid things.

"I realize that there was some prejudice in my memory—large family, Italians, superstition. Surely the president's daughters represent a different kind of Irish Catholic young woman . . . So self-possessed and determined."

"And bossy."

She actually smiled.

"No doubt about that."

"We have no monopoly on poltergeists," I observed, "despite the *Times* editorial. Most of my sister's clients were of other religious backgrounds."

A thin smile appeared on her lips.

"Of course, I should have known that! It is so hard to get rid of one's prejudices . . . In any event, I ache for this child that's right here among us, suffering perhaps worse than my neighbor did. Surely there is something that we can do for her!"

Ah, the liberal heresy—for every problem there must be a solution which men and women of goodwill can devise.

"I'm not about to walk among the denizens of the West Wing with a Holy Water stoop," I said, "as much as it wouldn't hurt most of them and might do them some good. I don't think it would have any effect on our friend. She might indeed grab the aspergillum—that's what we Papists call the water sprinkler—and heave it at the president."

"Do you think she's Catholic?"

"I hadn't thought of that . . . It's a good question. When she tries to disturb me, there's an implicit plea for help, such as a Catholic adolescent might make to a priest."

All my women suspects, from Dr. Genovesa on down, were Catholics except this woman. Even Francesca Jackson, about whose religious identification I was uncertain, had received Communion on Saturday evening.

"You must save her, Bishop Ryan," Jane Effingham insisted. "That young woman is going through enormous torment, even worse perhaps than my neighbor."

"I'll try," I said.

"I should like to be able to pray for your success, but I'm afraid I cannot."

"Wouldn't hurt," I said, getting up and walking down the corridor towards the Oval Office. "Address the prayers 'to whom it may concern.' "

"You can go right in, Bishop Ryan," Ms. Chan said. "The president looks like he needs a priest."

"Blackwood!" he said. "Come in and sit down. I feel like I should talk to a priest."

"Ms. Chan suggested as much. China?"

"China . . . there's a block of maybe twelve senators and perhaps twenty congressmen who are staunchly anti-China. They're against free trade with them, want us to arm Taiwan so they could invade the mainland, impose sanctions, do anything we can to eliminate the yellow peril. Send gunboats up the Yangtze, land the Marines. They are frightened at the number of Chinese who have moved into our country. Warn that they're enemy agents. It's like it's 1950 all over again."

"They really want you to land the Marines? Do they know anything about the size of the People's Liberation Army, even if it is currently divided?"

"They're not sure what they want me to do, only I have to do something now when China is weak and divided. If any Americans are killed in the fighting, they'll want revenge. They'll demand that we get all our people out of China, even if we have to use nuclear weapons."

"They don't have the votes."

"A perfect Chicago reaction." He grinned. "The voice is the voice of Blackwood, but the words are of Richard M. Daley. No, they don't have the votes . . . Unfortunately, Claire tells me that the Taiwanese are thinking of landing some of their own forces in Hong Kong and Shanghai. There's no trouble in Hong Kong yet, but Shanghai, the most important city in China, is in flames."

"What would happen?"

"Who knows? The rebels might welcome the help. Or they might resent it. The loyalists, if we can call them that, might say it's an American-backed invasion, maybe even toss around a few of their nuclear bombs."

"Ah."

"I'm meeting with the National Security Council and some of the Pentagon people in an hour. They'll argue back and forth. The generals and admirals will want to unleash the Kuomintang. The civilians generally won't. It's not quite the Missile Crisis, but it's a tough one."

"And you have made up your mind that, at the present time, you will not permit the unleashing of the Kuomintang?"

"Sure, what else? We'll put patrols in the South China Sea to prevent any outside interference. The Taiwanese won't like it, but they won't do anything either. I'll explain that at the present time we must leave the mainlanders to clarify their own problems."

"What else could you do?"

"Not a thing . . . The outcry from the right, especially the missionary religious right, is going to be ugly. We didn't need it right now . . . By the way, you hear anything from Mike Casey?"

"The project progresses well. I may have more for you shortly . . . Tell me, does Claire get to you?"

"She's first-rate on China. She and Marianna are a great team. You mean her shuffling back and forth into black English?"

"Not so much that as her talking about spirits in this building?"

"Gives me the creeps . . . Do you think . . ."

"Not really. I'm just interested in those in the building who seem to be in touch with the spirit world."

"Like my prospective daughter-in-law?"

"I was unaware that it was that serious."

"It's not really, but it might be. Travels By Night is cute and sweet, and those deep eyes of hers give me the creeps."

"You will then," I changed back to the original subject, "insist that we maintain nonintervention patrols and direct that the navy begins them and you announce that today."

He sighed.

"No choice is there, Blackwood? The most powerful country in the world should err on the side of restraint, shouldn't it?"

Patently.

Back in the corridor I sought out the wondrous Travels By Night.

"Can you make medicine that will help a president?"

"What kind of medicine?"

"Medicine which will bring him a little peace and ease his pain?"

"I can . . . But I'd have to give it to him. I'd be afraid . . ."

"No problem. Just put it together, march down to Ms. Chan, and tell her that Father Ryan said you should have two minutes with the president."

"Really?"

"Really."

"He won't fire me?"

"Not a chance."

My cell phone beeped. After a considerable struggle I found it in my jacket pocket.

"Father Ryan."

"Mike, Blackie."

"Indeed."

"It will go down tonight."

"Capital, you'll arrange to photograph it."

"We have a video camera that fits into a pin on one of our agent's sweater. We pick up the signal in a van outside."

"They will be taken to the Chicago Avenue Station?"

"They'll get their Miranda rights and an offer of

probation if they cooperate. That'll be tricky, but we'll play some of the tapes for them."

"Do you have enough evidence now that they're conspiring to suborn perjury?"

He hesitated.

"Enough to get an indictment, maybe even a conviction because people are so fed up with this stuff. However, Snodgrass and Sleidel have the money for good lawyers that might get them off. We're going to try for more tonight. If Drew and Carrie want to keep their law licenses or lose them only a few years and they cooperate, we'll have enough for a conviction of all involved, which means plea bargains. Otherwise, we have enough on the tapes to sink their whole conspiracy."

"Capital."

"You tell the president yet?"

"Not yet . . . He's busy with China. I'll tell him later."

"We'll let you know."

Out of the corner of my eye, I saw Travels By Night walking solemnly down the corridor towards the oval office with a bowl in her hands. Agent Wholley stopped her, then waved her on.

It was the kind of pick-me-up that Jack McGurn needed.

Might that lovely young Yaqui be the playful spirit?

There were fires within fires in her depths. The Yaqui were a tribe that gradually slipped across the border from Mexico in the last century because they were often on the wrong side in the revolution—the hypocrisies of which they had seen through. They had materialized without warning in Arizona and

New Mexico and eventually demanded that they be added to the register of American Tribes. It took them a long time to persuade the Bureau of Indian Affairs that they were entitled. Eventually they built their own gambling casino. They were a mysterious and secretive people who trusted no one. Germaine Connelly had broken out of the tribal culture and probably could return to it only with great difficulty. Yet she had brought with her mystery and secrets and fear. Maybe somewhere in the depths of her soul there lurked a playful spirit longing to be free of what she thought was a tribal curse—bad medicine.

Maybe, but probably not.

And Jane Effingham, a guilt-ridden liberal of the kind we don't grow among the Chicago Irish. Might the story she told so vividly be in fact autobiographical? Italian she was certainly not. Yet her family could well have been some kind of fundamentalist Protestant who could have reacted the same way. The very intensity of her manner when she was recounting the story to me seemed inappropriate for a stern upstate New York Protestant. Did she expect me to help her?"

She was a little old to be regressing to the poltergeist syndrome. For that matter so too was Mari Genovesa. Both their names, however, would remain on my imaginary list.

I spotted Luisa Peña. She was smiling happily and humming to herself as her fingers danced across a computer keyboard transcribing for some dignitary in the building who did not have high enough rank to have his own assistant.

"Do you always hum when you type, Luisa?" I asked.

She jumped in her chair and spun around. Then she saw who it was.

"Hi, Bishop Blackie! I didn't think you knew my name."

"A good priest tries to learn everyone's name."

"I sing because I love my work. I love being in Washington and in the White House and in the West Wing. I love the things I type. I don't always understand them, but it's still fun. I don't know how I got the job. Maybe because my uncle is a Democratic congressman from Arizona and there's only two of them. They wanted someone who was bilingual. I work a lot with Rita Suarez, who knows so much about Latino Americans. She's bilingual too . . ."

"Not as quick as you are?"

"She's pretty quick," she said, showing that she had acquired some political smarts form her uncle. "Germaine is really trilingual, except there's not much need for Yaqui around here is there?"

"Perhaps someday soon there will be."

"I hope so," she said, her round, open face showing concern. "I didn't know Germaine till we both came here. My parents wouldn't want me hanging around with a Yaqui girl in Tucson. She's such a nice person, isn't she?"

"A little mysterious perhaps."

"They're a lot closer to nature than we are and have a better feeling for the elemental forces in the world. My parents think that's just pagan superstition, but Germaine is a good Catholic, just like I am."

Not exactly, child. But I won't say that.

"She seems to be more aware of the presence of our poltergeist trickster?"

"Naturally! She takes time to sense everything that's happening. She knows all the strains and tensions in the White House and I think she suffers terribly because of them, poor thing."

"Indeed."

"So she knows what the poor poltergeist is going through and suffers for her too."

At the beginning of our conversation I had wondered what I had seen in the picture of this effervescent young woman which made me think she might be our troubled player. Now, however, her brown eyes were troubled and her smile disappeared.

"I wanted to cry for her yesterday when I heard your sister talk. Who would do that to a young woman? I want to help her. I know I can't. Yet I really want to help her."

"You think someone else is forcing her to play her little games?"

"She wouldn't want to do it on her own, would she? I don't ask Germaine about it, because she suffers so much because of it. The person who is forcing her must really hate her."

An interesting insight. Was there a malign power behind the poltergeist? Someone who was using her like she was a plastic fork to poke at the president? Who could be that cruel?

I chatted a few more moments with Luisa Peña, then retreated to my cubiculum in the basement, pausing to pick up a plate of pasta, a cheese sandwich, and two bottles of iced tea in the White House mess. While I was there, the player knocked over two chairs and turned the lights on and off. So used to her clowning around were the staffers in the mess that they paid no attention.

Maybe it would all end not with a bang but with a whimper.

After consuming my meal and making as little mess with it as I could, I wrote out a list of my suspects:

Deirdre McGurn
Granne McGurn
Marianna Genovesa
Claire Jones
Rita Suarez
Germaine Connelly aka Travels By Night
Jane Effingham
Luisa Peña
Francesca Jackson

I pondered the list. The last named I would have to interview tomorrow. As for the others, the Daughters were unlikely candidates, though madam my sister had not pointed out yesterday that there is some suggestion in the literature that these Teutonic leprechauns can leave some of their tricks behind them to work when they're not physically on the premises.

Marianna by her own admission has psychic interludes though only rarely. Might the sexual frustration of working every day with a man she loved who would not or could not be responsive to her have unleashed some deeply hidden energies?

Claire Jones kept talking about the spirits in the building, apparently bad spirits from earlier administrations.

Rita Suarez, vice president's daughter by her first marriage. Pretty, perhaps fragile, and not quite as forthcoming as she might be.

Germaine Connelly aka Travels By Night, deep, mysterious, medicine woman, though she did only good medicine according to herself and the Daughters. Perhaps beloved by the press secretary. Yaquis were reputedly a deep people who held long grudges. According to Luisa Peña she suffered greatly with the player. Would be my prime suspect if she weren't so sweet and good.

Jane Effingham narrated a story of a flawed exorcism in her neighborhood when she was growing up which might well have been her own story. Jumpy, nervous, guilty liberal.

Luisa Peña. Like Rita Suarez an ebullient young woman delighted to be working in the White House but more afraid of and perhaps for the poltergeist than was willing to admit.

All women that were likeable and in their own different ways attractive.

Making such lists and considering them was what real detectives do. I am not, however, a real detective. I see solutions in sudden bursts of light. The elevator doors hadn't opened for several days.

No light. And no reason to think that these nine suspects (counting Ms. Jackson) exhausted the possibilities. They were either people that might be the player or whose records I had picked almost randomly out of the stack.

Maybe it was a man, maybe the steadfast Stefan. Who was I trying to kid?

I glanced over the record of Francesca Jackson, the last of the current crop. Not much there.

I piled up the files and carried them upstairs in the general direction of the Oval Office.

The members of the National Security Council

were straggling out of the Cabinet Room. The secretary of state extended his hand. "Found any ghosts lately, Blackie?"

"A couple of British officers with torches in their hands who talked like they were from Arkansas."

He laughed enthusiastically.

"You and I may be the only ones in the building to know that they probably did."

"How did it go, Claire?" I asked a gloomy Claire Jones.

"Spirits all over the place, Mr. Preacher."

"Good or bad?"

"Bad, what else. They were all looking over our shoulders playing the roles they did back in the nineteen sixties—McNamara, Bundy, Rostow, Rusk, Wheeler, Lemay, the whole bunch of them."

The joint chiefs emerged and strode out, silent in lockstep—broad shoulders, perfectly fitting uniforms, ribbons on their chests. I wondered if they knew how silly they looked in their funny clothes. They were probably good men who had learned a lot from the mistakes of their predecessors. Yet, while I got along fine with and even admired lower-level folks in the military, these people always made me suspicious—too polished, too articulate, too confident.

Libera nos domine.

"Dr. Genovesa is in with the president and Mr. Horan." Stefan looked up at me. "Should I tell her you stopped by?"

"Perhaps."

I walked across to Ms. Chan.

"The president is decompressing with Mr. Horan and Dr. Genovesa, Bishop Blackie. You can go right in."

I did.

The three of them were pondering the bowl that Travels By Night had brought to his office.

"So she offers it to me like it's a sacred chalice and says this is medicine for a weary president. You don't drink it, though it's not poisonous. There are no narcotics in it, only herbs and things. It's aroma and colors help to bring peace. If you don't mind, I'll leave a new one every day with Ms. Chan. You can think of it as a kind of votive candle reminding you that nature is beautiful and that God loves you and that Travels By Night prays for you and that you should pray for yourself. Then she kind of bows and walks out just as if she were a priest and had finished distributing the Eucharist. Then she stops at the door and looks at me with her big black eyes and says don't tell the press secretary who gave it to you . . ."

Then my cloaking shield (or whatever) turned off and he saw me.

"You put the poor kid up to this, Blackwood, didn't you?"

"Good therapy."

"For me or her?"

"Arguably both."

"It does have a certain benign, soothing power," Mari observed. "Nice after that meeting."

I gave her the files.

"Any help?"

"Not yet anyway . . . The meeting was difficult?"

Ms. Chan brought me my glass of iced tea and two oatmeal raisin cookies.

"Boring mostly," the president said. "Everyone had to say their piece, as if they didn't know that I had already made up their mind. There was pretty much of a consensus that the best thing to do is to do nothing, a hard saying for Washington people. No one wants to land the Marines, especially not the Marines. They admit that they have no contingency plans for extracting—their word—our civilians out of there. The military are in favor of letting the Taiwanese eventually become involved under some circumstances. They don't want to do it now, however. They favor our signaling that to them quietly instead of setting up patrols, which makes some sense. Candidly, Blackwood, no one knows what the hell we should do."

"Fortunately," Marianna added, "both sides are being careful of our people now."

"Tomorrow we have to talk to congressional leaders," Tommy took up the story. "They'll go along too, though they'll reserve the right to complain constantly."

"And give advice," the president concluded. "If only we could shut them up like we can the military."

"They all figure they know more about China than you do."

"More than Marianna and Claire and me put together."

"There have been some developments in Chicago," I said, "that might be of some interest. Perhaps you should summon the trusted Jesus Maria as well as the press secretary and of course Ms. Rosen."

Senator Lopez, as he was always called, appeared shortly, Ms. Rosen right after him, and then Sean Patrick.

He noted the bowl of liquid on his father's desk.

"Germaine bringing you her medicine. Be careful, it works!"

"She's a very interesting young woman," the president said casually. " . . . Blackwood, do you want to set the scene?"

"It occurred to me that the worthy Dr. Rhea Snodgrass of the Christian Family Union might want more testimony to use against the president to bring pressure to bear on the president to seek a settlement before the case came to trial. An eventuality that Dr. Snodgrass perhaps does not want to face. It also occurred to me that the logical place to look for such testimony was at Loyola Law School, where only a couple of years ago the president was teaching.

"I therefore suggested, with the president's permission, to my relative Superintendent Michael Casey that he direct some of his employees, preferably part-time women cops, to be on the lookout for persons who might be seeking evidence against the president, or more precisely for women who might be willing to provide such false testimony in return for the payment of monies.

"Mr. Casey in fact has such agents on his staff who also attended Loyola Law School's evening sessions. With permission of their regular employer—the Chicago Police Department—and a judge in the Cook County Circuit Court these women donned wires to record their conversation with such investigators if they were able to find them.

"They did so and found the investigators with remarkable ease. They were not in fact practiced secret agents. Once they learned the phone number of these clumsy investigators, by name Drew and Carrie, they also sought and obtained a permit to put a tap on their phone.

"They recorded many conversations with the investigators in which it was made clear that they were not especially interested in the truth of the charges against the president, only that there be more charges. The investigators also communicated frequently with Dr. Snodgrass and once with Mr. Julius Sleidel who, it may be remembered, is picking up the bill.

"I am assured by Mike Casey that there is enough material on the tapes to get an indictment. However, he desires to collect enough to make it clear to the various actors in this little farce that they face conviction and jail time unless they plead. The thought is that the ineffable Drew and Carrie will be the first to jump ship. There has been a delay over the last several days while the final details of the payoff were to be arranged. Tonight is the agreed time for it all to go down. A video recorder will be involved to capture the exact words and expressions of the investigators as they conspire to suborn perjury. After that we shall have to see what happens. I caution that much could go wrong. However, if we fail tonight, the reason won't be that the investigators or the Christian Family Union were all that clever. Quite the contrary—they are bumbling idiots who thought they were not only above the law but smarter than the law."

"Thank God that's over." Marianna sighed.

"What will the media have to ask me about every day?" Sean Patrick asked.

"It all sounds to me," the president said cautiously, "like a cut-and-paste job. If I were their lawyer, I could get them off. Julie Sleidel will have first-class lawyers, maybe Snodgrass too. They'll claim that they're being railroaded by Chicago justice, which will delight the editorial writers at the *New York Times*. I'm not so sure we're out of the mess . . ."

"I assume," Jesus Maria asked, "that the Chicago police will leak some of the more choice excerpts from the various tapes."

"I don't doubt that," I said, "especially if Carrie and Drew plead guilty."

"That's the important point, Mr. President," Mae Rosen insisted. "In the eyes of the public, which likes you anyway, those tapes clear you. Subsequent legal moves will bore them. You must not, however, seem to be involved in them. You always said that you were innocent of the charges. Now that's been proven."

"Maybe Jesus could appear at a press briefing," Tommy suggested, "and tell them that we are surprised and delighted by the news that the frivolous charges against the president have been discredited. However, we will leave it to the state's attorney of the County of Cook to prosecute the case. We will not be involved. In due course, the president's personal lawyers will determine whether he will seek further relief."

Jesus nodded.

"I was thinking of something like that. Is it true that we knew nothing about it until now?"

"I have been informed every day," I admitted, "but then I'm not on the White House staff."

"It just seems that way," Mae said.

"I spoke at the beginning with Mike Casey and told him to go ahead with the investigation. Blackwood hasn't told me anything since then."

"Well, then," Jesus said, "it's fair to say that the White House has not been directly involved in the Illinois investigation and that we were informed only yesterday of the outcome."

Lawyers have their own language.

"Are you going to sue them personally?" Marianna asked.

"I have better things to do. Once the dust settles, we'll make a brief statement saying just that."

"What about the inevitable attacks from the media about Chicago justice?" I asked. "The claim will be made that the accused cannot obtain justice in a Chicago courtroom."

"We'll point to the confessions," Sean Patrick said.

"I'd bet by this time tomorrow," the president concluded, rising from his chair, "Dr. Rhea Snodgrass will want to plead."

"I'll be in my office in the residence," the president told me. "Come down and tell me what happened."

"Oh, yes."

Sean Patrick dipped his finger into the medicine bowl and rubbed his face with Travels By Night's concoction.

"What are you doing that for?" his father demanded.

"It smells good. Didn't she tell you that the serenity would travel with you?"

"No, she just said she'd bring a fresh bowl every day."

"She'll tell you about wearing it everywhere one of these days. It might have soothed things during the NSC meeting today."

"You're sure there's no narcotics in it?"

"Germaine use dope! No way."

"Not scheduled narcotics anyway," I observed.

Much laughter.

Then a chorus of "Thank you, Mr. President."

The portrait of President Washington fell again. Marianna replaced it as she did routinely. No one seemed to notice.

"This will take a lot of pressure off him," Mari remarked, as we walked away from the Oval Office.

"Now all we have to do is get rid of the Teutonic leprechaun."

"Any progress on that?"

"Not the slightest."

"It couldn't be that sweet Apache girl, could it?"

"Yes, it could be, but it could be almost anyone. And she's a Yaqui."

The waiter brought me a delicious chicken à la king dinner in the Solarium, which reminded me that even cliché foods were splendid when provided by a skilled chef.

I watched television for a few minutes, then retired to the Rose Room to work on my e-mail backlog on the second line into the room.

I had cleared it all up and still no call from Mike the Cop.

I don't know whether you approve of this stuff, I informed the deity, but consider your servant Jack McGurn with compassion and love and free him from this unnecessary burden.

At 11:00 it seemed appropriate to retire, though I knew I would not sleep.

Then the phone rang.

"Got 'em," Mike the Cop said happily. "Everything on tape. Clear evidence of an intent to conspire to suborn perjury. They're at the Chicago Avenue Police Station and are watching the video and listening to a selection of the audiotapes. I'm told their bravado is collapsing. The state's attorney himself is there offering them a misdemeanor charge and no jail time if they will confess and agree to testify. The grand jury will convene this morning. The State's Attorney's Office will play enough snippets of the tapes to leave no doubt of what was going down. Tell the president to get a good night's sleep."

I walked down to the president's private office in the old library room on the second floor.

He was sound asleep, his head on the desk over a stack of papers.

"Jack," I said gently nudging him.

"Hmm . . . Who . . . Blackwood! What happened!"

"Got 'em! Plea bargaining now!"

He sighed.

"Thank God there's one less problem. I'd better call some of the folks, Tommy, Sean Patrick, Mae, Jesus . . ."

"And?"

He blinked his eyes, still trying to wake up.

"Whom have I forgotten?

"I won't tell you . . ."

"Mari? I really couldn't call her at home at this hour. I don't want to wake her up . . ."

He looked up at me sheepishly.

"Okay, I'll call her right away."

Sometimes we make progress.

14

With the same predictability as the rising sun, Milord Cronin was on the phone first thing the next morning with his usual question.

"Blackwood! What the hell is going on!"

I noticed that the sun had not risen this morning. Or rather it was modestly hiding behind low clouds and a driving rain.

"Actually it's raining."

"It's all over the papers and TV. Two private investigators arrested last night for trying to solicit perjured testimony against the president. Are cooperating with the state's attorney. Grand jury convenes today. Link seen with D.C. charges. Fundamentalist clergyman and rich recluse may be involved. Snippets from audio and video recording! You behind this?"

"How would that be possible? I am currently in the Beltway."

"And Mike Casey has a telephone."

"True enough."

"Do they have enough to clear Jack?"

"Oh, yes, more than enough."

"Like I say, get rid of those poltergeists and you can come home."

"I've grown accustomed to the excellent food here."

However, he had departed.

The television sets in the Solarium all featured the Chicago story, usually with Chicago reporters who, while generally semiliterate carpetbaggers, knew more about the city than their counterparts in New York, Washington, and Atlanta. Their theme was that the Chicago police naturally responded quickly to the report that people were seeking dirt on the president.

"Is there any suggestion in Chicago," an anchorperson asked, "that this might be a frame-up?"

"This is not Bosnia, Teddie. The police apparently have hours of tape and confessions."

I chuckled.

Then my friend Mary Jane Quinn appeared.

"There is a sense of elation here in Chicago this morning," she said, "over the arrest of the two young spies who had come here to gather evidence against President McGurn. Even police sources, proud of the quick professionalism with which they handled this case, said that the two young people who are charged with conspiracy to suborn perjury, are, as one cop put it, extreme dumb. It may be that with enemies like that Jack McGurn doesn't need friends."

I applauded.

A spokesman for the Reverend Dr. Rhea Snodgrass said he would never submit to a trial in Chicago.

Good luck, fella.

I descended to the West Wing on an elevator with two young men who were extremely professional, crew cuts, cleanly shaved, well dressed.

"You gentlemen are patently not Secret Service."

"No sir."

"Marines?"

"Close, Bishop. We're navy. One of the three teams of navy medical personnel who are assigned to the White House full-time. We serve on eight-hour shifts. Our task is to protect the president's health."

"How provident," I murmured.

"With President McGurn there's no problem, but they have to get that swimming pool in working order soon."

"Yes, sir. Or we won't be responsible for him."

When I arrived at the Oval Office, Travels By Night was just leaving.

"You leave the medicine with Ms. Chan?"

"The president wanted to see me himself and thank me personally. He was upset that I hadn't told him that he could put it on like cologne."

"Someone else must have told him."

She blushed.

"I can't imagine who."

The president, in conversation with the inevitable Tommy Horan, was very happy.

"I just talked to the state's attorney, Blackwood. He told me the evidence they have. Snodgrass and Sleidel had better think about pleading. They're in deep doo-doo."

"Ah."

"How's the search for the poltergeist coming?"

Please clean up all my problems now, Blackwood.

"No progress. Yet I am not pessimistic. There is a picture in the back of my head that is slowly coming into focus. When it does we'll know the truth. It should require no more than a couple of days."

"No rush, take your time. I'd like you on my staff as the permanent chaplain. Am I not entitled to one?"

"You might apply to Milord Cronin. He could perhaps find a plausible candidate. It would not be me. He needs a harmless and almost invisible auxiliary around to sweep up his little messes."

"Like poltergeists in the White House?"

"Arguably."

In the bull pen, Francesca Jackson zeroed in on me.

"When are you going to talk to me, Bishop?" she demanded with a broad grin. "You've interviewed two white girls, a Latina, and that Apache witch doctor. What's the matter, don't you think we sisters can do any magic?"

"One white girl and two Latinas. Travels By Night is actually a Yaqui."

"Is there a difference?"

"Oh yes, the Yaqui are reputedly more dangerous than the Apache."

She made the sign of the cross, not altogether unseriously.

"Who's the other Latina?"

"Rita Suarez."

"Nice kid, but she's a honky."

"Latina on both sides."

"No shit? Well, don't you think we sisters can do poltergeist?"

"My sister tells me that she doesn't know of a single case."

"Maybe we're being dissed again?"

"More likely less adequate medical treatment and

resources, which is, I concede, a form of being dissed."

"Buy you a cup of tea?"

"My tastes are patently well-known."

"Can't imagine why."

Down in the mess she brought me the cup of tea and three donuts.

"This is a good place to work," she said. "Most of my life I spent all my time with brothers and sisters, even when I'm working in Springfield. Now I get to know honkies and Latinos and Yaqui . . . I got that right?"

"Yep."

"It's cool. Extreme cool. Everyone's different and everyone's the same, even that cute little witch who's got her eye on the big redhead."

"I would have thought it was the other way round."

"I tell her she done put a hex on him and she starts to cry and I tell her I'm only kidding. She say she'd never put a hex on a man and I said she'd probably never have to."

"That was nice."

"Who's the poltergeist, Bishop Blackie?"

"Don't know yet."

"It's creepy. You know that we brothers and sisters don't like spirits much. That nice old woman downstairs sees them all around here."

"The national security advisor."

"That what she is? She's really smart, but she says there's ghosts all around here from the old days. You think they are?"

"I think she means memories."

"More than memories, Bishop, more than memories."

What did I know?

"Anyway, I axe myself whether the memories make it easy to be a poltergeist, know what I mean?"

I note that she followed the West African custom of pronouncing sk as x, a custom that infuriates white racists.

"I hadn't thought of that, but you might very well be right."

Not likely, however. What was the girl up to?

"I think I see her, Bishop. I see the poor little thing."

So.

"What does she look like, Francesca?"

"Fran . . . she's little and she's scared and she's always running and then she kind of disappears. And she scares me."

"Do you recognize her?"

"I know her and I don't know her. She's there and then she's not . . . You think I'm bullshitting you?"

"No, Fran, I'm sure you're not."

This was a new wrinkle and I was not sure I liked it.

"Sometimes I see her running out of the Oval Office and then she's not there. You gotta help her, Bishop Blackie. I think she's going crazy. Someone of these days, she's just going to stop running and collapse on the floor, know what I mean?"

"The spirit will or the woman who's part of her."

"There's no difference, Bishop. They be the same person, only I don't know who she is."

"If you find out, Fran, let me know."

"I sure will."

Back in what was allegedly my office, I called Mary Kate and told her about Fran.

"Gives me the shivers," I admitted.

"That's a zoo you got down there, Punk, all kind of psychic folk."

"Maybe the poltergeist brings out the little bit that's in everyone."

"Messy stuff. Last case I had I said I'd never do it again."

"So what about Fran?"

"One of my cases—unlike yours but like the others—we knew who it was. There was a little sister, a toddler, who saw her running and a dog who barked whenever she went by. I agree that it gives me the shivers."

"Is there a shrink in the area we should bring this child to when and if she finally breaks down?"

"Let me think . . . Yeah, there's a great one at American University Hospital. Len Graymont. First-rate. He's written up the case he had, a very successful treatment it seems. Why don't I give him a call and tell him the White House might send a case over sometime. He probably saw me on TV . . ."

"Didn't everyone?"

"Same old Punk." She laughed.

I hung up the phone and it rang again.

"Mari, Blackie. Jesus is doing his press briefing in a few moments. See you in the Corner Room."

"I'll be right up."

Marianna and Sean Patrick were waiting in the Corner Room. Both of them wore the soothing, entertaining cologne that Travels By Night seemed to manufacture in a cave beneath the White House every night.

"She could make millions if she marketed that stuff," I observed.

"Use nature to make money?" Sean Patrick scoffed. "Sacrilege!"

I gave my slip of paper with Leonard Graymont's name on it to Marianna. "A shrink at American University whom my inestimable sister recommends, if we should contain the Merry Prankster. She will call him and ask him to be ready for us."

She nodded and put it in her pocket.

Jesus, smoother and slicker-looking than his usual Zorro persona, appeared with Mae Rosen.

"Piece of cake!" Mae said.

"I don't know why I should be scared of those ghouls." He smiled, smoothing his mustache. "Not the first time I did this."

Sean Patrick led him out to the podium.

"We have a statement to make about the arrests in Chicago," Sean Patrick announced. "I have asked Jesus Maria Lopez, senior counselor to the president, to describe our position and answer any of your questions which are answerable."

I marveled at his smoothness. If you were his size, you probably weren't intimidated by anyone.

"We are surprised and delighted," Jesus began, "by the news that the frivolous charges against the president have been discredited. We congratulate the Chicago police on their alert and professional response to this clumsy conspiracy, which in truth sounds like something from a nineteen thirties film. However, we will leave it to the state's attorney of the County of Cook to prosecute the case. We will not be involved. In due course, the president's personal lawyers will determine whether he will seek further relief. The president's present inclination is to think that it may not be necessary, but he reserves the right to wait till the present criminal trials are finished."

"Any questions?" Sean Patrick asked.

"Sir, Dr. Rhea Snodgrass says he will not subject himself to a trial in a Chicago court."

"As I understand the law of this country, if he is indicted by a grand jury in Cook County, he won't have much choice."

"Is it true that the state's attorney has issued warrants for the arrest of Dr. Snodgrass and Mr. Sleidel?"

"I have no knowledge of that."

"They have," Mari whispered to me.

"Don't you think, sir, that the American people will be suspicious of a trial carried on in a Cook County court?"

"No, I don't."

"Can an enemy of the president get a fair trial in Chicago?"

"I don't know what evidence the state's attorney really has. In a matter like this he wouldn't seek an indictment unless the proof of guilt was overwhelming. I believe he has confessions."

"Wouldn't it be better to bring the case to the District of Columbia?"

"The law was broken in Illinois. That's where the trial of first instance should occur. We do have appellate courts in Illinois, should the Cook County court misuse its power. Some of the judges in the appellate courts are in fact Republicans."

"Thank you very much, Senator Lopez," Sean Patrick ended the press conference.

"He called me last night to tell me," Marianna whispered to me. "He was shy and very sweet. He said he didn't want to wake me up, as if I could sleep. Do you think it's over, Blackie?"

"This one is over. Those who want to try the same thing will think twice about it. I'm not sure how much more will have to go down before no one seriously questions the legitimacy of his presidency . . . Does he have the votes to beat a filibuster against the payroll tax bill in the Senate?"

"Conrad says he does and that's Conrad's job."

"Good news."

"It means we can get back to serious stuff again."

Dr. Rhea Snodgrass and Julius Sleidel were arrested the next day by the FBI and, despite their refusal to waive extradition, were extradited to Chicago the following week. Dr. Snodgrass found it to his interest to agree to a plea bargain. He would have to confess the entire plot to a jury and to the public. Good enough for him. Suzy Schmidt and Elaine Walsh withdrew their complaints against the president but were still on notice that they would be called as witnesses in the Chicago trial.

Only the *Wall Street Journal* had the audacity to suggest that it would be a "show trial worthy of the old Soviet Union."

However, Mari was wrong. There was more to be suffered before the McGurn administration could settle down to the serious business of leading America and the world. That would not happen before blood was shed.

15

The next big event was to be a dinner in the State Dining Room.

"Prime minister of Slovenia and his wife," Marianna told me. "Good people, moderates, which means far to the left of our guy. Practicing Catholics. Probably would love to have a bishop at the dinner."

"I'll get in touch with Cardinal Cronin and see if he has time to come . . ."

"We don't need to do that. We have a bishop in residence." She smoothed her silken hair.

"I thought you meant a *real* bishop."

"I thought you were a *real* bishop."

"Not in the ordinary sense of the word."

"And don't say you lack your vestments. We know that they're still here."

"The player rearranges them every day."

"Purple buttons and zuchetto," she demanded. "And cummerbund. If you don't have them, I can get them."

"Indeed."

"You're supposed to be my dinner partner."

There were many pseudo funny things I could have said. Instead my mother intervened from her place in the empyrean, and made me say, "That settles it. I will certainly attend the state dinner. I'll direct Milord Cronin himself to find a cummerbund for me."

Mentally I cursed John Patrick McGurn for a blind fool.

The Chicago arrests disappeared off the front page. Shanghai had fallen to the rebels. Hong Kong had joined them peacefully. Two massive armies were converging on a plain two hundred miles south of Beijing. The Social Security Fairness Bill was subject to a filibuster in the Senate. However, the president's forces clearly had the votes to break it.

The West Wing was temporarily serene, if not exactly peaceful.

"I have a personal problem, Bishop Blackie," Sean Patrick McGurn informed me.

"Ah?"

"You know I'm the president's son."

"I am aware of that fact."

"So I have to attend that dinner tomorrow night."

"A grave inconvenience."

"And I can bring a date."

"Have to or can?"

"Don't absolutely have to . . . So I'm trying to make up my mind whether I should bring a date."

"Any prospects?"

"You know who I'm thinking about?" His face turned a darker shade of crimson.

"Should I?"

"Everyone knows."

"Then I guess I do."

"I don't know whether she would want to come to a state dinner or whether she would like it. She is a kind of unusual person, you know."

"Germaine unusual? I never noticed that."

"How can my father introduce us to the Slovenes, 'This is my son Sean Patrick and this woman in her tribal dress is Travels By Night. She's a medicine woman.' "

"I don't think your father would say that. Nor do I believe she would wear a tribal dress."

"I don't know."

"Faint heart, Sean Patrick, as the cliché puts it, never won fair lady."

"I know." He sighed and wandered away.

I spent much of my time that day meandering around the West Wing, waiting for lightning to strike (in fact the rain which had begun yesterday was still falling) or the elevator door to stay open long enough for me to witness the scene inside.

Nothing happened.

Marianna found me sitting disconsolately in the mess, viewing dyspeptically a chocolate fudge sundae—with whipped cream but without nuts.

"Elevator door hasn't opened yet?"

She sat next to me with a bottle of fruit juice.

"Quite the contrary, it opens repeatedly, but not long enough for me to see what's inside."

"It will stay open sometime, won't it?" she said, smoothing back her hair.

"It has before . . . There's always a first time . . . Am I correct in assuming that we will be sitting with Sean Patrick and his date?"

"Has he asked her yet?"

"He will . . . or he will be in extreme trouble."

"She's waiting patiently for the invitation. Then I

must help her find a dress . . . She should be striking, shouldn't she, Bishop?"

Her bottle of juice rose from the table, sailed the length of the room, and smashed into the machine from which it came. Fran Jackson picked it up and brought it back to our table. No one else seemed to notice. The women behind the counter didn't even look up.

"As to your question, how could she help but look striking?"

"I was thinking of shimmering silver, spaghetti straps, a little décolletage, and some sort of Hopi jewel around her neck. No other jewelry, only a slight touch of makeup."

"Will she wear it?"

"If I tell her it's all right."

"Incidentally, she's a Yaqui not a Hopi."

"Got it."

"She probably has an appropriate brooch already."

"Yes, Bishop."

I retreated to my office and waited for the elevator door. Claire Jones appeared at the door.

"Things are quiet in the Situation Room?"

"Yep. Nothing happening 'cept Chinese killing one another. Nothing new about that."

"Any developments there?"

"Well, it seems that the rebel generals are revolting against the big brass in the People's Liberation Army more than against the government, though they figure they have to get rid of the government before they get rid of the marshals. Apparently some of those folk are really nasty. Also they have been planning their own coup against the government, which they think is too friendly with us."

"What are we going to do about that?

"We ain't gonna do nothing, Mr. Preacher Man, cuz there's nothing we can do."

I gave up on the West Wing. It was time to return to my home away from home and check on my e-mail and perhaps rest my eyes against the exhaustion of a state dinner in my full purple splendor.

Marianna caught my eye as I entered the outside walk on the West Portico. She held her thumb up. Poor Sean Patrick had at last invited Travels By Night to the state dinner. She smiled and said she'd love to. To herself she had wondered what kind of good medicine she could bring. Unquestionably she would be the most striking woman there. Mari, for all her good looks, lacked the dark skin, the high cheekbones, and the dark, dark eyes that exuded mystery and magic.

The Teutonic leprechaun had hid my laptop in the bathroom of the Queens' Suite, under the wicker container, which for some reason covered the toilet. She had also scattered my papers all over the room and worked her usual mayhem on my episcopal vestments.

After I had sorted out the papers, one of the ushers came with a FedEx box from a certain S. Cronin at 730 North Wabash (which is also the home of the North Wabash Avenue Irregulars of which he is not a member). Not only the required cummerbund but also a cape of watered silk. I was reminded of the stratagem of the wife of G. K. Chesterton, who, unable to make her husband handsome, decided that she would make him picturesque.

I looked out the window. As the weather channel had threatened, the rain was turning into snow. How fortunate that the cherry blossoms had not been taken in by the false spring.

I sighed and turned to my e-mail. The leprechaun elected not to interfere.

What would she do at the state dinner tomorrow night? I did not want to think about it.

At the preprandial reception before the appearance of the president and his guests, we mingled in the lobby of the White House and in the Blue Room. My dinner companion—in a quite overwhelming, light blue, off-the-shoulder gown—and the press secretary and his date hovered close to me, assuming that there was some protection in being close to the comic figure of the evening. Or perhaps they assumed that the two beautiful women would cancel out his comedy.

An octet of the Marine Band in dress uniform played waltz music.

Travels By Night glittered, even more with her smile than with her glowing gown. She was utterly self-possessed, a woman of the world who attended state dinners every week.

"How long did you have to meditate, Germaine," I asked her, "to attain the proper mood for this evening?"

"Only an hour," she said. "Well, maybe an hour and a half."

Her Irish Viking date devoured her with his eyes as well he might.

"I'm intrigued," I whispered to Mari, "by what you consider a bit of décolletage."

"Don't be a prude, Bishop Blackie." Mari dismissed my cavil with a wave of her hand and a

smoothing of her hair. "It's perfectly appropriate for
a young woman with her figure."

"I would not deny that," I conceded.

"She give you a hard time about it?"

"You don't understand her spirituality, Bishop
Blackie. The human body is part of nature. If we live
close to our bodies, we are close to nature. She
wouldn't dress like that all the time. Once I explained
to her the custom, she was eager to wear it."

I sighed to myself. Mari, black hair falling to the
tops of her swelling alabaster breasts, should be walking down the stairs to "Ruffles and Flourishes."

Jack McGurn, whatever his emotional problems,
was a complete jerk.

Then the orchestra did strike up "Hail to the
Chief." The president appeared on one side of
the prime minister's wife and the prime minister
on the other side.

Tacky.

By dint of skillful positioning we managed to elbow our way into the front of the receiving line.

"This is Dr. Marianna Genovesa, my deputy chief
of staff and China consultant," the president introduced Mari.

The guests favored her with an appreciative smile.

"And Bishop John Ryan, one of the most brilliant
of American bishops, John Blackwood Ryan of Chicago."

"The man who writes the wonderful books?" the
Madame Prime Minister asked. "How good to meet
you."

Patently a woman of great good taste.

"Our press secretary and my son, Sean Patrick
McGurn and Germaine Connelly. Ms. Connelly is a

member of one of our Native American nations, Yaqui, I believe."

"What a lovely stone, my dear, is it part of your culture?"

"Made from desert rock, ma'am. It has much good medicine."

The president rolled his eyes, but added "Travels By Night, you are extreme gorgeous as the Daughters would say."

She blushed deeply but was evidently pleased.

"Thank you, Mr. President."

Jack McGurn, who knew how to read the auguries, probably resigned himself to having a medicine woman as his daughter-in-law.

"Well, that's over," Mari said, "I think I need a drink of wine."

She was trembling. Had some kind of signal, too faint for me to perceive, passed between her and the president?

"I'll get one for you," Sean Patrick said, "Bishop? Germaine?"

We all opted for a glass of red wine. Entirely civilized.

"You sure do attract beautiful women around you, Bishop Blackie," said a young blond with short hair and a skimpy white gown.

"And one more," I said. "You're not Agent Wholley?"

"Reckon I dress up different . . . Agent-in-Charge Chick Walker has some of us mingling with the crowd like we belong here. I don't know why, but figure it's a good idea. I kind of like it but don't tell Agent-in-Charge Chick or he'll bust me off this detail. 'Scuse me, I'm supposed to drift . . . Both of you women really look scrumptious."

"Well, she still didn't smile," Mari said sadly. "Her humor is kind of deadpan."

"I'd trust her more than any agent in this place," Sean Patrick mused.

"There is much good medicine at this state dinner," Travels By Night said, "much gentle mystery."

Sean Patrick put his arm around her bare shoulders.

"Wherever you are, Germaine, is always good medicine and gentle mystery."

She turned and winked at me.

A chime sounded discreetly. Time to eat. I did not argue.

We found our places halfway down the left wing of tables radiating from the head table, reserved for the guests, the presidents, and the major ministers of both governments.

"I am reminded by this polished grace of films about the Hofburg in the time of Hapsburg or Versailles in the era of the Louis or the Escorial or St. Petersburg," I observed to Marianna. "And then I reflected that this is the ultimate imperial capital and that, though it is only a small house, we do the imperial thing better than any of them did."

"Democratic and reluctant imperialism," she said, "and with lots of practice at state dinners."

The orchestra played "Chicago (That Toddling Town)" as the presidential party entered the State Dining Room.

"I wonder if Bishop Ryan would ask for God's blessings."

He had not of course warned me of this assign-

ment. I had, however, assumed he would make the
request.

Well, ineffectual and comic little bishop that I was,
I needed notes no more than Machine Gun Jack did.

"Heavenly Father and gracious Mother, look
down on this gathering of the leaders of two democratic societies, one quite old and the other very new.
Bless the leaders and their countries, bless Slovenia's
entrance into the European Union and grant them
the peace and freedom to which the small countries
of the world have a right and bless also this battered
but resilient American democracy and help us all to
be true to our best instincts. Bless this marvelous
food we are about to eat through the work of the
White House staff whom you should doubly bless—
and through your bounty. Through Jesus the Lord,
Amen."

The president winked at me.

"Always the joker," Mari said admiringly.

"You are a multiple jerk," I whispered to Jack
McGurn.

Astonishingly the player did not intervene.

"Now, if I may." The president rose again. "A
brief toast to the Republic of Slovenia and to all its
people. Welcome into NATO and the European
Union and welcome to your prime minister, and his
lovely wife on their first visit to the White House,
which I hope will not be their last."

He said some words in Slovene, then apologized
for his Russian accent.

"Show off," Mari observed with a proud sigh.

The woman had it bad.

The prime minister replied in Slovene, then in
good English. He assured the president that all he

noticed in his Slovene was a Midwestern American, which he was familiar with from his days at the University of Michigan.

We then began to eat. The waiters brought seemingly endless courses of healthy food (and in small portions) and of splendid American and Slovene wine.

It was a grand evening altogether as the Irish would say. Even the obnoxious presence of the TV cameras at the door of the State Dining Room did not interfere with the relaxed dignity and good taste of the evening.

I noticed that beside me Marianna was suddenly uneasy, restless, nervous.

"Not feeling well?"

"Something's wrong, terribly wrong."

"Bad medicine," Germaine agreed. "Terrible medicine."

I have often watched tapes of what happened then. I cannot believe that it was all so quick. Quicker than it is to describe it.

One of the TV cameramen shoved his camera aside, and his face glowing mystically, dashed towards the head table gun in hand. Agent Wholley threw herself against him. He shot her and threw her aside. She fell to the floor, blood flowing from the waist of her white dress. He was dashing towards the president for a close and lethal shot.

Marianna, who had risen before the man charged, bolted over the table, grabbed his gun arm, and wrestled him to the floor. A shot rang out. The president winced and fell against the table. Marianna locked a stranglehold on the would-be killer with one arm and slapped the gun out of his hand. He screamed obscenities as the Secret Service swarmed all over him. Only then did I notice that everyone was screaming and I was leaning over POTUS.

"Kerryman is down, repeat Kerryman is down," someone shouted into a walkie-talkie. "Secret Service agent down. Condition red. Kerryman down."

A navy doctor and medical corpsman were leaning over the president with me.

"I'll be all right," he protested, his voice tight with pain. "Take care of her."

"Flesh wound," the doctor said to the corpsman. "See about the agent."

"Blackwood," the president said through clenched teeth, "give me absolution, just in case. I've only one serious sin and you know what that is already. Then see to her."

Then it all became a nightmare, sirens sounding outside, more medical personnel rushing in, the Secret Service dragging out the obscenity-shouting cameraman, stretchers for the president and Agent Wholley.

"You two go with him," I told Mari and Tommy Horan. "I'll go with her." As I followed the stretcher-bearers out of the East Room, I noticed Travels By Night, kneeling on the floor next to Agent Wholley's blood, her head bowed in furious prayer. Or meditation. Or something. Whatever.

16

The Navy medic worked feverishly on Agent Wholley in the ambulance as we rushed through the falling snow. He poured antibiotics over the wound and pumped plasma into her bloodstream.

"Your first name isn't Agent, is it?"

"Elizabeth Ann." She grinned painfully. "Liz."

I held her hand. "You're sorry for all your sins, Liz?"

"Oh my God, I am heartily sorry *for* having offended Thee because of fear of loss of heaven and pains of hell . . ." She groped for the rest of it, then concluded, "but most of all because I love You and I know You love me."

I gave her absolution. She made the sign of the cross.

"Am I going to die, Bishop Blackie?"

"Maybe, but I don't think so."

"I'm not afraid to die. But I'd rather live if God doesn't mind."

"Don't give up," I urged her. "Fight it all the way, Liz. The God you love wants you to fight to save the life He gave you."

The corpsman nodded enthusiastically.

"The president . . . ?"

"You saved his life. Only a flesh wound in his shoulder."

"I'm glad . . ."

Tears formed in her eyes.

It is extreme unacceptable, I told the deity, that You take back to Yourself this brave young woman so early in her life.

We said the rosary together in the eternity it took us to get up to Georgetown Hospital.

The medics eased her onto a gurney. A surgeon with gray hair and a young face took one look at her.

"Bring this woman into surgery immediately. The president has only a flesh wound. Let's save this kid's life."

He turned to me.

"We'll do all we can, Bishop, all we can. With God's help we will save her."

"That's all we can ask, Doctor."

How, I wondered, did he know I was a bishop?

Then I realized the answer: I was still wearing my comic little bishop suit.

I wandered around the emergency ward and found the president, a couple of Secret Service men, Mari and Tommy, and several medical people who were probing the presidential shoulder.

"How is she?" he demanded.

"The hotshot surgeon they brought here for you is taking care of her. He says maybe."

"Ouch." The president winced and grabbed for Mari's hand.

"Got it," said the doctor, holding up a slug.

"Twenty-two," said one of the Secret Service men.

"All the better to smuggle in inside a camera bag,"

said the woman agent. "Does Liz really have a chance, Bishop?"

"She's a fearsomely determined young woman. I wouldn't bet against her."

"Mr. President, this is not a serious wound," the doctor assured him. "You were very fortunate. I propose to cleanse it, insert some sutures, give you a strong dose of antibiotics, and then some more painkillers to enable you to sleep. I would like to keep you here overnight as a precaution to watch for infection and possible delayed shock. We'll let you go back to the White House tomorrow morning."

"I don't think . . ." he began.

"Yes," the rest of us said together.

"You see, Doctor, how much power a president has? Okay, you win, but before the painkiller, I'll have to talk to the press and let the world see I'm still alive and well."

During the process of cleaning and binding the wound, the president grimaced painfully several times and clung to Marianna's hand.

"Sorry, Mari," he murmured.

"A man in pain reaches for the first womanly hand available," she said tenderly.

"Especially when the rest of the woman is so beautiful . . . Ouch!"

"That's all, Mr. President. Now your few moments with the media."

"You'd better be prepared to explain to them what you did. Show 'em the slug. They always like show-and-tell. Okay, guys, let's get this over with. No, first let's see how Liz is doing."

The doctor led us to the door of the surgery. A woman emerged briefly, a nurse perhaps; no, more likely a surgical resident. You couldn't tell these days.

"Mr. President!" she exclaimed.

"How she's doing, Doctor?"

The woman hesitated.

"We're making good progress, Mr. President. She has a fighting chance."

Then we went down to the lobby, where a podium was set up. The president shrugged off the support of Tommy and Sean Patrick and strode out to the podium on which he leaned.

"They only nicked me," he said, imitating John Wayne. "Sure does hurt though for a little nick."

The media laughed despite themselves.

"This, gentlemen"—he pointed to the doctor—"is James Hennesey, MD. He will tell you shortly about the delicate and challenging surgery that was required to remove a .22-caliber slug from my shoulder. I don't know what will happen to my golf game . . ."

"It won't make it any better, Mr. President. But when the wound heals, your game won't be any worse."

"I was afraid of that."

More laughter.

"Most important news," he plugged on, "is that I was able to talk to one of the surgeons operating on Agent Liz Wholley. She has, I was told, a fighting chance. I'm sure everyone in America will pray for that very brave young woman . . . And for this young woman too." He actually put his arm around Mari and drew her into the picture. "She proves that a president is a wise man if he has an all-American point guard on his staff."

He then released her.

"More seriously, I'm here talking to you guys so that the people of America will know that I am still conscious, still president of the United States. The doctors want me to stay here overnight so they can watch for infection and delayed shock. My senior staff will be with me here, kind of the Georgetown University Hospital White House. They say I can go home first thing in the morning. I'll see you in the Briefing Room then. Now I better go to bed like the doctors want me to. Dr. Hennesey, it's your podium."

"Thank you, Mr. President," the media said, like they really meant it.

We were shown to a suite of three rooms: bedroom, parlor, and media room.

"A man who's been wounded reaches out for a woman's shoulders if they happen to be available," Marianna remarked.

"Especially if they're bare. Blame it all on the medication, Mari."

"Saving it just for me," he said to the nurse, who was apparently in charge of him, as he looked around the suite.

"May I inject you with the pain medicine, Mr. President?"

Tommy's cell phone rang.

"Just a minute," the President said.

"What?" Tommy said, his voice more emotional than usual. "I can't believe it. I'll see what the president wants to do."

"Who?"

"Jesus, he's in charge over there. He says that the vice president stormed into the briefing room ten

minutes ago and announced that she was in charge.
Told the country that she was the acting president.
Then marched in and took over the Oval Office. She
has been ordering people around. Blair and Putin
both called. She insulted them both. She ordered the
secretary of state and our Slovene guests out of the
Yellow Oval Room. Said he had no right to be there
anymore. They didn't go. She may be on drugs."

Jack McGurn bowed his head and grimaced.

"That bitch . . . Tell Jesus that I'm still president.
Tell him to go out and tell the media there that I'm
not incapacitated. I'll send someone over to get rid
of her."

"Yes, Mr. President."

"Tommy . . . No, Sean Patrick . . . No, I need both
of you here . . . Mari, would you mind . . . ?"

"I'd love to, Mr. President."

"I'll go with her," I said.

No one seemed surprised.

Our Secret Service driver negotiated the streets of
Washington carefully on our return. The snow was
piling up.

"You saw it coming beforehand?" I suggested.
"You were halfway over the table."

"Yes . . . And I wasn't all-American."

"It's now part of the folklore."

"How will I get her out of there?"

I told her exactly how she could do it.

"Are you sure?"

"Yes," I said, with less confidence than I felt.

The driver pulled up at the back door of the
White House. I pulled off my comic costume,
dropped it in the Diplomatic Reception Room, and,

in Roman collar, shirt and trousers, trailed along after Marianna.

Ms. Chan sat in her office in tears.

"She's terrible," she told us. "She's insulting everyone."

"Stefan around?"

"Yes, Dr. Genovesa."

"Get him for me."

We entered the Oval Office. The vice president sat behind the president's desk, a triumphant glow on her face. Rita, shoulders sagging in humiliation and defeat, leaned disconsolately on the couch.

"Get out of here, you whore," she told Marianna. "You're fired."

"Ms. Cruz," Mari said softly, "in the name of the president of the United States, I order you to leave this office at once. He is conscious and in no way incapacitated. You saw that on television. You have no right to be here."

"Fraud!"

"Again, I order you to leave."

"Fuck you!"

"For the third time . . ."

"You can't make me leave."

"Actually we can. If you don't leave at once, we will leak the truth to the media about your daughter. When she was young she was under a doctor's care for some considerable time because of a poltergeist syndrome. We can prove that. When you learned that she was working here for President McGurn, whom you hate because you think he stole the presidency from you, you caused her to revert to that condition and forced her to haunt the White House. By so doing you hoped to drive President McGurn out of office, regardless of the terrible damage you were doing to your daughter's mental health."

"You can't prove any of that."

"I'm afraid, Genie, that we can prove all of it."

Rita screamed, a terrible, anguished wail. The Oval Office was possessed by psychic energy. The windows swung open and shut. The lights flickered on and off. The president's desk was swept clean. Lamps fell over, books flew from their shelves in huge salvos, all the pictures fell from the wall in one quick movement. The walls rattled and shook. Chains clanked across the room.

"For God's sake and your own, Rita, stop it!" I ordered her. "Stop it now. You're on the edge. Don't let her push you over it."

Rita rolled off the couch onto the floor and sobbed.

"Tell the president I'm sorry! Please! I really am sorry!"

"Is that enough, Genie?" Mari demanded implacably. "Get out of here now with something of your reputation intact. Or stay and we will destroy you."

"I'll go to court about this," the vice president responded. "You have no right to do this to me!"

Unsteadily she walked towards the door of the Oval Office.

"I don't want to go with her." Rita cried out.

"You don't have to . . ." I assured her.

"Just a minute, Genie," Marianna said, as the vice president reached the door of the office. "There's one more thing."

"What?" the vice president snarled.

"On tomorrow afternoon before the close of the business day, we want your letter of resignation on

the president's desk. You've been disloyal to him
from the beginning. Your behavior is intolerable.
You say in your letter that you realized tonight that
you did not want the terrible burden of the presidency and are therefore resigning from the office of
vice president."

"You can't make me do that!"

"You know what we will do if you don't."

"You wouldn't dare!"

"Resign and you can get on with your life. Perhaps
run for the House or even the Senate. If you don't
resign, you will be forever disgraced."

"Jack will never back you up!"

"You know he will!"

"We'll see about that!"

She stormed out of the office. We watched the TV
screen. She didn't stop in the briefing room.

"That's one very mean lady," Stefan observed.

"Extreme mean . . . Stefan . . . What do I want you
to do? . . . Get Jesus and Mac and Germaine Connelly for me, if she's still around."

"She's still around, praying up a storm."

"Good for her."

As she talked, Mari sat on the couch and cuddled
the weeping Rita in her arm.

Jesus appeared first.

"Didn't see you come in, Mari."

"Came through the portico. We got rid of her."

"You sure did. Congratulations."

"Yeah . . . Tell the press that the vice president left
as soon as she was assured that the president was
able to discharge his duties of office."

"Yes, ma'am . . . He's all right?"

"What you saw on TV is what he is—hurting, but

his old crazy self . . . Mae, the line is that the president will be back in the morning as he said. The vice president went back to her home because she realizes he's not incapacitated."

Mae had entered as she finished the instructions to Jesus.

"Anything you can think of, Mae?"

"Any change in the Secret Service woman?"

"None that I know of."

"We're going to need a lot of information on how the man got in with the gun in his camera bag."

"Yes, the Secret Service is investigating that . . . Do we know anything about him, Jesus?"

"They've searched his apartment already. Drugs and anti–World Bank, antiglobalization literature. Other media types say that he's been acting a little strange lately. Not so bad that they thought they should tell the Secret Service. Nice guys, huh?"

"A left-wing loony this time?"

"OK, I better phone the hospital."

"Thank you, Mari," they said as they left.

Not quite "Thank you, Ms. President."

"Hi, Sean Patrick, what's happening? . . . Sound asleep . . . Sure I'll tell her, but I don't think she minds . . . Let me talk to Tommy . . . Tommy, we got rid of her . . . Don't want to talk about it on the cell phone . . . Yeah, tomorrow, it's not a problem . . . I'll get Stefan to make those calls . . . No, I don't want to talk to Blair and Putin . . . Jesus will be delighted I'm sure . . . Thanks, Tommy, I appreciate that."

"That's all right, dear," she said to the weeping child in her arms. "We got it in time."

"Stefan, start making calls to Mr. Blair and Mr. Putin. Tell Senator Lopez and Ms. Rosen to figure out what we should say to them in addition to apologizing for the vice president. She was under great stress."

"Yes, ma'am."

"Travels By Night, Dr. Genovesa."

"Thank you, Ms. Chan."

In jeans and a White House sweatshirt, the Yaqui woman almost crept into the battered Oval Office.

"Yes, ma'am . . . Oh my, you poor kid." She rushed to Rita and folded her into her arms. "It will be all right. We all love you so much!"

Mari slipped away and sank into a chair opposite the sofa.

"First of all, Sean Patrick sends his apologies for abandoning you."

The young woman smiled.

"He's such a sweet boy."

"Secondly, the president is fine."

"Yes. I saw him on television. He had his arm around you."

"He was already heavily sedated . . . We have hope for Liz too."

"Oh, she will recover, Dr. Genovesa. She has great energies flowing through the organism. She is very strong. Very powerful medicine."

Mari was not about to debate that.

I had seen Travels By Night kneeling by the pool of drying blood. I was prepared to accept her judgment.

"I have some traveling by night for you to do, Germaine. First of all, I am appointing you temporarily a special assistant to the president."

"Yes, ma'am."

I doubted Mari had the authority to do that, but I wasn't going to argue.

"Then I'm calling a Service car to take you and

Rita over to American University Hospital."

She searched for one of her cards and couldn't find one.

"Ms. Chan," she shouted, "do you have one of my business cards?"

"I always have one," Ms. Chan said, coming into the Oval Office. "My there's a terrible mess here."

"Thank you, Ms. Chan. We'll get it cleaned up before the president comes back tomorrow ... Now, dear, you give this card to them in the emergency room at American. You tell them that the White House has sent you with this young woman. They should call Dr. Leonard Graymont—I'm writing his name on the back of the card—and tell him that Dr. Mary Kathleen Murphy from Chicago recommended him and has probably talked to him. It is very important that he come at once."

"Yes, ma'am."

"You stay there until he arrives and take care of Rita. The car will wait for you ... Wait a minute ... Ms. Chan, can you still make cards?"

"Certainly." She appeared at the door with her usual bright smile.

"Germaine here is temporarily a special assistant to the president. Can you make a card?"

"Certainly!"

Rita had fallen asleep in the Yaqui woman's arms. Good medicine.

The card was produced. The Secret Service car appeared at the back door. Mari took the two young women out the Rose Garden door and along the South Portico to the White House itself, oblivious of the snow.

"I don't see any reason why she can't handle it,"

she said to me when she returned, shaking the snow-flakes out of her hair. ". . . It's cold out there."

"Especially in a light blue evening gown."

"With the president's blood on it. I guess that makes it a historical gown."

"I think there was a historic hug tonight too . . ." She blushed.

"Come on, Blackie, give me a break . . . When that man hugs, he really hugs."

Several minutes later Mae and Jesus returned.

"I talked to both Blair and Putin. They're de-lighted that the president is well and that there was no increase in security precautions because of the incident."

"I guess we didn't think of that."

"Where are the United States Marines when we really need them!" I asked.

"Is there anything else I should do?" She glanced at me.

"Except maybe get some sleep."

"No chance of that . . . I know I'll go to my own office, put on some proper clothes, and retire this historic gown. Then I'll straighten up the office . . . Blackie, you go get some sleep. Better call your Car-dinal first."

"Won't the poltergeist come back and mess it up again?" Mae asked.

"No, the poltergeist is gone," I said.

I began, with considerable lack of success, to at-tempt to rearrange the mess.

Mari returned.

"Blackie"—she smiled—"you're a man of many gifts, including a frightening insight into the workings of the human heart. A housekeeper you're not. Go get some sleep and call your poor Cardinal."

Why should I be the only one in the White House to disobey her orders?

"I was waiting for your call," the Cardinal said patiently. "What the hell is going on?"

"An anarchist assassin this time. Apparently working alone. The president is recovering at the hospital, just as he said on TV. The Secret Service woman will recover too, though the doctors don't know that yet."

He didn't bother to question that pronouncement.

"Blackie, did you see that woman jump the gunman as he headed for the president? She saw him coming before he was coming."

"Mari has some psychic propensities about when people are in danger."

"Good thing for Jack she does . . . Did you see him hug her on television? Maybe a little healthy lust is stirring up inside him."

"There was medication in his bloodstream. However, I anticipate a gradual return to full male Eros for him."

"Yeah . . . Well what about the poltergeist?"

"Oh, that's been dealt with."

"Dealt with! How?"

"Not on the phone. When I come home."

"Which will be when? Tomorrow?"

"More likely the next day."

"The Megans say that I'm a better Cathedral administrator than you are."

"The Megans are utterly unprincipled," I replied.

He laughed enthusiastically.

I, however, went to sleep. There would be no poltergeist tonight. I prayed for her.

17

The president entered the Oval Office the next morning through the outside door. His arm was in a sling, but he was clean-shaven and beaming, albeit pale and a little unsteady on his feet.

"I tell you, Ms. Chan, Mari, there's nothing like these painkillers to make the world look bright even on a day with snow all over the place."

"Don't take too many of them," Ms. Chan warned. "You don't want to become an addict."

"Yes, ma'am."

Tommy and Sean Patrick were unshaven and exhausted.

"I better go out there and let them see me and then come back here and see what wonders you worked last night—Jesus talked to Tony and Vladimir?"

"Of course, Mr. President."

"Naturally . . . Now if you two guys will just guide me to the Briefing Room."

"Wait till he finds out about Genie," Mari said. "I may be out of a job."

"Not very likely."

Out of force of habit we went down to the Corner Room.

Just as we got there, the president walked out on

the stage and leaned against the podium. The press applauded.

"Better the devil you know than the devil you don't know, huh?"

Laughter.

"First of all, the best of the good news. The surgery on Agent Liz Wholley was a complete success. She is now in intensive care and her condition is about to be upgraded from critical to serious. However, the doctors assure me that she's going to make it. I saw her this morning. She said she sends her best to all of you. The Daughters, who managed to come to D.C. last night despite all the snow, figuring that I don't need any more supervision, are taking care of Ms. Wholley, who does not have a family of her own. I get reports from them every fifteen minutes. As was obvious last night, she saved my life. She will receive the Secret Service Medal and we'll have new work for her when she comes back.

"Secondly, I owe my life no less to our all-American point guard. Every president, as I think I said last night, should have one. I have the impression from some of my staff that she did a better job last night than I would have. I don't doubt it. Thank you very much, Mari, for all you've done for us."

In the Corner Room, Mari bowed her head in acknowledgment.

And he didn't know the half of it yet.

"To turn to another matter, I realized last night when I saw that gun pointed at me and thought I would certainly die, that I have let myself for a number of reasons become less of a person than I should be. I'm afraid I let myself become partially deadened by grief and self-pity, two of the worst temptations that God permits us to succumb to. I'm going to do my best to reform myself in that regard."

We looked at each other in bemusement in the Corner Room.

"Finally, I am deeply concerned about the climate of partisanship which has grown during the last twelve years. As I have said before, I deplore it and try not to be part of it. To the extent that I have failed, I am sorry. Once again I call on the leaders of the two major parties, especially the congressional leadership, to damp down the appeals to hatred and payback. I also ask the religious leadership to condemn those who in the name of religion preach violence. I would hope that the major media outlets reconsider some of their policies and perhaps even some of the editorials they permit.

"When I saw the blood pouring from Agent Wholley's body last night, a stream of red on her lovely white dress, I blamed myself for not taking a harder line on these matters. I violated my own political instincts. I am convinced that the ordinary American is fed up with such hatred. Realistically, I know that none of the changes I would like to see take place could have stopped directly either of the two assassination attempts of the last week. Yet I believe that they did take place in a mode of far more intense partisanship in this country than is normal. I suppose that only time will diminish this intensity. However, an administration should strive not only to avoid the attack and payback politics but also to see that suggestions of the violent overthrow of the government be restrained. We distributed a dossier last week of articles and newsletters that seem to support such strategies. Many of these seem to my legal

advisors to violate the law against inciting to the violent overthrow of the government and to go far
beyond the boundaries of free speech. I am asking
the attorney general to monitor these incitements to
violence and to take appropriate action. I'll answer
two questions."

"Mr. President, do you believe that the editorial
in the *Wall Street Journal* the other day, along with
the op-ed piece, incited to violence?"

"I think in combination they come awfully close
to it. However, we will not take action against previous attacks. I hope the owners of the *Journal* caution their editorial writers to greater restraint."

"Sir, is there any evidence of a larger conspiracy
linking these two attempts on your life?"

"In a way, I wish there were. You could search
out a conspiracy and destroy it. You can't do the
same thing to a culture of partisanship and hatred
which creates an atmosphere in which these attempts
become routine."

Later, relaxing in the Oval Office, he poured himself a drink, then gave it to Tommy.

"Doesn't mix with pain medicine," he said sadly.

"Now I want to hear the whole story of how you
got rid of Genie last night. Mari, how did you do
it?"

So she told him and Tommy and Sean Patrick the
whole story.

"Blackwood, how did you know?"

"I must confess, Mr. President, that I have been
unconscionably dense, even by my own lenient standards of incompetence. I knew from the beginning
that someone was managing these phenomena to embarrass you. I assumed that it was either Republicans

or fringe opposition groups. I should have guessed from the public record and from her attempt to get down here at the time of the rocket attack that she was an enemy within. Then, when I began my patrol of the building, waiting for troubled people to appear, Rita was the first to seek me out. That should have been a revelation to me. She was asking for help and I didn't hear her cry. She seemed sweet and innocent, which she is. I could not imagine a mother, no matter how ambitious, who would do that to a daughter. When I heard of her attempt to seize control of the Oval Office, I knew we were dealing with madness as well as ambition, drug-induced madness most likely. I was almost criminally negligent not to have seen the truth before."

The president grinned.

"Yeah, but you saw it before anyone else. And now, thank God, the poltergeist is gone . . . Where is the girl?"

"I sent her over to American University Hospital," Mari said. "There is a psychiatrist there whom Dr. Murphy recommended. Germaine went along to take care of her."

"Germaine?" The president was startled. "Why her?"

"There was no one else around. I couldn't go myself. She is good with troubled people. I appointed her a special assistant to the president and Ms. Chan printed up a card for her."

The president threw back his head and laughed.

"Well, I guess I'd better confirm that appointment . . . Unless you object, Sean Patrick."

That tired young man smiled happily.

"I've always thought she was special . . . Is she back yet?"

"I told her not to come back until she personally turned poor Rita over to this Dr. Leonard Graymont . . . Maybe I'd better see what's happened."

She pushed a button on the president's phone.

"Any news about Germaine Connelly's car?"

"They just reported they were returning from American University. She said if you asked, we should tell you that it took a while, but everything is fine now."

"Patently," I said.

"There's one more thing I must tell you, Mr. President, perhaps I should say confess."

"That's Blackwood's field, Mari."

"He was here when I did it."

"What did you do that was so bad?"

"I fired the vice president. I told her that she should have a letter of resignation on your desk by the end of business today or we would leak the whole poltergeist story to the media and then she would have to resign. She said she would call you to protest."

"That was certainly ruthless, Mari," the president said slowly.

"I'm sorry, Mr. President, if you are upset. You can always decline to support me."

Jack McGurn looked puzzled.

"I wouldn't think of doing that, Mari." He reached out and placed his hand on top of hers. "Your decision was proper and brilliant . . ."

"Sure was," Tommy agreed. "Congratulations, Mari!"

"You save me the necessity of firing her. I would

have procrastinated and equivocated. Thank God I am surrounded by women who have more courage and intelligence than I do."

"Aren't we all," Tommy agreed.

"Thank you, Mr. President," Mari said, tears glistening in her eyes.

All very nice.

"Ms. Connelly's car is approaching the gate, Mr. President," Ms. Chan informed us.

"You want to go meet her, Sean Patrick?"

"I might as well."

"Bring her down here and we'll give her a letter of appointment. She can have charge of good medicine in the White House."

At that point it seemed wise for Blackie Ryan to slip away.

I arranged with Secret Service for a car to drive me to the airport the first thing the following morning.

"You have to get over this habit of smiling all the time, Agent Wholley," I said during a brief stop at Georgetown University Hospital.

"New game face, Bishop . . . Are you going home now?"

"I have another job."

"We'll miss you. I'm sorry I'm not taking you out to the airport."

"Next time."

"May it be soon."

"You are recovering?"

"It feels like an elephant walked over my belly, but otherwise I'm all right . . . How's the president? Are they telling the truth about him?"

"One might go so far as to say that the experience

has actually improved his outlook on life."

She nodded, as though we understood one another.

"Thank you very much for all you did for me that night. I knew I was going to die. You persuaded me to keep fighting."

"You'll never stop fighting, Elizabeth Ann."

"Spare me a blessing?"

"Almighty God, source of all our life and all our nourishment, look down on this very brave young servant of Yours who showed that no greater love of being ready to die for a friend. Take care of her and protect her, bring her back to her friends and colleagues as quickly as You can and guide and protect her on her journey through life. Now bless her and keep her, Father, Son, and Holy Spirit."

Which was as good a way as any for Blackie Ryan to end his undistinguished term in the West Wing.

Epilogue

The Daughters kept me informed about the events in the White House and the West Wing during the next couple of months by intermittent e-mail. Daddy was much better now that the swimming pool was in operation. It was an entirely cool pool, reserved for the president every morning for an hour and then open to the staff for the rest of the day. "Everyone harasses him if he doesn't use his hour. That includes us when we're in D.C. Mari is extreme gorgeous in her two-piece suit, so awesome that Daddy stares at her, which is an improvement, don't you think? Rory is a big hit here, though he is one humongous white wolfhound. He is friendly with everyone, except those who are scared of him. When he's in the West Wing he spends his time curled up in the Oval Office or sitting next to Travels By Night, who now goes to the White House movies with our big brother. Rory follows Daddy out to Marine One. Someday they're going to get confused as to who is president and leave Daddy on the South Lawn.

"He also greets the tourists and lets all the little kids pet him.

"Liz Wholley sort of has charge of him, though she's deputy Agent-in-Charge around here. She's still a little thin and gets tired easily, but she smiles now, which she never used to do.

"There's an extreme great photo of Rory and Daddy on the terrace outside the Oval Office, both apparently concerned about something they see in the distance. We want Mari in a picture like that soon. Daddy is certainly nice to her since she saved his life. But he's always been nice to her.

"The senile crowd over on the Hill (as we say around here) is nice to Daddy all the time now because they know the people like him so much. Even the media goons are nice.

"They were extreme nasty only when he made your sister Judge Kane a Supreme Court Justice. They wrote stuff about "Daley Cronyism" as if the mayor had chosen her when we kinda told Daddy that he should. She is extreme cute.

"Daddy talks about an Era of Good Feeling, which if you don't know, Bishop Blackie, was the last time people were nice in Washington. James Monroe was president then.

"Nothing much else has changed since you left us (Please come back!). Daddy looks much better now that he's swimming every day and all his bills and things are going through Congress.

"Oh, yes, we hear that Rita Suarez has recovered and has flown off to California to be with her daddy. It was really smart of our daddy to get rid of that awful woman, though if he had listened to us he would have gotten rid of her a long time ago, Constitution or not. Senator Garcia from Montana is an entirely neat vice president.

"Anyway this place is still extreme weird, but a lot better than it used to be."

With that information, I was not entirely surprised on a radiant morning in late April when I returned from my hospital calls and Milord Cronin informed me at the breakfast table, "I see your friend has lost her job."

"Dr. Genovesa?"

"You knew?"

"It was inevitable."

"It says here in the *New York Times* newspaper that she has resigned as deputy chief of staff to pursue other interests."

"Indeed."

"Listen to this: 'Dr. Genovesa, along with National Security Advisor Dr. Claire Jones, has been credited with devising the president's apparently successful China policy. White House staff sources discount the rumors of a brief romance and then a serious tiff between the president and Dr. Genovesa, who is single. More likely, sources say, is that she grew weary of playing second fiddle to taciturn Chief of Staff Thomas I. "Tommy" Horan. Dr. Genovesa is expected to return to her faculty position at the State University of New York at Stonybrook this autumn.' "

"Fascinating," I said in a tone of voice indicating that I thought it was extreme dull city.

"Well, I suppose you need some kind of hiatus between being deputy chief of staff and first lady."

"Arguably."

I was not surprised by this analysis. Milord Cronin understands the ways of the human heart better than most.

"Get out of the West Wing before they exile you to the East Wing?"

"Possibly so."

"When do you think the wedding will be?"

"Middle of June at the latest."

"Figures . . . East Room?"

"Arguably. That's where the fabled Alice Blue Gown was married. No president's married there yet. So it would be a historic first."

"I'll do the ceremony and you can tell your strawberry story of which I am a little tired but people love it."

I continued to eat my Belgian waffles.

"There's but one problem."

"Oh?" Sean Cronin frowned. Like all humans he liked happy endings.

"Your good friend and brother bishop, His Gracious Lordship, the Angel to the Church of Washington, may refuse permission for the projected ceremony, save in one of his churches."

Milord grinned, I might even say wickedly.

"Tell you what, Blackwood." He folded his *Times* and rose from the ornate chair reserved for him at the Cathedral breakfast table. "We won't ask him!"

Tucson
Holy Week 2001

Afterword

My remote research involved long interest in the mechanics of presidential decision making stirred up by Irving Janus's excellent book *Group Think*. My visits to the White House during the Clinton administration gave me the idea of sending Blackie there for an exercise in wits, even before the fabled (as Blackie would say) TV program with Martin Sheen (who would make a great Blackie). For the fun of it I made the president an Irish Catholic from the South Side of Chicago (though I am from the West Side and hence more civilized and refined).

And a Cub fan!